## PRAISE FOR TITANS

"Though the kids all have special powers, they also have regular teenage problems, and O'Hearn uses humor to lighten the mood. The teens' endeavors to understand those from different worlds may inspire readers to do the same here on Earth. . . . Fans of Rick Riordan's series will be taken with these characters who learn to be heroes in order to rescue those they love." —*SLJ*

## PRAISE FOR THE MISSING

"Book two of the Titans series, the sequel to *Titans* (2019), is a thrill ride of episodic encounters, with a new danger or confounding wrinkle every couple of pages. The action includes snakes as allies, life-threatening injuries to favorite characters, time travel, planet hopping, and clashing personalities that threaten missions, yet somehow O'Hearn syncs it all together for a fast-paced, satisfying adventure. This is more of the same for her fans, especially of the Pegasus series, which shares characters with the Titans series. Give this also to young Percy Jackson fans, and try it with readers of Michael Carroll's Super Human series." —*Booklist*

## PRAISE FOR THE FALLEN QUEEN

"Constant action makes for a fast-paced read as Mimic mythos is unveiled to raise the stakes, lending this volume the most weight of the trilogy . . . A big, flashy, and—most importantly—fun finale." —*Kirkus Reviews*

# ALSO BY KATE O'HEARN

## THE TITANS SERIES
*Titans*
*The Missing*

## THE PEGASUS SERIES
*The Flame of Olympus*
*Olympus at War*
*The New Olympians*
*Origins of Olympus*
*Rise of the Titans*
*The End of Olympus*

## THE VALKYRIE SERIES
*Valkyrie*
*The Runaway*
*War of the Realms*

## THE ATLANTIS SERIES
*Escape from Atlantis*

# TITANS

## - BOOK 3 -
## THE FALLEN QUEEN

## KATE O'HEARN

### Aladdin
NEW YORK   LONDON   TORONTO   SYDNEY   NEW DELHI

ALADDIN

An imprint of Simon & Schuster Children's Publishing Division
1230 Avenue of the Americas, New York, New York 10020
First Aladdin paperback edition July 2022
Text copyright © 2021 by Kate O'Hearn
Cover illustration copyright © 2021 by Winona Nelson
Also available in an Aladdin hardcover edition.
All rights reserved, including the right of reproduction in whole or in part in any form.
ALADDIN and related logo are registered trademarks of Simon & Schuster, Inc.
For information about special discounts for bulk purchases, please contact Simon & Schuster Special Sales at 1-866-506-1949 or business@simonandschuster.com.
The Simon & Schuster Speakers Bureau can bring authors to your live event.
For more information or to book an event contact the Simon & Schuster Speakers Bureau at 1-866-248-3049 or visit our website at www.simonspeakers.com.
Cover designed by Karin Paprocki
Interior designed by Mike Rosamilia
The text of this book was set in Adobe Garamond.
Manufactured in the United States of America 0522 OFF
2 4 6 8 10 9 7 5 3 1
The Library of Congress has cataloged the hardcover edition as follows:
Names: O'Hearn, Kate, author.
Title: The Fallen Queen / Kate O'Hearn.
Description: First Aladdin hardcover edition. | New York : Aladdin, 2021. | Series: Titans ; 3 |
Audience: Ages 8 to 12. |
Summary: "Astraea and Zephyr venture to the Mimic home world in order to save Titus and defeat the Mimics for good in this third book of the Titans series."—Provided by publisher.
Identifiers: LCCN 2020045528 (print) | LCCN 2020045529 (ebook) |
ISBN 9781534417106 (hardcover) | ISBN 9781534417120 (ebook)
Subjects: CYAC: Titans (Mythology)—Fiction. | Animals, Mythical—Fiction. |
Mythology, Greek—Fiction. | Adventure and adventurers—Fiction. | Fantasy.
Classification: LCC PZ7.O4137 Fal 2021 (print) | LCC PZ7.O4137 (ebook) | DDC [Fic]—dc23
LC record available at https://lccn.loc.gov/2020045528
LC ebook record available at https://lccn.loc.gov/2020045529
ISBN 9781534417113 (pbk)

*For Kenneth O'Hearn*
*My best friend and the greatest dad in the world*
*I just lost you, and now I am lost*

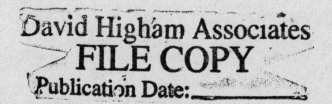

# 1

"ZEPHYR, I'M SCARED," ASTRAEA SAID SOFTLY.

"Me too," Zephyr agreed.

They were standing on the edge of the jungle just outside the Temple of Arious. It was their turn to keep watch for any new Mimic attacks. So far, their shift had been uneventful, but things could change in an instant.

The massive snake Belis was beside Astraea, his tongue dipping in and out of his mouth as he tasted the air for Mimics. Every few minutes, Astraea would look at him. The moment Belis became aware of the deadly Mimics, his scales would turn from colorful stripes to black.

Around them the trees were filled with cheerful birdcalls, but they found no joy in the songs. The beauty of Xanadu was missed as they stood watch.

Since arriving on Xanadu and clearing the temple of the shape-shifting Mimics, everyone was on edge. There had been several more attacks, but now that the Titans had security patrols carrying slingshots with rocks covered in snake venom that killed the invaders, the Mimics were quickly driven back. It was the Shadow Titans controlled by the Mimics that proved to be the most dangerous. Their arrival was always brutal and was happening more often. It was obvious—the deadly Mimics were fighting back.

"Do you think Jake is with my brothers?" Astraea asked as her keen eyes watched the jungle. "You don't think the Mimics killed them?"

Fear for Jake and her missing brothers had been pressing down on Astraea like a lead weight. Despite her best hopes, her four brothers hadn't been in the Titus prison, while Jake had been abducted from Earth by the Mimics and had vanished without a trace.

Not long ago, she, Zephyr, Tryn, and Pegasus had decided to go to the Mimic home world to try to rescue Jake and the others. But that was before the attacks had become bolder and more intense.

Zephyr snorted and shook her head. "Of course they're not dead. If the Mimics wanted to kill them, they wouldn't have bothered taking everyone. I think Jake was taken because he can talk to the snakes."

"Why would they care? All Mimics want to do is kill the snakes. Look what they did to Belis." Astraea looked along the snake's body to all the scars from the Shadow Titans' swords. "Every time they attack us, he seems to be their main target."

The snake could now understand them completely and raised his head higher for Astraea to stroke. "But we won't let them hurt you again," she cooed.

"I still don't get it with you two," Zephyr said, and snorted in disgust. "But it seems that's the only reason the Mimics would go for Jake. I mean he's human. Why else would they care, if not for Nesso?"

Zephyr looked slyly at Astraea, then winked.

Astraea chuckled softly. Zephyr was still making a show of not liking Jake because he was human, but she was ready to go on the secret rescue mission to save him. "Maybe. But I'm just so worried about him."

"I'm worried about all of us!" Zephyr said. "Seriously, I never imagined we'd ever be going through anything like this. Our lives have been turned upside down. Titus is overrun with Mimics, and they want Xanadu as well."

"They want our worlds, but not us," Astraea said.

Tryn appeared out of the temple and flew over to them on his skateboard. "How's it going?"

"So far it's been quiet," Astraea said.

"Quiet?" Zephyr snorted. "I can barely hear myself think with all the jungle sounds around us."

"I'm glad for the sounds," Tryn said. "Haven't you noticed how it goes quiet when the Mimics are here? It's as though everything in the jungle is frightened of them."

"Does it?" Zephyr said.

Astraea looked at her friend in shock. "Seriously, Zeph, you haven't noticed?"

"Hey, I'm too busy trying to stay alive to notice stupid things like that."

"Those stupid things could help save your life," Tryn said.

Astraea was about to say more when Jupiter, a

herd of centaurs, and several other Titans ran out of the temple. They were followed by multiple Shadow Titans being controlled by Tryn's people that were racing behind them. Everyone vanished into the jungle behind the temple.

Triana ran out of the temple and up to her brother. "We all have to go back inside right now!"

"What's happening?" Tryn asked.

"They're back!" Triana cried.

Astraea looked all around and saw only the calm jungle. She looked at Belis, who was still striped. "Where are they?"

"They're attacking the nectar orchards," Triana cried. "Jupiter says they are going after our food."

"That's low!" Zephyr cried.

"That's war," Tryn said.

Triana caught hold of her brother's arm. "Come on, Mom says we have to get inside. This is a big attack."

It didn't take more prompting to get them running. They entered the temple just as more fighters rushed out. Hercules and Mercury, the messenger of Olympus, were among them. Hercules paused long enough to call, "Get to Arious and seal yourselves in."

"Maybe we should help them," Astraea said.

Belis was still at her side and hissed loudly. When Astraea looked at him, the snake was jet black.

"Uh-oh," Zephyr said. "That isn't good."

Moments later, a blaring siren sounded. It was Arious, the mainframe computer, warning of Mimics arriving within the temple.

"This is huge!" Tryn cried. He pulled out his slingshot and opened his pouch of venom-covered rocks. Astraea and Triana did the same as they ran deeper into the temple.

"I wish I had hands," Zephyr cried.

"You don't need them," Astraea called above the siren. "You can stomp the Mimics' Shadow Titans into oblivion. That's way better than hands."

"Yes, but I can't stomp Mimics."

"We'll take care of them; you just go after the Shadows." Astraea entered the stairwell going down toward the entrance to Arious and looked back at Zephyr. "Be careful here."

"How?" Zephyr complained as she followed behind. "Would you please tell me how I'm supposed to be careful on stairs? And why are there always so many of them? Here, back on Earth, Tartarus, even Titus—they're everywhere. Don't architects think about those of us with hooves? What's wrong with ramps?"

"You can tell them when this is over," Tryn offered.

"Don't think I won't," Zephyr finished.

Tryn and Astraea linked arms while bracing against the stairwell walls to keep Zephyr from slipping down the long flight of stairs. When they reached the bottom, Zephyr neighed, "Thank you."

The siren was still blaring as they moved deeper through the cavernous corridors of the temple. Belis was directly beside Astraea and still as black as night. She held her slingshot at the ready but knew that the snake would move on any Mimics long before she could fire it.

With each step, Astraea felt more and more on edge. Perhaps it was the blaring siren, or the confines of the temple. But the fear that she'd felt earlier was now turning into terror as she kept looking all around. It wasn't a question of *if* there were Mimics in the temple—it was a question of where. It was not knowing that was making her terror worse.

When they approached a junction, Zephyr's ears sprang forward and she stopped. "I hear something."

Belis didn't stop. The snake lunged forward, hissing loudly as he slithered down the corridor. Just then, a group of four Shadow Titans rounded a corner. The large warriors were bright green and looked like walking sea turtles. Standing side by side, they formed a large, impenetrable wall blocking the corridor.

When they saw Astraea and her team, they paused. But then a gray, blubberous Mimic appeared behind them. Seeing Belis, it raised a small silver cylinder to its mouth and gave the command "Kill that snake!"

Belis hissed again and slithered toward the Shadow Titans.

"Belis, no!" Astraea cried, but the snake wouldn't stop.

"We have to have a serious talk with that snake!" Zephyr whinnied as she charged forward behind Belis. As the Shadow Titans whacked at the snake with their swords, Zephyr arrived, spun around, and started to buck. "It's stomping time!"

"Zephyr, be careful!" Astraea shouted.

"Go for the Mimic!" Zephyr called. "Get the controller!"

As the Shadow Titans focused only on killing Belis, Zephyr managed to kick the first one to pieces.

Astraea, Tryn, and Triana took aim with their slingshots and started to fire on the Mimic controlling the Shadows. But the Mimic was blocked by the large fighters. It held up the controller and shouted, "Kill the snake *and* the winged horse!" Two of the Shadow Titans stopped hitting Belis and focused on Zephyr. They charged forward with their swords held high.

"Winged horse?" Zephyr spun again and reared high, kicking out with her front hooves. "I'll show you a winged horse!" With her rage focused, she kicked at the attacking Shadow Titans and drove one to the ground. Zephyr slammed down on it, stomping it to pieces.

The second Shadow slashed at her, grazing across the chest and knocking her to the ground.

"Zephyr!" Astraea screamed.

"I'm all right," Zephyr called. "Keep going for the Mimic; get his controller!"

The Shadow Titan advanced on Zephyr as she struggled to regain her feet on the slippery stone floor. Standing above her, it raised its weapon high.

"Leave her alone!" Tryn sprang forward and used his skateboard like a bat to knock the Shadow Titan's descending sword away. Then he struck the massive Shadow in his armored head.

With only one Shadow Titan left trying to kill Belis, Astraea had a clear shot at the Mimic. She drew back her slingshot and fired. The small rock passed right through the Mimic's gelatinous body, but the poison covering the rock worked. As the Mimic cast out its deadly tendrils, it started to melt.

There was just a puddle on the ground by the time Belis arrived from his fight with the Shadow Titan. But the snake didn't stop; he charged forward and slid around the next corner.

Triana ran forward past the broken Shadow Titans and reached the melted Mimic. She kicked the controller out of the goo and cleaned it off with a piece of fabric torn from her top.

"Stop fighting!" she called into the controller.

The turtle stopped just as Tryn gave it a final whack.

"Belis!" Astraea cried as she watched the tip of his long tail vanishing around the corner into another corridor. Running after him, she made it to the junction and was met with four more Shadow Titans with drawn swords.

"There are more here!" Astraea shouted.

Belis was braver than she'd imagined, but the snake was being struck and cut by the relentless Shadow Titans. She feared by the time the others arrived, he would be dead.

"This is dumb, Astraea," she muttered as she charged forward. She approached the tail of the snake and threw herself down on the floor. Loading her slingshot, she drew back the elastic vine and waited for a clear shot at the Mimic controlling the Shadow Titans.

"Astraea, what are you doing there?" Zephyr cried as she charged around the corner.

Astraea heard her friend but didn't look back. The Shadow Titans were weaving back and forth as they attacked Belis. But with each movement, there was a moment when she had a clear shot.

Astraea fired. The rock struck a Shadow Titan

and bounced harmlessly off its arm. Cursing silently, she pulled out a second rock and loaded it.

Tryn arrived, threw himself down on the ground beside her, and raised his slingshot.

"Astraea, Tryn, get away from there!" Zephyr whinnied. "Belis might crush you!"

"Just a moment more," Astraea called. "Belis, move a bit!"

Belis finally moved, and for the briefest moment, Astraea and Tryn had a clear shot. "Please . . . ," she uttered as she took aim.

They both fired at the same time, and two rocks shot between the Shadow Titans and straight through the Mimic.

With a double dose of venom, the Mimic melted quicker. But that didn't end their troubles. The Shadow Titans were still trying to kill Belis.

Astraea sprang to her feet and looked at the wall of fighters before her. There was no way through.

"Astraea, come here and get on my back!" Zephyr cried.

Astraea leaped onto Zephyr's back. Without pausing, Zephyr turned and ran down the opposite corridor. Then she turned again and galloped toward the Shadow Titans. "Tryn, move!" she shouted.

When Tryn stepped back, Zephyr spread her wings wide in the confines of the corridor, leaped into the air, and flew awkwardly over the heads of the Shadow Titans.

Zephyr and Astraea touched down on the opposite side. Sliding off Zephyr's back, Astraea peered into the puddle of dead Mimic and saw the silver controller. She knocked it out of the goo with her foot and cleaned it off. Pressing the button, she shouted, "Stop fighting!"

The four Shadow Titans stopped immediately. Two were midswing with their swords, but now stood stone-still as though they'd been turned by Medusa.

Astraea ran up to the snake. Belis raised his head and looked at her. His eyes were clear, but there was an angry wound running the length of his head.

"He's a mess," Tryn called as he approached. He reached out and patted the snake. "Belis, I know you can understand me. You must stop doing that. You're the one they're after."

"Yeesh, I think I'm going to be sick," Zephyr said

as she looked at the snake's wounds. "They really wanted to kill him."

"You're not much better," Astraea said as she approached Zephyr and inspected the slice on her chest. "This is deep."

"It looks worse than it is," Zephyr said. "It will heal quickly. But Belis is hurt badly."

"We have to get him to Arious. He needs treatment," Tryn said.

Astraea nodded and lightly touched the snake's snout. "Come on, Belis, let's get you taken care of." Belis closed his eyes briefly; then his body tensed and started to slowly turn around in the corridor.

When they were halfway to Arious, the grating siren stopped and the whole temple fell into overwhelming silence.

"Thank you!" Zephyr said. "That alarm was really getting on my nerves."

"At least it means there are no more Mimics inside," Triana said.

They heard footsteps in the corridor next to theirs. Soon a large group of armed night dwellers arrived. Several were wearing pieces of armor taken from destroyed Shadow Titans. They approached Belis.

"How is he?" a woman Astraea knew as Paye asked. Her long white hair was tied back, and she had a deep wound on her cheek.

"He's alive," Astraea said. "But the Shadow Titans hurt him. We're taking him to Arious."

"How bad was the attack?" Tryn asked.

"Bad," another night dweller said. "Really bad."

Paye sighed. "I fear they are attacking us here to keep us occupied while they go after the nectar orchards."

"We were ordered to go to Arious," Astraea said. "But I'd rather go to the orchards to help. We can fight from the sky." She looked at Zephyr. "Are you well enough to do that?"

"It's not a question of whether I'm well enough," Zephyr said. "It's if I want to."

"Do you?" Astraea asked.

"Not really, but we're going to go anyway, aren't we?"

When Astraea nodded, Tryn stepped forward. "We're coming too."

"The trouble is Belis," Astraea continued. "He needs help. We should get him to Arious first."

An older night dweller came forward. He also had several wounds. "Go join the battle for the orchard. We'll take care of Belis."

Astraea nodded and patted Belis again. "I know you want to stay with me, but please go to Arious with Paye and the others. We'll be back soon."

Belis lifted his head weakly and leaned against Astraea.

"Please, Belis, do this for me," Astraea coaxed.

Finally he started to turn around in the corridor and move toward Arious.

Astraea looked at her friends. "Come on, let's go. They need our help."

# 2

FROM THE MOMENT JAKE HAD EMERGED from the Solar Stream, his life had become a nightmare of unimaginable terror. The only time a Mimic talked calmly to him was to tell him he was now on their home world and was at their mercy—which, he quickly discovered, they didn't have any. He was constantly ordered about or threatened, and when he didn't cooperate, they touched him and knocked him out.

Jake and Nesso were locked in a small cage that sat on a table in what Jake could only describe as a laboratory. The walls were as gray as the Mimics themselves. The lighting above them was nothing like he'd ever seen before. There were no light fixtures or bulbs—it seemed the ceiling itself was glowing. Across from his cage was a silver table that looked like the kind he saw on TV detective shows where they did autopsies. Beside the long table was another that held trays of instruments that would have scared the most avid horror fan.

The walls of the room were lined with shelves that contained hundreds of specimen jars. Some of the jars were filled with dead snakes taken from Nesso's home world, Zomos. Seeing the unfortunate snakes upset both Jake and Nesso. Other jars were filled with more terrors than Jake could bear. Unfortunates taken from the worlds the Mimics were invading.

Had they done that to a Titan? Was he next to be put in a specimen jar?

While in the cage, Jake was fed twice a day. It was a kind of strange-looking fruit that under different circumstances he would have really liked. At first, Nesso refused to eat because she wanted him to have it all. But when he stopped eating until she did, she finally agreed.

On their second day, or what Jake thought was a

second day, he and Nesso were witness to an experiment that shocked them so badly, Jake was sure he'd have nightmares about it for the rest of his life—however much time he had left.

Mimic doctors or scientists or whatever they were caught hold of a small snake in one of their gloved hands. Then another Mimic entered the room. The new Mimic didn't react, didn't fight. It was directed to lie down on the table. When it did, the doctor Mimic forced the snake to bite it.

Jake gasped as the Mimic melted. After that, the goo was collected and studied. Seeing the Mimic killed was bad. But when they killed and dissected the sweet, innocent snake, Jake started to scream and shout at the Mimics.

They didn't react at all.

On the third day, the dissection table was cleaned until it sparkled in the horrible light. One of the Mimic doctors approached Jake's cage and opened the lock.

"Get out," it ordered.

"Oh, no, you're not putting me on that table!" Jake shied back in the cage.

"Get out," the Mimic ordered again. It didn't raise its voice, and somehow, that was even worse.

"No," Jake said. Was this it? Was it his turn on the terrible table of death in this house of horrors?

"I will tell you one more time," the Mimic said. "Get out or we will drag you out."

"You're gonna have to drag me out, because you aren't doing to me what you've done to the snakes!"

Without another word, more glove-wearing Mimics arrived and hauled Jake out of the cage. Despite their gelatinous bodies, the Mimics were surprisingly strong as they carried him over to the steel table.

Struggling all he could, Jake was strapped down. He looked at Nesso. "Whatever happens to us, whatever they do, you know I love you."

*"I love you too, my bessst Jake. . . ."*

The Mimics examined Jake while speaking in their strange language. No matter how he shouted, screamed, or struggled, they didn't react or speak to him. He was nothing to them, and they were letting him know it.

Samples were taken. Pieces of his hair, fingernails, skin, blood, and so much more. All without pain relief, all while he was conscious and terrified. No matter how painful it was, how loud he screamed, they didn't stop. But after the physical examination, nothing they did hurt as much as when they dragged Nesso away from her place around his neck.

"Nesso, no!" Jake howled at the top of his lungs, straining against the restraints. "Bring her back! Don't kill her! Please, please don't kill her!"

"*Jake . . . ,*" Nesso hissed. She squirmed in the gloved hand that held her and tried to bite the Mimic. "*Jake . . .*"

Nesso was taken away and put in a small jar. She was across the room, striking against the glass walls that imprisoned her, but at least Jake could still see her.

After that, another snake was brought in from somewhere behind him. It was a little bit bigger than Nesso and was hissing loudly.

"Where are you getting all these snakes?" Jake cried.

His question remained unanswered as the Mimics held the new snake up to Jake's arm, but the snake refused to bite. Finally, they pried open the snake's mouth and forced the two fangs to bite down on Jake.

Just like the first time Nesso had bitten him, pain coursed up Jake's arm, and it felt like his whole body was on fire. Then the pain reached his head. After a single, sharp intake of breath, the world went black.

Jake awoke back in the cage. He hurt all over but was surprised to realize he was still alive. There were pains he'd never felt before coming from the back of his head. When he touched his hair, it was sticky and matted. Looking at his fingers, he saw drying blood. Jake wondered what else they had done to him while he was unconscious. For as much as he'd hated them before, there were no words to describe what he felt about the Mimics now.

The room was quiet and dimly lit, and it was what he now recognized as night on this terrible world. His head was pounding, and his arm stung from the snakebite.

Coming fully awake, Jake instantly knew that Nesso wasn't at his neck. The pain of her absence was genuine and physical. He peered over to where the Mimics had placed her and saw that the jar was missing. "Nesso, Nesso," he called. But he couldn't see her. Panic set in at the fear of what they might be doing to her. Finally he remembered what he'd done on Zomos, the jungle world, to find her. Jake closed his eyes and reached out all his feelings for her. He cried aloud when he felt her life force. She was away from him and in pain, but at least she was alive.

Then he thought of the other snake that had been forced to bite him, and he felt no trace of it. He started to grieve. Somehow, he knew it was dead. Perhaps they'd killed it to try to understand his relationships with them, or maybe they just liked to kill things.

Whatever the reason, all he felt was Nesso.

Now more than ever, Jake was desperate to get out of the cage. There was a lock on the outside of the door that looked basic enough. The trouble was, he had nothing to pick it with. What he wouldn't have given for Tryn's lockpick set.

While he had been unconscious, the Mimics had changed his clothes. His jeans and T-shirt were gone. Instead he was wearing what looked like a kind of nightshirt made of a coarse woven fabric. There were no pockets, or anything to help him escape.

Across from him was the table of torture, and

beside it, a fresh set of instruments. He shivered looking at them, realizing he now knew what half of them were for. But among them was a long, slim probe-like thing. Just perfect to fit in the lock. He just had to figure out how to get it.

Tearing up his nightshirt to make a lasso wouldn't work—it was too light. He needed to reach the instruments. Finally he set on an idea that was simple enough but would be painful. But if it got him out of the cage and back to Nesso, he would do it. He would do anything to reach her.

The cage he was in was small. Maybe four feet by four feet. He couldn't stretch out in it and certainly couldn't stand. But as he inspected it in the dim light, he confirmed that it wasn't attached to the table it was on.

Pausing to listen, Jake heard nothing but his own breathing. If there were Mimics around, they were being completely silent. Though something told him there weren't any. They were too arrogant, believing they had him contained.

Convinced he was completely alone, Jake grabbed the front cage bars and started to rock. Back and forth, back and forth. When he put all his weight into the forward thrust, the cage started to slide.

As he moved faster, the cage slid steadily toward the edge until it flipped off the table and crashed noisily to the laboratory floor.

"Ouch," Jake moaned as he hit the floor hard and landed on his knees, which slammed against the bars of the cage, hurting worse than he'd expected.

At least he was closer to the instrument table.

Taking a calming breath, Jake started to rock back and forth again, to move the cage closer to the tray. It was crude, and it was slow, but with each forward rock, he slid closer to the instruments.

When the cage was as close as he could get it, Jake pushed his arm up through the top and strained to reach the probe. "Please," he begged aloud. "Just a bit farther . . ."

His fingers landed on the various instruments that had been used against him. Finally he grazed the probe. Snatching hold of it, he brought it down.

Jake needed to flip the cage over again to give him access to the lock. Just one flip. But when he did it, he somersaulted with the cage and landed painfully on his back and head. It hurt, but not nearly as much as coming off the table had.

With the lock now accessible, Jake's hands were shaking as he inserted the probe into the keyhole. This was so important. Perhaps the most important thing he'd ever done in his life, and he had to get it right. After a few minutes of wiggling the probe, he heard a single click.

He nearly cried aloud when the lock opened.

Jake could hardly believe what he'd just done. A moment later, he was out of the cage and standing up stiffly. His legs were throbbing from the crash down to the floor, and his back killed because of the somersault in the cage and because he hadn't straightened up in what felt like forever. Pulling up the hem of his nightshirt, he saw the damage to his knees. Peeled skin and bruising that was starting to show.

But he was free.

Looking around the room, Jake searched for any snakes, but there were none. He did find his clothes and shoes and was grateful to change back into them.

Once he was dressed, Jake stood very still, and he reached out to Nesso again. He felt her. She was close, in a room adjoining this one. Listening for any sounds of movement, he crept up to the lab's only door. It was larger than doors on Earth or even the ones he'd encountered on Titus. Meaning it was built for the bigger Mimics. Meaning they lived in buildings.

Pressing his ear to the door, Jake listened carefully. He heard nothing. There was no handle, but when he pressed against the door, it pushed open easily.

The adjoining room was as dimly lit as the laboratory itself. But as his eyes adjusted to the light, he could see it was larger than the lab. Although there were no dissection tables, there were other tables and shelves. In the center of the room on a massive island counter were two containers that he recognized from the Mimic camp on Zomos. He and the others had used these containers to transport the snakes back to Earth.

Had the Mimics gathered more? Or were these the Earth snakes? Without Nesso, there was no way for him to find out.

Jake closed his eyes again and reached out for Nesso. She was close. Very close. Moving forward, he followed his feelings until he reached a counter against the wall. Jake had to put his hand to his mouth to keep from screaming.

Nesso was there. She had been pinned down to the surface of an examination board. The pins went right through her tiny body. Jake could feel her suffering coming at him in thick waves.

"Nesso," he cried softly. "Nesso, it's me."

*"Jake . . . ,"* Nesso hissed weakly.

Jake's hands shook even more than before as he pulled the pins out. When Nesso was free, she coiled tightly around Jake's hand. He lifted her up to his cheek, unaware that he was crying until his tears dripped onto the snake.

"I'm so sorry, Nesso. . . ." He wept softly.

*"Thisss isss not your fault,"* Nesso said weakly. *"I am ssso glad you found me. Pleassse, take me out of here. Take all of usss out. . . ."*

Cradling Nesso, Jake found other snakes pinned down to boards. Some had been dissected and were dead. Others, like Nesso, were still alive and suffering greatly.

"Please tell them I'm here to help. Don't let them bite me."

*"They know you and won't,"* Nesso said weakly.

Jake gasped. "Are these the same snakes that we took to Earth?"

*"Yesss,"* Nesso said. *"The Mimicsss brought them here from Xxxanadu."*

"Xanadu?" he repeated. "These snakes were on Xanadu?"

There were so many questions Jake wanted to ask, but no time. He freed the snakes pinned to the boards and then crossed over to the containers. The lids had been sealed down. Breaking the seals, he opened the containers and tipped them over for the snakes to climb out.

Jake felt great sadness when he saw that many snakes had died at the bottom of the containers, crushed by the weight of the others on top. Even so, there were a lot of snakes now slithering along the countertop.

"Can you all understand me?" Jake asked.

The snakes stopped and all peered up at him. Their tongues flicked in and out of their mouths.

*"Yesss they can,"* Nesso said softly.

Jake lifted Nesso. "Are you strong enough to go back around my neck?" he asked her.

*"Pleassse,"* Nesso said.

Jake helped settle Nesso around his neck. She then asked if he would allow the other wounded snakes to join her. Before long, Jake had four wounded snakes coiled lightly around his neck. Somehow, having Nesso back gave him the courage to go on.

"All right, everyone, we are going to get out of here together. I don't know where we are or where we can go, but we can't stay here. Will you follow me?"

Again the snakes all stopped and peered at him. Nesso didn't have to translate for him to understand. "Great," he said. "First, let's see if we can get out of this room. Then, and this is very important, if they come after me, I want all of you to run. Get away. Find places to hide and stay there. Will you do that?"

The air filled with soft hissing.

Nesso said, *"They are grateful to you. If the Mimicsss come, we will all protect you."*

Jake sighed. That was the last thing he wanted. He needed the snakes to escape. But he knew there would be no reasoning with them. Instead he moved forward through the room toward the exit. He motioned for the snakes to follow.

The survivors slid off the counter and gathered behind him, all looking up at him expectantly. Jake was stunned by just how many there were.

"Well, this is it," he said as he reached for the door and pushed it open. "Let's go."

# 3

JAKE STEPPED THROUGH THE DOOR OF THE Mimic lab and found himself in a long corridor. Like in the other rooms, the lighting had been dimmed. And in the faint light, he saw many doors lining the wall. It looked like a hospital. But this was not a place of healing. It was a place of suffering and death.

As Jake held the door open, the snakes silently slid forward until they were all in the corridor. Jake looked around, not knowing where to go next. There was no writing on the doors and nothing to indicate an exit.

Jake turned back to all the snakes and held up his hand. "Stay here," he said softly. "I'm just going down to the end to see if there's a way out."

Hundreds of tiny tongues flicked out of small mouths.

*"They will ssstay,"* Nesso said softly.

Jake nodded and started to run. When he reached the end of the corridor, there was no exit that he could see. He ran back toward the snakes and then to the opposite end. He was grateful to see a large set of stairs. By the time he ran back to the snakes, he found them all gathered outside one of the doors.

"There's a way out. All of you, follow me."

The snakes refused to move.

"Please, we have to hurry. It's this way."

Once again, the snakes refused to move. They looked up at Jake, and then back to the door.

"What's wrong with them?" Jake asked Nesso.

*"They want you to open the door. They need to get in there. Sssomeone ssspecial isss inssside. We mussst help her."*

"Who?" Jake asked.

*"The one insside is frightened. We mussst help her. Pleassse open the door."*

Jake instinctively reached up to his neck and stroked Nesso and all the wounded snakes coiled there. Nesso was still suffering, but she was worried about others. He looked down the corridor toward what could be freedom, and back at the door.

"All right, but if we get into trouble, it's you guys' fault."

The snakes parted to allow Jake through. He pushed the door, and it opened easily.

The room was another laboratory. In the center was a dissection table just like the one he'd been on. Beside it was a cage. A young girl, perhaps his sister's age or a bit younger, was curled up in the corner of the cage and crying. When she saw Jake, she crawled up to the bars and pointed to a counter against the wall. "Help them, please. The Mimics are killing them to punish me."

Jake followed the girl's finger to the counter. Several snakes were pinned down, just as Nesso and the others had been. Others were in jars with the lids sealed tightly shut. They were losing their color as they slowly suffocated. Other jars were filled with water that was deeper than the small snakes. Two were already drowned, lying pale and dead at the bottom.

Jake reacted instantly and ran over to the counter.

He unscrewed all the lids on the jars to allow air in. Then he reached into the bottles of water to free the snakes. Finally he freed the pinned snakes. Like Nesso, they coiled themselves up when the pins were removed.

"Those monsters," Jake muttered. "Why are they doing this to you?"

"It's my fault," the girl wept. "I am a snake charmer, but when I couldn't explain how it worked, they punished me by hurting the snakes."

Jake looked back at her and saw that all the snakes from the corridor were in the cage with her.

"Who are you?" Jake asked, walking closer.

"Angitia," the girl said softly. "I come from Titus. Who are you?"

"I'm Jake." He approached her cage and looked at the lock. It was the same as his. "I'm from Earth. I'm friends with Astraea and Zephyr. They're from Titus too."

"I know Astraea and Zephyr," Angitia said. "Will you please let me out of here?"

Jake looked around the room. "Do you know where they keep the key to the lock?"

Angitia nodded. "Over there, beside the door."

Jake found a strange-looking key hanging on a

hook beside the door. It took a bit of fiddling, but soon the lock was opened and Angitia was free.

The first thing she did was throw her arms around him and weep into his chest. "Thank you, thank you. Will you take me home?"

Jake embraced the young girl and could feel her trembling. "I really wish I could, but the Mimics took my Solar Stream ring. What I can do is get you and all the snakes out of here. Then maybe we can find somewhere safe to hide until we figure this out."

Angitia nodded and waited for Jake to move.

Looking into her pale, young eyes, in that one instant, Jake felt the last of his childhood end.

Everything about him had changed. It wasn't so long ago that he'd been in California and the most difficult thing he'd had to worry about was learning a new skateboarding trick. His whole life had been only about himself. What he'd wanted or thought he needed. He hadn't really thought about his sister or mother that much. It had been all just Jake.

Now he was on a strange planet filled with Mimics that could kill with a touch. Angitia said she was a snake charmer. By the looks of the snakes around her, she was. Despite that, and the fact that she was a Titan and would be much stronger than him, she was young and vulnerable. Somehow, she reminded him of his sister, Molly. He was instantly protective of her.

He smiled at her and wiped away her tears. "Can I call you Angie?"

When she nodded, he continued. "Great. Angie, we have to stick together. All of us." He included the snakes gathered around them. "I don't know where we are or what is out there. But if we look out for each other, we might just make it. Okay?"

Tears still trickled down Angie's face, but she wiped them away and nodded.

"Good," Jake said. "Can you carry some of those injured snakes for me?"

Angie went over to the counter and picked up the snakes. Those that had been pinned and were badly hurt, she wrapped around her neck, just as Jake had done with Nesso and the others. She cradled other snakes in her hands. "We're ready," she said softly.

"Good stuff." Jake walked back to the door and pressed his ear against it. There were no sounds from the corridor. He looked back at Angie. "There are stairs at the end of the hall. That's where we are going. Are you ready?"

Angie nodded and took a step closer. When she did, all the snakes moved with her.

"Wow, you really are a snake charmer," Jake said. "Okay, everyone, let's go."

Jake held open the door as Angie and all the snakes made their way into the long corridor. As they started toward the stairs, Jake pushed open every side door along the way, looking for more prisoners. They were all laboratories, but luckily, they were empty.

They entered the stairwell and started down. On the next level, there was a window. Jake and Angie approached it and peered outside.

Jake gasped. He wasn't sure what he'd been expecting of the Mimic home world, but this certainly wasn't it. The sky was mostly dark, but there were soft yellows on the horizon, promising that dawn was on its way.

With what little light there was, he saw other buildings that looked like the industrial estates back home, but not quite—they were very ornamental and only climbed three or four stories high. Beyond them were homes. Beautiful homes with pointed roofs covered in brilliant blue tiles and ornate decorations. There was a canal weaving through the area, with charming arched bridges that crossed it. In the distance, he saw the start of some woods.

"I don't believe this." He looked at Angie. "Are we in Bruges?"

"Where?" Angie asked.

"Bruges. It's a small city in Belgium."

There was still a look of incomprehension on Angie's face. "It's in Europe, on Earth. Before my parents got divorced, they took me and my sister there."

"I've never been to Bruges," Angie said softly.

"Trust me, it looks like this." Jake continued to peer out the window. "No one's moving out there. I thought the Mimics would be out."

"They don't see well in the dark," Angie said.

Jake looked at her. "How do you know?"

"Astraea told me when she and Zephyr came back to Titus to get us. It was night. There were very few Mimics out and they needed bright torches. They don't like the dark."

"That is great news," Jake said. "It gives us an edge."

"What is an edge? Like a knife?"

Jake smiled. "No, it means it gives us an advantage over them. If they don't like the dark, then that's when we'll move. But looking out there, it won't be dark much longer. Come on, let's go."

They moved together down the stairs. Jake's heart pounded with each step. Now it was more than just his own life he was worried about. It was Angie's and the snakes'.

When they reached the bottom, Jake was thrilled to see a set of glass doors. Looking at them, he was once again reminded of his home. The Mimics continued to surprise him with how ordinary they were in all their weirdness.

Jake approached the doors and pushed against them, and they opened easily. "The Mimics are obviously not big on security," he said. He looked back at Angie. "But then again, they're kinda like bees. They're not individuals—they only work for the hive, so I guess they don't have thieves."

"Is that good?"

He grinned again. "That's very good. Meaning we shouldn't encounter a lot of locks."

They walked outside and were greeted with the

most fragrant air Jake had ever smelled, just like lilacs when they first bloomed. There was a slight chill, like Michigan in spring. But it wasn't cold enough for him to need a jacket.

He looked back at the snakes. "I hope you guys can move fast, because we gotta go."

Jake started to jog. Angie was keeping up with him easily. When he looked back, all the snakes were too. Although, there was one snake lagging farther behind.

Angie stopped and ran back to collect it. "Don't worry, you're safe," she cooed to the snake.

They started to run again. But after a short while, Jake was out of breath and very tired. He stopped and bent over to breathe. "We—we haven't gone that far, but I'm exhausted. What did those Mimics do to me in the lab?"

Angie was breathing hard, but not nearly as bad as Jake. "I don't think that is the problem."

Jake looked at her. "What do you mean?"

"This is another world," she said. "My father told me that before he was locked in Tartarus by the Olympians, he would use the Solar Stream to go traveling to explore new worlds. Sometimes they went to worlds where they couldn't breathe and had to leave quickly. There were other worlds where the pressure was so much, they couldn't stay without getting sick or weak. We are on a different world here. Maybe it's not good for us."

After all the sci-fi movies he'd watched, Jake should have realized the same thing. This was an alien world. He was amazed he could even breathe at all. "I think you're right. I just hope it's not poisonous for us."

"If it were, wouldn't we be dead by now?" Angie said.

Jake looked at the young girl and smiled. She was small and vulnerable-looking, but she was smart. Very smart. "That's true." He looked back toward the horizon and the yellow dawn. It hadn't changed much.

"Sunrise is really slow here," he commented. "This must be a huge planet. The gravity could be different. But even if it is difficult, we have to keep moving."

Jake started to jog again. He had no idea where, just away from that building of horrors. But with each step, his heart was pounding violently in his chest. Finally he had to slow to a walk.

There was a film of sweat on Angie's brow. She was feeling the pressure. "How long have you been here?" Jake asked.

As they walked, Angie told him about meeting Astraea, Zephyr, and Darek on Titus and the big prison break. Then how they'd traveled to Earth in the middle of the fight with the Mimics, and finally how they'd made it to Xanadu with the snakes but were attacked there as well.

"You were taken just after me," Jake mused. "Have they given you any food, like ambrosia or nectar?"

Angie shook her head. "Just this strange fruit."

"Me too," Jake agreed. He didn't say more but knew that Angie would need ambrosia or nectar soon if she was going to stay strong.

They pressed on, looking for somewhere to hide. As they walked, Jake noticed that everything about the Mimic world was immaculate. There wasn't a trace of trash or graffiti to be seen anywhere. The one thing he did notice, though, was that there were planter boxes containing rock-hard, dried soil. But no flowers or plants remained.

There were no vehicles on the road, none parked

along the pavement. But if there were no vehicles, why did the Mimics need roads?

"This really looks like Earth," he commented, turning around and looking at all the buildings. "But how is that possible? It just doesn't make any sense. Had the Mimics been visiting Earth before they visited Titus, so they copied our architecture?"

"I don't know," Angie said softly.

Reaching another corner, to their left they saw an open square. A fountain sat in the middle of the area. There was a statue made of metal at the top of the fountain.

Jake felt pressure to keep moving, but something about the fountain drew him closer. "Come on," he said to Angie. "I need to see something."

As they approached the fountain, the statue became clearer. Jake gasped. The figure wasn't a Mimic. It looked like a human or a Titan. There were two legs and a body with two arms reaching skyward. There was a large head. As they walked around it, the only difference they saw was on the face of the statue. It had three eyes in a line across the forehead, and the nose was much flatter.

Jake looked at Angie. "That definitely isn't a Mimic."

"What do you think it is?" Angie asked.

"I don't know." Jake looked around again. "But for as much as I know about the Mimics, this place doesn't look right for them. It's too pretty. Yes, the Mimics are clean freaks, but they don't seem to appreciate beauty. I mean, look around, there are planters with no plants. There's no water running in this fountain, and there are roads, but no cars or trucks or anything."

"The Mimics didn't originate here," Angie said softly.

Jake looked at her in surprise. Then he nodded. "I bet you're right. But if it's not their world, whose is it?"

Angie pointed to the statue. "It was theirs. The Mimics probably stole it, just like they're stealing Titus."

"Maybe," Jake said softly. "We'd better keep moving."

"Where?"

"Good question," Jake responded. "I saw out the window that there were some woods just past the houses down there. From what I could see, the area looked bigger than a park. Maybe we can hide in there."

"I don't care where we go," Angie said. "Just as long as it's far away from the Mimics."

"Me too!" Jake agreed.

They left the square and headed toward the canal. The cobbled walkway was made up of colorful stones. Lined up along each side of the water were beautiful, ornate homes. The doors on the houses were bigger than on Earth or on Titus. Whoever the people were, they were bigger than humans. The houses all had large windows, but all the curtains in them were drawn.

Jake, Angie, and the snakes approached the edge of the canal and peered into the water. It was crystal clear and teeming with shoals of tiny fish and other water creatures.

"It's so quiet here," Angie mused. "There are no birds singing. I can't even hear insects."

"Maybe the Mimics have eaten them all," Jake said darkly. "We've seen what they eat. It's disgusting. Just dry, flattened animals."

"They haven't taken all the fish yet," Angie commented.

"They probably don't want to get wet. Maybe they melt in water too. . . ." Jake said it, but his own casual comment brought back a memory he'd suppressed. When he'd been taken from Earth, it had been snowing out. He'd been in such a panic as the Mimics had dragged him away from his father's plant that he'd forgotten how they'd complained that the snow was hurting them. Snow. Snow was water. Could it be true? Were Mimics sensitive to water as well?

"Angie, does it rain on Titus?"

She looked at him and frowned. "Yes, I don't think we could live without it."

"So have you ever seen any Mimics, or people you thought were Mimics, out in the rain?"

Angie stopped. "I—I don't know. It rained during the day when Astraea, Zephyr, and Darek came back to Titus. My parents wouldn't go out, even though they'd promised to walk me to school and loved rain. That's when I started to wonder if something was wrong. Then when Darek was talking to other students about the Mimics, I got scared and went with him to meet Astraea and Zephyr."

"So your parents are missing? Do you have any brothers or sisters?"

Angie looked like she might cry again. "It's just me and my parents. I need to find them."

"We will," Jake promised. He looked again at the empty planters and dry fountain and mused, "So, Mimics don't like water. . . ."

*"How can that be?"* Nesso said. *"The Mimicsss are mossstly water. They are nothing but a puddle after we've bitten them."*

"A puddle of what?" Jake asked the snake. "They appear to be gelatinous and filled with water, but it can't be water. It's too dangerous for us to touch." They started walking again. "But if they can't stand water, why would they live near a canal?"

"Maybe they don't live in these houses?" Angie said.

"There's only one way to find out, and I don't want to do it," Jake said. "Let's just keep moving."

Jake checked the sky every few minutes. The light was getting brighter, so the sun did move, but it was slow. He just hoped they had enough time to find somewhere to hide.

Feeling the pressure of time, he forced himself to jog again. But he could only sustain it for a short time before the effort became too great.

After a while, the canal swerved to the right. As they continued along it, Jake looked up and cried aloud, "Thank you!"

"What is it?" Angie said fearfully. "What are you seeing?"

He pointed. "Look, it's a marina."

Angie followed Jake's finger. "I can't see it. All I see are boats."

Jake looked at her and laughed. "That's what I mean. A marina is a place for boats. Maybe we can hide there. If Mimics don't like water, we'll be safe."

For the first time since he'd met her, Angie's face lit up. "Can we?"

He looked at her and grinned. "I'll race you there!"

It wasn't much of a race. After a few steps, Jake was too tired to continue. Angie slowed to allow him to catch up. She put the wounded snakes in her right hand and caught him by the arm. "I'll help you."

Jake didn't fight her help. He knew that Titans were much stronger than humans. But it seemed their strength also included moving in different gravities.

*"Jake, hurry,"* Nesso hissed at his neck. *"I can sssmell Mimicsss."*

Nesso's warning put more speed in Jake's walk. Soon they were approaching the marina. As they got nearer, he could see that most of the boats were in a terrible state of decay. Those with wooden hulls were not much more than rotting shells. But there were two moored further out in the water that had hulls made of something else. Not wood, not metal. He didn't know if this world had plastic or fiberglass, but whatever it was, two boats still looked seaworthy.

"Over there," Jake said. "If we can get to that one, we might be safe."

"I can swim," Angie said.

"So can I," Jake said. "But Tryn warned me that if you're on a world you don't know, you have to be very careful. There might be people eaters in this water. Or the water itself could be poisonous."

"So, what do we do?" Angie asked.

Jake frowned and looked at the rotting boats against the pier. "How are you at climbing?"

"All right. Why?"

Jake checked the sky again. It was definitely getting lighter, and if Nesso was right, the Mimics were starting to move. "Because I think if we climb over these two rotting boats, we might just reach that one further out. Follow me."

Jake started first. He approached the edge of the water and looked at the rotted hull of the first boat. At any other time in his life, he would never have attempted this. But these were dangerous times and he had no choice. Stepping out onto the deck of the rotting boat, he pressed his foot down lightly. The wood creaked, but it held.

He looked back at Angie and gave her a reassuring grin. "We can do this."

When he put his second foot on the board, the wreck listed to the side but stayed afloat. He started to move. Little by little, he inched around the rotted deck of the ship. When he reached the other side, the board he was on gave way.

Jake tried to right himself, but the boat started to rock and sway. Soon he heard cracking, and he looked down just as the board broke. With nowhere else to go, Jake fell into the water.

# 4

ASTRAEA, ZEPHYR, TRYN, AND HIS SISTER made it out of the temple. As always, the air around them was sweet and filled with birdsong. It revealed none of the horrors happening now within the temple and out.

"Astraea, get on," Zephyr called.

While Astraea climbed up onto Zephyr's back, Tryn laid down his skateboard and invited his sister on. "Hold on tight. Let's see what's happening at the orchard."

Zephyr looked back up at Astraea. "Did you know there was a nectar orchard here?"

Astraea shrugged. "No, but it makes sense since so many Olympians live here all the time."

"True," Zephyr agreed. She opened her wings and began a trot that turned into a gallop. Leaping gracefully into the air, she started to fly.

Astraea looked over at Tryn and Triana beside them. It didn't seem right that Jake wasn't there. He should have been.

Astraea was about to ask Tryn to have the skateboard lead them to the orchard, but the sudden loud booming of thunderbolts led the way.

"That's Jupiter!" Astraea cried. "Zeph, follow those sounds."

They followed the intense booming as Jupiter used his best powers against the Mimics. Flying over the top of the temple itself and farther ahead, Astraea saw very familiar flowers growing on extra-large trees.

"Look how big they are!" Zephyr called. "They've got to be at least double the size of the nectar trees on Titus."

"It's the rich Xanadu soil; everything grows well here," Tryn said. "Even plants from our world."

As Astraea looked around for Jupiter, she saw a tree fall. Then a second one and then a third, in the middle of the orchard. Flying closer, they saw Jupiter surrounded by Shadow Titans. He was summoning his lightning and thunderbolts and firing them at the Shadows as they focused on destroying the trees. On contact, the Shadow Titans exploded.

"His powers are working!" Astraea cheered. "Jupiter is destroying Mimic Shadow Titans!"

"Yes, but look how many Shadows are going after him," Tryn cried.

As they flew over the battle, the fighting became more intense and violent. While Jupiter fired at the Shadows in front of him, others attacked from behind and he was knocked to the ground.

"Jupiter's in trouble!" Tryn cried. "We have to help him!"

"No! We will go," Pegasus whinnied as he swooped down from above. "Zephyr, Tryn, stay up here where it is safe. Use your weapons against the Mimics, but do not go down there!"

Minerva was seated on the stallion's back. They landed in the large group of Shadow Titans attacking Jupiter. While Minerva slid off his back and used her sword, Pegasus started to buck and kick the ferocious fighters to pieces.

"Wow, look at him go," Zephyr said. "He's good."

"So are you," Astraea said. Within minutes, Pegasus, Minerva, and Jupiter had managed to destroy most of the Shadows attacking them. But the orchard was filled with hundreds more, as well as the Mimics controlling them.

The most powerful Olympians and Titans were able to gain some wins against the invaders, but the sheer number of Shadow Titans and Mimics was making progress difficult.

Tryn looked back at his sister. "Triana, turn around on the board and sit down. I don't want you falling off while we fight. We must go for the Mimics and get their controllers. It's the only way to defeat them."

Triana did as Tryn asked and sat down on the back of the board so she could fire her slingshot without needing to hold on to her brother.

Astraea was using her own slingshot when she saw Cupid soaring across the sky above the battle. He was dipping down close to the fight, then back up before the Mimics' tendrils could reach him.

"I wish my wings were bigger," she sighed. "I could be doing that too."

"You're fine right where you are," Zephyr said.

As they flew over the battle, shooting all the Mimics they could hit, Astraea thought she would have been prepared for this. But she wasn't. The orchard was a gruesome battleground. Titans and Olympians were fighting side by side. Centaurs, satyrs, and other beings of all shapes and sizes. Her eyes also landed on a group of silver Rheans. They were wielding swords and using their strength against the Shadow Titans. The Rheans were morally opposed to violence, but since the Shadows weren't alive, they were able to fight them, leaving the Mimics to be fought by the Titans and Olympians.

When a Mimic went down, a fighter ran forward, pulled the Shadow Titan controller from the goo, and turned the invaders' Shadows against them.

Although many Mimics were being defeated, a great number of defenders were also falling beneath their tendrils. As Astraea watched, Hercules was felled by two tendrils from the same Mimic. Astraea hoped he and the others were only stunned, but based on the brutality she was witnessing, she couldn't be certain.

"It's a slaughter down there," Zephyr cried.

"There are just too many—we have to take out the Mimics to stop the Shadows! Stay up high, Zeph. I don't what you hit by a tendril."

"Well, it's not on my list of things to do today, so yes, I'm staying *way* up high."

Astraea focused on one Mimic at a time as she drew back the slingshot and fired. Each pebble she shot passed through a Mimic, and they started to melt. But there was no time to celebrate—there were too many others down there.

It seemed to take the better part of the afternoon to finally get on top of all the Mimics and Shadow Titans trying to destroy the orchard. More kept coming through the Solar Stream, but soon the Titans had an army of Shadows on their side that were able to drive back the invaders and defend the nectar trees.

By the time the sun had crossed the sky and was starting to descend, the remaining Mimics had been reduced to puddles, and their Shadow Titans were being taken by the defenders. There were no cheers, no celebrations. The exhausted fighters simply put away their weapons and carried the fallen away from the orchard, back to the temple.

Guards were posted to keep watch on the trees, with a full complement of Shadow Titans ready to defend against further attacks. Everyone knew it wasn't the best fix and that there would be more battles. The Mimics didn't seem to care if they were killed. They fought down to the last, every time.

When Zephyr landed and walked with the others, Astraea sighted her mother waiting to greet the returning fighters. She had been badly hurt on Earth when she'd been struck by a police car—it was only getting her to Arious that had saved her life.

"Mom!" Astraea slid off Zephyr's back and ran to her mother. Throwing her arms around Aurora, Astraea never wanted to let her go. "I'm so glad you're all right!"

"I am fine," Aurora said softly into Astraea's hair. "I saw you and Zephyr out there. You were so brave." She released Astraea and put her arms around Zephyr's neck. "I couldn't be prouder of the both of you."

"We just did what we could," Zephyr said.

"Which was more than I could have ever dreamed," Pegasus said, clopping up to them. Minerva was no longer with him. "You flew very skillfully, Zephyr; I too am proud of you."

Astraea watched Zephyr shuffle on her hooves. Though her best friend would never admit it, she was flattered by Pegasus's compliment.

When Tryn and Triana arrived, Aurora embraced them too. "You were all so brave."

Astraea noted that the haunted expression was back on Tryn's face. He'd done what was necessary to protect the orchard. But it was taking a terrible toll on him. Triana appeared to be dealing with the battle much better.

Astraea stepped closer to Tryn and whispered, "I know how you are feeling, but the Mimics aren't giving us any choice. We have to fight to defend our worlds, or they will destroy us."

He smiled at her, but it was still shadowed. "I just never thought I would ever see war. It is more terrible than I imagined. So many were hurt and killed."

Astraea nodded. "I know. I can hardly remember what my life was like before the Mimics."

"That is why we try our best to avoid conflict," Pegasus said. "I have seen far too many battles in my life. But this fight is not over yet. I fear the worst is yet to come. . . ."

Astraea knew what Pegasus meant. They would soon leave to go to the Mimic world to try to rescue everyone that the Mimics had taken. But with the Mimics attacking Xanadu so often, they hadn't been able to go.

They walked back to the temple to find Jupiter and Juno calling everyone forward. Jupiter's fight with the Shadows had left him with a deep wound on his arm and face. Juno was nursing a fair few wounds of her own.

Tryn's parents were also at the gathering. Astraea noted that Tryn's mother had the same haunted expression as Tryn. When she embraced her children, silver tears trickled down her cheeks.

It was then that Astraea noticed how many Rhean fighters there had been. Granted, they'd mainly fought the Shadow Titans, but they had fought, which went against everything they believed.

Cylus clopped up to Astraea with Darek, Render, and more of his herd just behind him. Astraea was stunned when Cylus put his arm around her shoulders. "Saw you and Zephyr in the sky shooting those goo-filled monsters. Well done."

"Uh, thanks, Cylus. We just did what we could."

"Shooting from the sky is definitely the best way to get them," Render said. "It makes me want to fly even more. I could have taken out so many that way."

Cylus turned quickly to him and looked like he was going to say something curt, but then nodded. "Me too, I guess. It's the safest way." He looked back at his herd. "All of you fought well on the ground. You melted loads of those squishy liquid bags."

Astraea realized that Cylus had been a lot nicer lately and his change of attitude was working. More people spoke to him and included him in their conversations and plans. At one point, his mother came up to her and said she was grateful for the change of demeanor she'd started to see in her son and hoped it would continue.

Astraea did too.

"But," Cylus continued softly, "we've got to get to the Mimic home world soon if we want to save Jake and the others."

"I was thinking the same thing," Astraea said.

Further conversation was cut off as Jupiter climbed painfully onto a quickly erected platform. Astraea noticed a tiny dot of light beside him and recognized it as Arious Minor, the mobile version of the supercomputer.

Jupiter raised his hands to gain everyone's attention.

"My friends and family, this has been a very difficult day with many losses. But we managed to defend our precious nectar orchard. The Mimic attacks are happening more frequently now and are much bolder. I have discussed this with Arious, who has had experience with these creatures for millennia. She fears the time of a great spawning is upon us. She says the Mimics see us as a threat, and as such, they are increasing their attacks to keep us occupied while the Mimic nation spreads."

"How can we stop them?" called Venus. She was standing beside her son, Cupid. "There are too many and we too few."

Jupiter lowered his head. "It is doubtful we can stop them. But perhaps we can slow them down. Right now, we are a divided people. We have our fighters here with the snakes and weapons that do work, but there are even more on Titus whom we could use and provision.

"Those of us that can still fight will return to Titus tomorrow. The time has come for us to reclaim our world."

Astraea had heard Jupiter talking about only saving Titus before, when he and Pegasus had been arguing. She believed Jupiter was wrong. They should have been looking to take on the Mimics on their home world. Perhaps even stopping the queen from spawning. Going to Titus would only delay the inevitable invasion.

Astraea was about to raise her arm and speak, when Pegasus put his muzzle on her shoulder lightly. "Say nothing, Astraea. Jupiter's mind is set. He will follow his plan; we have our own."

Without looking back at the stallion, Astraea nodded. "It's time, isn't it?"

Pegasus said nothing as Jupiter continued speaking about the return journey. When he finished, he stepped down. There was agreement with the plan, but gone was the normal enthusiasm for one of his speeches. Everyone knew deep in their hearts that they were fighting a losing battle.

Pegasus whispered to Astraea, "Yes, Astraea, it is time."

# 5

JAKE BROKE THE SURFACE OF THE WATER
and started to cough.

"Are you all right?" Angie called.

"Yeah, I'm fine." Jake cleared his throat. The water
was warm and sweet on his lips. "Well, at least it's not
acid," he said. He swam around the second wreck
and over to the boat with the intact hull.

His arms felt heavy as he reached for the side and
hauled himself aboard. When he was lying across the
deck of the boat, he looked back to Angie.

"Try coming over. I don't want you in the water if
you don't have to be."

Angie nodded. She looked at the route Jake had

taken and started to follow. Halfway there, she reached down and broke a large plank off the side of the rotted hull, then walked back the way she'd come.

"What are you doing?" Jake asked.

"I'm making a ramp for the snakes."

Jake realized that was why she was a snake charmer. She was even more considerate of the snakes than he was. He hadn't thought how they were going to get over.

Before long, all the snakes were sliding across the board and onto the first wreck. When they were safe, Angie lifted the board and carried it carefully to the other side to reach the second boat. She lightly hopped over the area that had given way under Jake's weight and made it to the second wreck. As the snakes followed, Jake called, "Angie, hurry up. It's getting dangerously light out."

"I am," she said. After laying down the board for the snakes to cross onto the intact boat, Angie leaped gracefully into the air and landed on the deck beside Jake.

"That—was—cool," Jake said. "Wish I could do that."

Angie grinned at the compliment. "Thank you."

Together they made their way toward the back of the boat.

*"Hurry, Jake,"* Nesso called. *"The sssmell of Mimicsss isss getting much ssstronger. They are near."*

Jake didn't need to be told twice to move. "Nesso says the Mimics are around us. We have to hurry."

Angie nodded and moved with an ease and grace that Jake envied. She made it to the back of the boat before him. "There's a hatchway here."

"Can you open it?" he asked.

Angie reached for a handle on the hatch. It was stiff, but with a bit of prying, she got it open. After peering down, she looked at Jake and nodded. "There's no water in there, and it looks comfortable and big enough for all of us."

"Everyone, down into the boat," Jake called.

The snakes slithered forward and slid down into the cavity below the deck. Angie followed them. Jake stayed on deck a moment longer to ensure they left no clues of their hiding place. He looked around and didn't see any Mimics either. Hoping they were safe, he climbed down the steps and closed the hatch, but left it open a tiny slit to allow the light in when the sun came up.

It was pitch-black belowdecks. "I can't see a thing," he said softly. "Can you?"

"Yes," Angie answered. "Keep walking straight; all the snakes are here with me."

Jake followed Angie's instructions until she told him he could sit. He hesitantly sat down and was surprised to find the seat cushioned.

"What's it like in here?" he whispered.

"It's lovely," Angie said. "Like a little house. We're in the kitchen area. There are chairs and a table. We're on a bench near the table. Across from us I can see some cupboards too. There's even a small sink. Farther back are beds with covers. The fabric looks a bit rotten, but otherwise, it's all very comfortable."

The way Angie described it was like the canal boats they'd seen in Bruges. His family had even had lunch on one that cruised around.

"I wonder if the engines still work," Jake said.

"I don't know," Angie said. "I can't see anything mechanical in here."

"I can't see anything at all!" Jake said. "You said there were beds?"

"Yes, at the back."

Jake started to yawn. "I don't know about you, but I am so tired right now, I can hardly keep my eyes open."

"Me too," Angie agreed. "I couldn't sleep in that cage. Do you want me to lead you to the beds?"

Jake held on to Angie's arm as she led him to the sleeping area. The boat was much longer than Jake had realized, and the ceiling was too high for him to reach.

"I really should keep watch," Jake said as he sat down on the edge of the bed. The cushion beneath him was soft, and even though the rotted fabric tore apart in his hands, it didn't smell musty at all. "But I'm too tired."

"Me too," Angie said.

Jake could hear her moving around but couldn't see her. He also heard the soft slithering sounds of the snakes following her farther back.

*"We will keep watch,"* Nesso said softly. *"You and Angie sssleep. If anyone comesss, we will wake you."*

Jake repeated Nesso's message to Angie. But he doubted she heard, as it sounded like she was already asleep. Lying down on the soft bunk, it wasn't long before he joined her.

* * *

Jake awoke with a sudden fright and couldn't see anything even though his eyes were open. "Nesso?" he called into the darkness.

*"I am here,"* Nesso responded. *"Lower your voiccce. Mimicsss are not far away."*

Everything rushed back to him. He was on the Mimic world, hidden in a boat with a Titan he called Angie. Snakes were with them. He raised his head and looked toward the hatch. A bright slit of sunlight was pouring down through the half-closed hatch and illuminating the snakes on the steps leading up.

"Are we safe?" he asked softly.

*"Yesss,"* Nesso said. *"There are Mimicsss on the water'sss edge, but we don't think they know we are here. Their voicccesss are normal and come and go. We have heard no ssshouting or alarmsss. But we mussst be careful. If they can't sssee well, they might have excccellent hearing."*

"How long have I been asleep?" Jake whispered.

*"A very long time. You are right. The sssun doesss move ssslowly here. Much ssslower than on my world."*

"Is Angie still asleep?"

69

"Yesss. Mossst of the othersss are with her. Ssshe hasss bad dreamsss, jussst like you. When ssshe criesss out, we wake her."

Jake's dream before waking had been a nightmare, but it was nothing compared to what his reality was now. "Let her sleep."

Part of him wanted to go forward to peek out the hatch, but caution told him not to. He didn't even want to move on the bed in case it rocked the boat. But lying there knowing that somewhere on this world other Titans were being held and maybe tortured left him wanting to do something. Anything. But all he could do was lie still and wait for the darkness.

Then what? What was he going to do? Yes, they'd found a place to hide. But they needed food. They couldn't last forever. They probably had water, because he'd swallowed mouthfuls when he'd fallen off the wreck beside this boat, and he was still feeling all right.

Food was now the big worry. Even more so for Angie. She needed ambrosia and nectar, and he was sure the Mimics wouldn't have any here.

"Ssshe isss awake," Nesso said softly.

Moments later, Jake heard soft movement. He sat up and felt Angie sit beside him. She didn't say a word. She just took his hand and settled down to wait for the sun to set.

Jake and Angie spent the better part of the long day watching the crack of sunlight from the hatch. It took ages for the spear of light to creep across the steps and finally vanish into the shadows. It took even longer for it to fade into complete darkness.

"Angie?" Jake asked. "Can you really see in this darkness?"

"Yes, why?"

"Because we need snake venom. Is there anything here in the boat that might work as a container to hold some? Then maybe we can find some sticks or something to use to defend ourselves."

"Let me look."

Just as she started to get up, Jake warned, "Move very slowly and don't rock the boat, just in case someone is out there."

"I'll be careful."

Jake felt frustrated and helpless in equal measures as Angie moved confidently around the boat. He heard her going through cupboards and pulling open drawers. Finally she returned to him. "I have a strange-looking container. It's not glass, but it has a tight cover."

Jake reached out and felt the container. It was very much like the ones his mother had at home for sealing leftovers in. "This is perfect," he said softly. "Now we just have to ask the snakes to . . ." Before he could finish, he felt snakes gathering at his feet, and some were climbing up his jeans.

Jake told Angie how they milked the snakes. Before long, they had filled half the container. When it was sealed, he said thank you to the snakes.

"Now what?" Angie asked.

Jake sighed. "Now we have to go back out." He focused on the snakes around his neck and carefully removed them and laid them down on the bunk. "Nesso, I can't see you. Would you climb back onto my hands? You other guys, stay here and relax."

He felt Nesso slip back into his hands. Jake brought her back to his neck, and she settled in her proper place.

"Nesso, would you ask the snakes keeping watch if they can see anyone outside the boat?"

Nesso hissed.

"They are moving," Angie said softly. "One has just gone outside."

Jake only realized he was holding his breath when he started to get dizzy. He let it out softly.

"He's back," Angie said.

*"Jake, there isss no one outssside. He did sssee a Mimic with a torch, but they were far away."*

Jake repeated the message to Angie. "They are looking for us."

"Maybe we should just stay here."

Jake turned to her, and even though he couldn't see her, he knew she could see him. "We can't. At least not at night. We need food for us and the snakes. And we should try to find the Titans taken from Titus and Xanadu. We might even find your folks."

"I know," Angie said softly. "But I'm just . . ."

Jake squeezed her hand. "I'm scared too. Let's give it to the count of two hundred, and then we can go look."

Jake and Angie counted very softly and slowly. When they reached two hundred, Jake squeezed Angie's hand again. "Would you help me find the way to the hatch? I really can't see anything."

Angie rose and, keeping hold of Jake's hand, led him toward the stairs going up. "Stay here," she said. "Let me look."

"Be extra, *extra* careful," Jake warned.

Angie moved past him and climbed the stairs. He heard her drawing back the hatch. His heart was racing in his chest as he waited to hear.

Moments later, Angie returned. "We're alone. I don't even see torches."

"Fantastic." Jake turned into the darkness and called softly to the snakes. "You all may want to come with us, but it's too dangerous. Please stay here. We are going out to get you some food. I promise we will come back."

There was hissing coming from all around.

*"They are not pleasssed with thisss arrangement,"* Nesso said.

"Neither am I," Jake said. "But we need to move around, and I don't want to be worried about you guys. Please do as I ask and stay."

*"They will ssstay,"* Nesso said. *"They are not happy, but they will."*

Jake stored the jar of venom in his waistband and

climbed the stairs. The sun was completely down and there was no moon. He couldn't see a thing.

"I think I'm going to swim this time," he said softly.

"But I thought you said it wasn't safe."

"I was worried it wasn't safe, but considering I fell in and swallowed some of the water, at least it's not poisonous. I don't know about monsters, but I just can't see anything. It'll be more dangerous for me to try to cross over those wrecks."

"I'll swim with you," Angie said.

"Good," Jake said softly. "Because you are going to have to be my eyes until I get used to the dark—if I get used to it."

"I never knew humans couldn't see well," Angie said.

Jake knew it wasn't meant as an insult. But it sure felt like one. "Yeah, I know. We're much weaker than you guys."

"But you're a lot braver," Angie said.

Jake smiled as he lowered himself to the deck and slipped quietly into the water. Angie entered beside him.

"Hold on to my back," she suggested. "I'll swim." Angie led his hands to her shoulders and moved confidently through the water.

"I love the taste of this water," she said softly. "It reminds me of nectar."

"It does, doesn't it," Jake agreed. "I wonder if it will work like nectar."

"I guess we'll see," Angie said.

When they reached the bank of the canal, Angie pulled herself out of the water and then helped Jake out.

"Where do we go?" Angie asked.

Jake looked around, hoping his eyes would adjust. They didn't. He was essentially blind.

"Can you see the woods we saw this morning?"

Angie looked around. "Yes, they're that way."

"Angie, I still can't see anything. It's just a black wall in front of me. Can you lead me and stop me from walking into something or tripping?"

"Of course," Angie said. She took Jake by the hand. "It's this way."

# 6

JAKE HELD ON TO ANGIE AS THEY WALKED in the darkness. None of the buildings around them had lights on, and there were no streetlights. Peering up, he gasped. "Look, there aren't any stars."

"How can there be no stars?" Angie asked.

"I don't know," Jake said. "But stars are just suns. So maybe this planet is all alone in this part of space and there are no neighboring solar systems."

"I don't understand how that is possible," Angie said.

"I haven't a clue," Jake said.

Each hesitant step gave him a deeper appreciation for blind people who bravely found ways to move around in the sighted world. It made him grateful that his problem was only a lack of light, and not permanent.

"How much farther?" he asked softly.

"Not far," Angie whispered.

*"The treesss are jussst ahead of usss,"* Nesso answered.

"Can you see too?" he asked the snake.

*"Yesss,"* Nesso answered. *"Ussse your other sssenss-sesss. Feel the ground beneath you. Lisssten to your ssstepsss. You can do thisss."*

Jake took Nesso's advice and closed his eyes. He felt the even ground beneath his feet and heard nothing but their soft tread. There were no insects or even a breeze to disturb the overwhelming silence.

But a while later, he felt a subtle change. The faint sound of what could be crickets started. Next there was a different smell in the air. Like pine trees.

"We're getting close, aren't we?" he said softly.

"Yes," Angie said. "We're about to leave the pavement. It goes to the right, but straight ahead of us are trees. What are you hoping to find in there?"

"I'm not sure," Jake said. "But we need food, and what they gave us was fruit. It had to grow somewhere."

"I hope you are right," Nesso said. "The otherss haven't been fed at all."

"I hope I'm right too," Jake agreed.

"Get ready to step down," Angie warned.

Jake stopped and hesitantly reached out with his foot. He felt the pavement dip down, and then the ground became softer.

"That'sss it, you're doing fine," Nesso coaxed. "Jussst keep moving."

This was the most surreal experience of Jake's life as he held on to Angie and walked into what could be woods or a forest on an alien world. He felt soft bristles of the pine needles brush against him.

But with each step, he started to hear more sounds. There was wildlife around them. He'd never been happier to hear scampering and buzzing than he was right now. He didn't let his mind linger on the fact that there could be very big, very dangerous animals lurking inside the woods as well.

"I think I see something," Angie said.

"You're seeing everything," Jake answered.

"No, I mean torches or something. Farther ahead."

Jake opened his eyes and again saw a wall of

blackness. But this time, his eyes did adjust. Before long he saw the hint of a glow filtering through the trees. "Can you see movement? Are there Mimics?"

"Nothing is moving around us," Angie said.

Jake was still holding on to her arm. "Take us there, but we have to be very quiet. Let's circle around it so we can see what's happening."

"It's this way," Angie said softly.

They moved as quietly as they could toward the glow. The closer they got, the more Jake was able to see. When they were nearer the lights, they ducked down and started to search the area. Inching closer, Angie gasped, and Jake had to hold in his own reaction.

"Sssh . . . ," Jake hushed softly. He glanced at Angie, and in the glow of the light, he could see the fear in her eyes. He felt the same way. Ahead of them were glowing lights high on poles suspended over what looked like a massive prison yard. It had to be at least the size of a football field, and it was filled with people.

Some were walking around, but their movements were sluggish. Others were sitting on the ground against the tall bars. They were all filthy, and their clothes were tattered and torn. Near the closest side of the yard was a centaur. He was seated on the ground, leaning against the bars. The skin on his bare upper torso was covered in dirt, and he was so thin, all the bones in his body stuck out.

"That's Chiron!" Angie gasped. "And look, over there, that's Diana and Apollo; they are Jupiter's twins." She turned to Jake. "These are the missing Olympians and Titans. Jake, my parents could be in there!"

"It's not just them," Jake replied softly. "Look, that tall one with three eyes—it looks just like the statue."

"What are they doing here?" Angie asked.

"I don't know," Jake said. "But we have to find out. Let's walk around but stay in the dark in case there are Mimics."

The lights were bright and enabled Jake to see as they moved deeper into the trees. As they circled around the prison yard, they found it was even bigger than they'd expected. There were other creatures in there that he couldn't identify—all mixed together. They all looked too sick and exhausted to do anything other than sit.

Outside the yard and attached to it by one wall was a cabin-like building. It was made of rough timber and appeared much bigger than the enclosure. There were no windows on the side, so they couldn't see what was in there. But as they neared it, they could smell it.

"What is that stink?" Angie asked.

"That's the smell of Mimic food," Jake said. "They eat these dried squished animals." He looked at the yard and then back to the cabin. "I hope they are making those people prepare the food . . ."

"That's not a nice thing to say," Angie said.

"You didn't let me finish. I was going to say, I hope they are making those people prepare the food and the people are not the food itself."

Angie gasped. "You don't think the Mimics are eating them?"

"I don't know what they're doing with these people. All I know is, we have to find out."

Angie started to move. "I'll go ask."

Jake caught her arm and hauled her back. "Don't!" He pointed up to the tall light posts. "Do you see that black box beneath the light? Back on Earth something like that could hold a security camera. If it does, and if we get too close, the Mimics might see us."

There was an expression of incomprehension on Angie's face, and Jake remembered she was from a world without electricity. "Cameras are machines that can watch us and then show the images to the Mimics. I don't know if those are cameras, but that town back there looks a lot like an Earth town. If the buildings have electricity, I bet the Mimics have cameras, too."

"What do we do?" Angie asked.

Jake shook his head. "I don't know yet. Just let me think."

He looked around the area. Up against the cabin was a line of short bushes. It wasn't great cover, but it was better than nothing.

"Let's try to reach those bushes; then we can call to the prisoners and hope they don't attract Mimics. Follow me."

Jake and Angie wove through the trees surrounding the prison yard and approached the dark end of the building. Jake lowered himself to his hands and knees and pulled Angie down beside him. "Now, stay close to me. We're going up against that building to stay hidden. When I duck down, you duck down too. Okay?"

Her weak "Yes" told him that she was terrified. "Would you rather stay here and wait for me?"

"No," Angie said quickly. "I'm staying with you."

He gave her hand a quick squeeze. "I'd prefer you with me too. Just promise me you'll be quiet, whatever you see or hear. Is that a deal?"

"Deal," Angie said.

*"Jake, be careful,"* Nesso warned. *"The sssmell of Mimicsss isss overwhelming. I can't tell if they are here now or if it isss from earlier."*

"Thanks for the warning. Tell me if you see or hear anything."

*"I will,"* Nesso finished.

Jake tried to sound brave and confident. But he was neither. He was terrified. But he had no choice. They needed to reach the prisoners to learn as much as they could. After giving Angie a reassuring thumbs-up, he started to crawl.

They made it to the side of the building. The

stink from inside was coming right through the boards. It probably was a good thing that he hadn't eaten. Anything in his stomach would surely have come back up.

Pressing on, they approached the bushes. Jake squeezed himself between them and the wall and looked up to the lamppost. The black box hadn't moved. But would it move? This was alien technology. There was no way to know what it could do.

No more than five feet away were the prison bars. A person was leaning against the bars. Another was lying beside them. Jake could see their backs, but no more. They could have been men or women; there was no way to tell. They weren't speaking or even moving. As Jake crawled as close as he dared, he wondered what he should say. The last thing he wanted was for the people to turn around.

Finally he softly called, "Hey, you against the bars, don't turn around. . . ."

The person reacted to the voice, and their back stiffened.

"We're behind you in the bushes. Cough if you can understand me."

The person coughed.

"Cough if you are a Titan or Olympian."

Another cough followed.

"My name is Jake," he whispered. "I'm from Earth. I have Angitia from Titus with me. We've been brought here just like you, but we've managed to escape. Can you turn around without looking or acting suspicious?"

The figure coughed again, then slid down the bars to turn around. They rolled over like they were preparing to sleep. It was a boy, a bit older than Jake, with shaggy brown hair. His face was filthy, pale, and gaunt, and he looked half-starved.

Angie peered around Jake and gasped.

"Do you know him?" Jake asked.

"Yes," Angie whispered. "He's one of the heroes of Olympus. His name is Paelen."

# 7

AS EVERYONE SET ABOUT DOING THEIR assigned tasks to prepare for departure the following morning, secret messages were passed between Astraea's team and Pegasus. They agreed to meet up on the glass lake later that evening.

Until then, Astraea and Zephyr were working together to gather as many small pebbles as they could. Zephyr carried two large bags draped over either side of her neck as Astraea filled them.

"I feel like a packhorse," Zephyr complained.

"Right now, you are one," Astraea said. "And I'm glad. We're going to need these to take with us."

"Yes, about that." Zephyr lowered her voice. "I've

had a really crazy idea that I need you to talk me out of."

Astraea looked back at her best friend and grinned. "Go on. . . ."

Zephyr caught her gently by the arm. "This way. I don't want to be overheard."

They walked deeper into the trees. Zephyr looked around to ensure no one was listening. "Well, I've been thinking. And I really need you to stop me—"

"Just say it!" Astraea cried.

Zephyr inhaled deeply. "I wonder if we should go back to Zomos and get Lergo and take it to the Mimic home world so it can eat them all!" She let out the remainder of her breath. "There, now I've said it, and we can forget all about it."

Astraea wasn't sure what she'd expected of her friend, but this sure wasn't it. Considering how Lergo had nearly killed Zephyr when they were on Zomos, that would be the last place she thought Zephyr would want to go. Astraea looked down and took a few steps.

Zephyr chuckled uncomfortably. "I told you it was crazy and stupid and extremely dangerous. . . ."

"And it's brilliant!" Astraea cried. She ran back to Zephyr and kissed her on the muzzle. "Zeph, this could really work. If we could get Lergo to the Mimic home world, the Mimics would be so distracted by it, we could slip in, get the others, and then get out again." She jumped up and down excitedly. "Wait, maybe we could even get the Mimic queen!"

"No!" Zephyr cried. "Astraea, you were supposed to talk me out of this."

"Why? It's perfect!" Astraea cried. "All we have to do is figure out how to get Lergo into the Solar Stream. After that, we just let it loose." She looked around. "We have to find Tryn and tell him."

Zephyr groaned, "Why did I open my big fat mouth!"

Astraea grinned at her. "Because deep down you knew this was a good idea. It could really save all of us."

"Or get us all killed," Zephyr said.

"If we don't stop the Mimics, that's going to happen anyway." Astraea put down the pebbles in her hand. "Come on, we have to find the others."

\* \* \*

Tryn, Triana, and the centaurs brainstormed with Astraea and Zephyr for the balance of the day. They were all shocked by the idea at first, but quickly came around to the logic of it.

"We just have to find a way to lure Lergo out of the cave," Tryn said.

Cylus looked at Render and Darek and nodded. "So one of you is going to have to be wounded for Lergo to chase into the Solar Stream. Who's going to volunteer?"

The centaurs turned around and found something very interesting to look at on a tree leaf.

"Cylus, we can't hurt one of you," Astraea said. "Lergo is too fast and too dangerous. We have to find another way."

"Well," Zephyr said. "It did bite me once. Maybe I still stink?"

Cylus grinned and opened his mouth to comment, but Astraea held up a finger. "Not one word from you!"

"What . . . ?" Cylus laughed.

"We still have time," Tryn said. "I am sure we can figure something out before we leave."

They hoped to tell Pegasus before their meeting on the glass lake, but the stallion was soaring high overhead, with Minerva on his back and Cupid flying beside him, keeping an aerial patrol over the temple area and nectar orchard.

As the day faded and night arrived, the patrols changed. Pegasus and Cupid landed, and Aurora and another flying Titan took over.

Astraea looked up, watching her mother gliding gracefully in the sky. She dreamed of the day when she would be able to fly beside her. If, she thought darkly, they lived long enough for that to happen.

They ate in silence, and as people entered the temple to settle down for the evening, Astraea, Zephyr, and the others left the protection of the temple and walked into the dark trees.

They made their way to the glass lake and found Pegasus already waiting for them.

"Good evening, everyone," Pegasus said formally. "The time has come for us to move against the Mimics in their home world."

Cylus nodded, then shoved Zephyr lightly. "Go on, tell him your idea."

The stallion's ears pricked forward. "You have an idea?"

Zephyr nodded. "But it's really dangerous and kinda stupid."

"It's not stupid," Astraea said. "It's brilliant and I think we should do it." She stepped closer to Pegasus. "Zephyr suggested we go to Zomos and get the giant snake, Lergo, and take it to the Mimic world. All the snakes seem to hate the Mimics, and we saw Lergo eat three Shadow Titans without stopping. It could really help us."

"Or it could kill us," Zephyr said.

Pegasus tilted his head to the side. "You thought of that?"

"Don't look so surprised, Pegasus. I do occasionally think," Zephyr shot back.

Pegasus chuckled. "You think a great deal, and in this case, I believe it is a wonderful idea. Tell me more about Lergo."

Tryn came forward. "Well, it's many hundreds of times larger than Belis and is a predator that wounds its prey and then follows it until it dies. If we plan this right, we can get it to follow us into the Solar Stream, and then we can let it loose on the Mimic home world. While they fight it, we can find the others."

Pegasus looked at each of them. "You all agree on this course of action?"

Cylus nodded. "We're not kidding. Lergo is huge. I mean *huge*. The Shadow Titans attacked him, but they couldn't hurt him. It would be a perfect weapon. If we could just get him there."

Zephyr snorted. "How do you know Lergo is a *him*?"

"Of course Lergo's a him," Cylus said. "He's big and strong and ferocious. What else could he be?"

"That's the dumbest thing I think I've ever heard you say. I'm not a him, but I can be ferocious!" Zephyr said.

"Only in smell!" Cylus responded.

Zephyr started a retort, but Pegasus whinnied, "This is not the time for fighting among ourselves. We do need help with this mission. I agree with your plan. We just need to find the correct bait for Lergo."

"I know what we can use," Cylus said. "I'll bring it with us."

"Oh no," Astraea said. "I told you, no hurting Render or Darek or any member of your herd."

"It's not a herd member," Cylus said.

"Then what?" Zephyr asked.

"You'll see," Cylus said. "When are we going?"

They automatically turned to Pegasus.

"We cannot waste a moment. How about we meet back here just before dawn. We can slip away before the others leave for Titus." They all looked at each other and nodded.

"It is decided," Pegasus said. "We leave before dawn."

# 8

"ARE YOU PAELEN?" JAKE ASKED SOFTLY.

"Yes," Paelen answered.

"Tell me, are there any Mimics or their Shadow Titan guards here right now?"

"Mimics?" Paelen asked.

"Yes, we call them Mimics because they can change shape and mimic others."

"No," Paelen said. "There is no need for guards— we are too weak to fight. How did you get here?"

"They had Angitia and me in a laboratory. We think it was because of the snakes and how they are helping us."

"What snakes?" Paelen asked.

Jake realized that Paelen and the others in the prison yard would have been taken from Xanadu before they'd ever heard of the snakes. He explained to Paelen as quickly as he could who he was, where he came from, how he'd come to be involved with the Titans, and how he'd found out about the snakes.

"This is Nesso." He pointed up to his neck. "She and all the other snakes are precious. If they bite a Mimic, the Mimic melts. If we put their venom on anything and touch the Mimics, that works too." Jake held up the jar of venom. "This is enough to kill a lot of Mimics."

"And you have more snakes?" Paelen asked.

Jake nodded. "There were a lot here that we've rescued from the laboratory as well. And even more on Xanadu. Jupiter and the others are fighting back."

"There is no fighting against these things."

"Yes, there is," Jake insisted. "Believe me, the snake venom works. My friends Astraea, Zephyr, and Tryn told me about girls called Emily and Riza, saying they are really powerful. If we can find them and they help, then with the snake venom and everyone fighting, I think we stand a good chance of beating the Mimics."

"They were powerful. . . ." His voice dropped. "But they are dead."

"Dead? How? They're supposed to be invincible."

"It was the Mimics. They surprised us on Xanadu. The first one arrived looking like Jupiter. When Emily and Riza went to greet him, it touched them, and they collapsed. Then more Mimics came through the Solar Stream. We tried to fight, to defend ourselves, but they overwhelmed us. No weapons worked against them. They killed so many. I saw them kill Pegasus—"

"Pegasus isn't dead," Jake interrupted. "I swear, I've met him. That big purple two-headed animal, Brue, buried him to save him. When Tryn and I went to Xanadu, Brue took us to him, and we got him to Arious."

"Pegasus is alive?" Paelen cried. "What about Brue? How is she?"

Jake said, "They're both alive. At least Pegasus was the last time I saw him. He and Aurora were chasing the car that I was in with the Mimics. Then they drove through the Solar Stream and brought me here."

"Why were the Mimics in a car?"

"I told you, we were all hiding in Detroit, on Earth," Jake said. "But then the Mimics found us, and I was brought here. The others know where we are, and I'm sure they'll be coming for us. We have to be ready."

"We are too weak; I cannot stretch out anymore. I can barely move."

"What do you mean, 'stretch out'?" Jake asked. "There is room in there. You can stretch out fine."

"You do not understand," Paelen said. "When I am healthy, I can stretch out my body. I would be able to slip through these bars easily. But not now. They feed us barely enough ambrosia to keep us alive so we can be their slaves, but not enough so we can fight. . . ." He looked over to the person lying beside him and lightly patted his leg. "This is my best friend, Joel. He has not awakened in two days. He lost his temper and tried to fight the Mimics. They grabbed him and held on for a while. Me and several others tried to stop the Mimics, but we were all touched. Two died, I recovered, and now Joel will die too."

"He needs ambrosia," Angie said.

Paelen pointed to the big wooden cabin. "There

is plenty in there, where we work. But the Mimics and Shadow Titans guard it well during the day, and we are locked in the cage at night. There is also fruit that we can eat. Some of us are forced to work in the orchard during the day."

"Where's the orchard?"

"Not far," Paelen said. "I have never been but have heard there are a lot of fruit trees growing there. Yet we are only given one piece each day."

Jake looked at Angie. "We have to get them more food."

When Angie nodded, Jake looked back at the cabin. "What else is in there?"

"It is where we are forced to prepare their food. The work does not require strength, but it is more dreadful than you could imagine."

Jake considered for a moment. "All right. Angie and I are going to see if we can get in to get some ambrosia. Are there any Mimics here?"

"No. They leave us alone at night."

"Good," Jake said. "We'll be right back."

"Be careful," Paelen called as he laid his head back down.

Jake and Angie crawled back into the bushes toward the front of the cabin. They were slowly getting used to the terrible stink, and Jake wasn't as nauseous as before.

"They're killing them slowly," Angie said softly.

"They don't care if they all die," Jake said. "There are other worlds full of people they can use as slaves. But this has got to end."

When they reached the front of the building, Jake looked around for any signs of security cameras. But he didn't see any boxes. This would be a risk, but they didn't have any choice.

Keeping low, they crawled along the front. They soon reached a door. There was no lock on it, and when Jake pulled it, it opened easily. The stink struck them like a solid wall. Jake's throat reacted and he choked. Angie was the same. But neither stopped. They slipped inside.

Jake's voice was stolen from him by the stench. He tried breathing through his mouth, but then he tasted the air. It tasted even worse than it smelled. "Vile . . ." was all he could manage.

They crawled in deeper. The big room was dark,

but there was some faint light coming in from between the gaps in the wooden sides. It allowed him to see shapes, but no details.

But when Angie started to whimper, he realized that whatever she was seeing, it had to be bad. "What is it?"

"There are so many dead animals in here," she said softly. "And others that are alive but in cages."

Jake could hear his sister's voice in Angie. Molly loved animals too and hated to hear of any abuse. "Angie, I know it must be terrible. But please focus on helping the others outside. Can you see any ambrosia?"

When she didn't answer, he looked down. "Nesso, can you smell ambrosia in here?"

*"All I sssmell isss death,"* Nesso said. *"But I will try."*

With each step into the room, Angie's distress grew. She started to weep. This was the first time he was grateful that he couldn't see in the dark. He had no idea the horrors the young girl was witnessing. "I'm sorry, Angie," he said softly. "If we stop these Mimics, this will end."

Angie sniffed, and he knew his words were empty and didn't help.

*"I sssmell ambrosssia,"* Nesso hissed.

"Lead us," Jake said.

Jake and Angie followed Nesso's instructions toward the right side wall of the building.

"What can you see?" Jake asked Angie. "Can you see ambrosia or nectar?"

"There are containers, like the ones the snakes were in." Angie moved away from him and approached the containers. She lifted the lid on the first one. "It's full of ambrosia cake."

Jake followed Angie's voice and bumped into the containers. "These have ambrosia?"

"Yes." Angie reached into a container and broke off a piece of cake and handed it to him.

Jake cautiously brought the piece to his mouth and took a small bite. It was sweet and delicious. Despite the stink in the room, it made him realize he was starving. "It's good," he said. "Have some. It will make you strong."

"I can't eat in here," she said sadly. "There is too much suffering."

Jake nodded. "I understand."

He took off his T-shirt and tied knots in the sleeves

and neck and turned it into a small sack. He handed it to Angie. "Take some ambrosia from several containers and put it in here. Make sure you don't take too much from any one container, or the Mimics might notice. We have to get food to the others."

As grateful as Jake was for not seeing the horrors of the room, he wished he could see so he could help. Instead, all he could do was listen to Angie moving containers around so she could take ambrosia from all of them.

"All done," she said.

"Perfect. Now please check the area. Make sure it looks like we haven't been here."

"I'm not stupid; I did already," Angie said.

"I'm sorry," Jake apologized. "I know you're really smart. I'm being paranoid, that's all. They can't know we were here."

"I know, but I was extra careful," Angie said. "Can we leave now?"

"You bet."

As they made their way out of the room, Angie called out to the animals, "I'm sorry for what they've done to you. We'll do all we can to free you."

"We will," Jake said. "Right after we feed everyone outside and get them out of that yard."

They went down to their knees again and left the cabin. Jake was grateful to take big gulps of fresh air. The smell was all around them, but it was so much better outside. Crawling around the building, they made it back to the bushes near the prison yard. Paelen was still there, waiting.

"We have ambrosia for you," Jake called. "You're right, there's lots in there." He took several pieces out of his T-shirt for him and Angie and then pushed the rest over to Paelen.

Paelen reached his arm out and caught hold of the bag. "Thank you so much. Can you get more?"

"Sure, but we don't want to let the Mimics know we've been in there." He looked at Angie. "You saw the containers, the way they were stacked. Do you think the Mimics would miss one or two?"

Angie frowned. "Not really. There was a whole wall full. I'm sure we could take more than two."

"Good," Jake said. When he looked back at Paelen, his cheeks were packed with food. "Aren't you going to share with the others?"

"Of course," Paelen said. "But I needed to eat a lot, so I can do this. . . ." He held up his hand, and the fingers started to extend.

"Gross!" Jake said softly. "Doesn't that hurt?"

Paelen nodded. "More than you know. But if I can do this, I can slip through the bars and we can all get more ambrosia for everyone else."

"Keep eating!" Angie said. "The less I have to go back in there, the better."

For the first time, Paelen grinned. His smile was crooked and infectious. Jake liked him instantly. "What about your friend?"

Paelen grabbed a handful of ambrosia and moved slowly over to his unconscious friend. "Come on, Joel, eat." Paelen pried Joel's mouth open and placed some ambrosia inside. He pushed Joel's chin to get him to chew.

"Won't you choke him, feeding him like that?" Jake asked.

"It is a risk, but there is no nectar here. It's ambrosia or nothing. Without it, he will die." Paelen kept making Joel chew. "Swallow, Joel. You must swallow it."

Because of the angle, Jake couldn't see if Joel swallowed. But when Paelen said "Good, now do it again," Jake realized Joel had eaten.

After a few minutes, Paelen returned to the cage bars. "Thank you for that. I am feeling much better. Move back—I am coming out."

"You gonna do that stretchy thing again?" Jake asked.

When Paelen nodded, Jake and Angie crawled farther back in the bushes. They watched Paelen's body stretch and lengthen. His bones snapped and cracked as he thinned down to the size of a thick snake.

*"He looksss like one of usss,"* Nesso said.

"He sure does," Jake agreed. Then he whispered, "But he's not as pretty as you."

"I heard that," Paelen said through his distorted mouth. Soon he was slipping through the bars and crawling up to them. He returned to his normal shape.

"Okay," Jake said softly. "That was one of the grossest things I've seen a Titan do."

"I am Olympian, not Titan," Paelen said when he was back to normal. "Now let us go get more food."

Jake stood back as Paelen and Angie worked to take four containers of ambrosia and then moved the others to make it look like nothing had been disturbed. When they were finished, they were all grateful to get out of the cabin.

They dragged the ambrosia back to the side of the cage. Paelen paused, looked up to the sky, and sighed, "I do not want to go back in there."

"Would they miss you?" Jake asked. "Could you stay with us?"

Paelen shook his head. "I would never leave Joel. Not to mention all the others. Now that we have ambrosia, this will help us all grow strong again. With your help, and the help of the snakes, perhaps we can fight back."

"This will get you started." Jake handed over the jar of venom. "Hide this somewhere inside. If things get really bad, cover anything you can with it and hit the Mimics. They will melt."

"Thank you. I will take it and bury it." Paelen put the jar back inside the cage. Then he started to stretch out his body again. Very soon, he slipped through the bars and was back inside.

The containers of ambrosia were emptied as the precious food was distributed to all the prisoners.

When Paelen came back to the bars to collect more, Angie asked him, "Are my parents in there? Their names are Aeetes and Idyia. I think they were taken from Titus."

"I have not seen them," Paelen answered. "Perhaps they were in the same place as you?"

"We didn't see anyone else," Jake said.

Paelen smiled gently at Angie. "I am sure we will find them."

On Paelen's fourth trip around the cage, Jake and Angie started to notice how the prisoners were moving. Jake told Paelen to warn them not to move too much or show changes. And they were careful. But they were growing stronger.

Just before Paelen was about to set off again, they heard a soft, deep moan from Joel. Paelen crawled over to his friend. "Be calm, Joel," he warned. "Do not move too quickly. The monsters might see."

Joel moaned again and sat up slowly. Paelen knelt before him to block the camera and handed him a large piece of ambrosia. "Eat all of it; you need it."

"H-how?" Joel moaned.

"I will tell you later. But we have friends on the outside and we stole it."

Joel looked up weakly to Paelen. "But I thought you weren't a thief anymore."

Paelen grinned over at Jake. "He will recover."

"Who are you talking to?" Joel asked.

"A human from Earth called Jake and a Titan called Angitia. I will tell you everything later. Right now I need you to stay here and recover. I have more ambrosia to distribute."

"No," Joel groaned. "I'm going to help."

Paelen looked over at Jake. "There is no stopping this one. He is even more stubborn than Emily."

"Who are you calling stubborn?" Joel crawled slowly to the bars and looked at Jake and Angie. "I'm Joel."

Jake frowned as he looked at Joel. He had a silver arm. It moved like normal, and the hand and fingers moved naturally too. Jake couldn't see any joints. It looked just like Tryn's silver skin.

Joel looked down at his arm. "Vulcan made this for me when I lost my arm fighting a Gorgon. It works just as well as the original."

"What's a Gorgon?" Jake asked.

"Nasty creatures that can turn you to stone with a look. But they weren't nearly as bad as these creatures."

"They are called Mimics," Paelen explained. "They took Jake from Earth and Angitia from Titus. . . ." Paelen quickly repeated what Jake and Angie had told him and what they'd done to get the ambrosia.

"You've been out of this cage?" Joel cried. "Paelen, why did you come back?"

"He came back for you," Angie said softly. "And to help feed everyone."

"Which we must continue to do," Paelen said to Joel. "Are you strong enough to help?"

"Let's do it!" Joel said.

When the containers were empty and everyone had eaten their fill, Joel and Paelen returned to Jake and Angie.

Jake said, "Now that you've eaten, we should get you all out of that cage and find somewhere to hide."

"Not yet," a voice called from behind Joel and Paelen.

The largest centaur Jake had ever seen staggered closer and collapsed to the ground.

"Chiron," Angie called.

"I am unharmed," the centaur said softly as he dragged himself closer to the bars. "Consider this a performance for the watching eyes."

"So, you're all right?" Jake asked.

"With many thanks to you two, I am better than I have been in a long time. On behalf of all of us prisoners, I want to thank you for what you've done for us."

"No problem," Jake said. "We just got you a bit of food."

"You have done more than I could have dreamed. It is likely you have saved many lives."

"For now," Jake said.

"True," Chiron agreed. "But with your continued assistance, we will grow stronger, and then with the venom from your snakes, we all stand a chance of escaping this cage and perhaps finding somewhere safe where we can take on these monsters."

"Mimics," Paelen said. "They are calling them Mimics."

"Mimics," Chiron repeated. "So, Jupiter knows where we are? What has happened? Is he coming for us?"

Jake nodded. "Jupiter knows we're all here. But

Xanadu wasn't the only place the Mimics attacked. They've taken Titus and are moving on Earth."

"That is grave news indeed," Chiron said. "Who are these monsters?"

"Arious knows them," Jake explained. "They are old enemies of the Xan. She's afraid the queen is going to use Emily and Riza to help her spawn powerful new queens."

"Does Arious think they're still alive?" Joel asked softly.

Jake shrugged. "She doesn't know how the Mimics use the Xan. Only that every thousand years or so, the Mimics would attack Xanadu and steal a Xan, who was never seen again. Arious figures it was about spawning."

Chiron was lying on the ground, barely moving. But Jake could see the lively sparkle in the centaur's eyes. His face was gaunt and filthy, but he was very much alive. "I feared something was up," he said softly. "We have been preparing more food than normal. A spawning might well explain it."

"Maybe you should poison their food," Angie suggested. "You have the venom."

"No!" Jake said back to her. "Not yet. It seems

like when one dies, the others know about it and how they died. If a Mimic died by snake venom, the others might kill everyone in the cage. We have to think of something else."

"Jake is correct," Chiron said. "We will take tonight to regain some strength. If you come for us tomorrow evening, we will leave here and find somewhere safe to fully recover. Then we will be prepared to start our reprisals against these Mimics. For now," Chiron continued, focusing on Jake and Angie, "I would suggest you two go back to where you are hiding. The night is very long, but it is passing. You must reach safety before dawn."

Jake nodded. "All right, we'll go. We're really not far from here—"

"Do not tell us your hiding place," Chiron warned. "If the Mimics touch us, they learn our thoughts. You and the snakes must be protected."

Jake nodded. "You're right. I just hate to leave you all here."

"It's cool," Joel said. "Get going. Just come back tomorrow night. We'll be waiting. . . ."

"We will," Angie promised.

Jake and Angie exited the bushes, carrying the empty ambrosia containers with them into the woods. Turning away from the bright lights of the cage, Jake was cast back into the world of darkness and had to hold on to Angie to guide him back to the boat.

It was still very dark out when they reached the water and swam over to the boat. Before going below, Jake and Angie stood on the deck looking around. At least, Jake tried to look around. In the solid darkness, there was nothing for him to see.

Angie helped Jake into the hatch and down the stairs. She led him over to his bunk and then took a seat beside him.

"You okay?" Jake whispered softly.

"I'm glad we could help them, but I'd hoped my parents were in there."

"I know. But if there's one camp, there must be more. Don't worry, Angie, we'll find them."

They fell silent for a while and sat in the dark. Finally Jake said, "I like Chiron. He sounds like he knows what he's doing."

"He's very smart," Angie said. "He was Hercules's teacher."

Jake figured that meant something important, so he didn't comment.

*"Jake,"* Nesso hissed. *"The othersss in here are very hungry. Would you pleassse give them the ambrosssia?"*

"I'm so sorry," Jake said. "Angie, the snakes are hungry. Can you give them some of the ambrosia we brought back?"

Angie left the bunk and started to move around in the darkness. Jake could hear all the snakes hissing as they waited.

"Come here," Angie called softly. "Time to eat."

Without seeing her, Jake was struck again by how much she reminded him of his sister. Thinking of Molly made him homesick. He had a baby brother he'd never met, and he missed his mother more than he'd thought possible. He even missed his stepdad. By now they must have settled down into thinking he was never coming home. Did they think he was dead? If only he could reach them and tell them where he was. But he didn't even know where that was. It was another planet, but one so far away, Earth's sun didn't even appear as a star in the dark sky. Without realizing it, he let tears stream down his cheeks. He wanted so much to get out of this nightmare and go home.

"Are you all right?" Angie said softly as she sat beside him.

Jake sniffed and wiped his eyes. "I just miss my home and my family."

"Me too," Angie said.

Jake put his arm around her, and the two sat in the dark, talking about their lives and what they used to do before the Mimics. Jake realized that although they were from different worlds, their lives weren't so different after all.

A while later, one of the snakes hissed louder. The sound was coming from the hatch area.

*"Dawn isss risssing,"* Nesso said. *"We mussst all be quiet now."*

Falling silent, Jake and Angie sat together, listening to the sound of the water gently lapping against the boat. Eventually fatigue set in, and they settled down on their bunks to sleep.

The horrific sound of screeching roused Jake from a dreamless sleep. It sounded close—too close. Across from him, Angie started to whimper.

"It's all right," he whispered softly. "They can't cross the water to get us." Jake had no idea if it was true, but he couldn't leave Angie to suffer in fear.

"Wha-what is that?" she asked.

"I don't know," Jake said. "But we can't go out to check." He called softly to the snakes, "Everyone stay here. Don't go above."

*"They won't,"* Nesso said.

The screeching and squealing grew in intensity and, if possible, sounded even angrier. But it didn't get any closer. They were like sound effects from a terrifying horror movie. But this was no movie. The fear coursing up Jake's spine was very real.

Once again, Angie moved and took a seat beside him. She wanted comfort from him, but having the strong Titan sitting beside him made Jake feel better too.

"What do you think it is?" Angie whispered.

Jake thought carefully. "Well, I think it's a giant with a cold and a very snotty nose. He's trying to blow it, but his hanky keeps blowing away. Then he screeches and has to chase it."

Angie's shoulders moved as she chuckled softly. "Or

maybe it's a sea monster that's angry and having a tantrum because Neptune said it had to go to bed early."

"Could be," Jake agreed.

As the sounds continued, Jake and Angie kept coming up with stories explaining the shrieking. That helped, but only a bit. Mixed in with the terrible sounds were others. A soft murmuring that could be heard between the screeching.

After a time, the sounds stopped, but the murmuring continued. Jake heaved a sigh of relief. His shoulders were aching, and he realized just how tense he had been.

"It's over, right?" Angie said softly.

She had just finished speaking when they heard more sounds coming from outside the boat. Mimic voices were getting closer. Jake tensed and reached for Angie's hand. Were the Mimics coming to the boat? Was this it?

# 9

THE MEETING AT THE GLASS LAKE ENDED, and everyone made their way back to the temple entrance via different routes so they wouldn't look suspicious. Astraea and Zephyr walked back in silence.

When they arrived, Tryn was waiting for them. As there were guards posted outside the temple, he didn't say anything and just motioned for them to follow him. Keeping close, they took the stairs down to the bottom and walked toward the entrance to Arious.

The door was open again, and the control room was empty except for Belis, who was still recovering from his wounds. The snake raised his head when they entered, and he immediately slithered over to Astraea and pressed against her.

"Hello, baby," she said softly, patting the snake's head.

"Baby?" Zephyr teased. "Oh please, that is not a baby!"

"He's a baby to me," Astraea said. She looked down on Belis. "Aren't you? You're my sweet baby."

"Yeesh . . . ," Zephyr said. "I think I'm going to be sick."

Tryn checked the corridor. "Arious, would you please close the door? We need to speak privately."

The lights on Arious flashed as the door closed. "Why have you asked me to close the door, Trynulus?"

"Because we are planning on doing something that is dangerous and will no doubt anger Jupiter."

"This sounds serious," Arious said. "Come closer."

"It is," Astraea agreed as she continued to stroke Belis's head. "Tomorrow, just before everyone leaves for Titus, we—Pegasus, Cylus, Render, and Darek—are going back to Zomos to try to get Lergo and take it to the Mimic home world, Tremenz."

Astraea never imagined that a machine could gasp,

but Arious did a very close approximation. "What? Please tell me you are joking."

"We're not," Tryn said. "Jupiter's plan is to take everyone back to Titus to try to defeat the Mimics there. It may work. But it won't stop the queen from spawning, and it won't free those taken by the Mimics. We need to rescue Jake, Riza, and Emily. Then we can stop the Mimics on their own world before they spread farther. Pegasus agrees with us and is coming too."

"I might have known Pegasus would be involved in this," Arious said. "He is desperate to get back to Emily."

"He's not wrong," Tryn said. "Going to Tremenz is the best option."

"But taking Lergo there?" Arious said. "I see the logic in the plan. But I do not need to tell you how dangerous and unpredictable that snake is."

"No kidding," Zephyr said.

"Yes, it's dangerous," Astraea agreed. "But with Lergo, we stand a better chance of success."

The lights on Arious continued to flash, but the supercomputer became silent. Finally she said, "I should try to talk you all out of this. Logically, the risks are too great. But I am desperate to have Riza and Emily returned, and if there is a chance this could work, I am grateful to you for trying."

A drawer opened, revealing Solar Stream rings. "You will be needing another of these."

"I still have mine," Tryn said.

"Astraea, please take one," Arious said. "In case you become separated from Trynulus."

Astraea reached into the drawer and pulled out one of the jeweled rings. She placed it on her finger. "Thank you, Arious."

"You are most welcome." The computer paused, and then the door behind them swished open.

Pegasus clopped in. "I thought I might find you in here."

Tryn nodded. "I am sorry, Pegasus, but I thought it best if Arious knew what we are planning."

"There is no need to apologize," Pegasus said. "I was about to tell her the same thing. It is good that someone knows where we have gone. There will be questions in the morning when our absence is noticed."

"Indeed," Arious agreed. "I shall inform Jupiter and all your parents of your plan. No doubt they will be furious, but I will try to explain your reasoning. Perhaps Jupiter and his fighters might change their minds and follow you. I agree that stopping the queen from spawning is the best option for stopping the spread of the Mimics."

"So I guess we're all in agreement," Tryn said. He looked at Belis. "But we're going to have to find a way to keep Belis here. He's going to want to follow Astraea, but it's too dangerous for him."

"I will make sure he stays," Arious said.

"Come, everyone," Pegasus said. "We must rest before we leave. We do not know what we are about to face, but it is going to be difficult and we need to be at our best."

"I'm too nervous to sleep," Astraea said.

"Me too," Tryn agreed.

"If you prefer, we could start out now," Pegasus said.

Astraea looked at Zephyr and then to Tryn. "I'm happy to go now. Waiting only makes it worse."

"I agree," Tryn said.

Astraea looked back at Belis. "We have to go. Please stay here with Arious. I don't want Lergo or the Mimics to get you. We won't be long, I promise."

The snake rose to Astraea's height and leaned closer. Astraea put her arms around him as much as she could and hugged the snake. "Stay safe, Belis."

"He is saying the same to you," Arious said. "As am I. Please, all of you, be on your guard every moment."

"We will be," Pegasus said. The tall stallion looked at the others in the room. "Come, we must collect the centaurs and then we can go."

After leaving the control room, they split up. Tryn went to find his sister and to gather extra food supplies along with their slingshots and extra rocks, while Astraea and Zephyr went to get the centaurs. They found them in the large room at the bottom of the temple. Cylus was sitting beside his mother, who was sleeping. When he saw Astraea, he nodded.

Astraea motioned for him to come. Cylus rose and then quietly gathered Darek and Render.

"We're leaving early, aren't we?" he whispered. When Astraea nodded, he continued. "Good, I couldn't sleep anyway." He and the others went back for their supplies.

When they had everything, they made their way quietly out of the temple. Pegasus was standing outside talking to the night guards. He nickered and came over.

"Are they going to try to stop us?" Astraea asked.

"No," Pegasus answered. "But they are not foolish. They realize we are up to something."

The centaurs were carrying their bows and quivers full of venom-dipped arrows, as well as slingshots and rocks. Astraea had her own supply of weapons and was wearing the bracelet that Vulcan made for her that held two volunteer snakes. She stroked the surface to reassure herself as much as them.

When Tryn and Triana arrived, Tryn was carrying his and Jake's skateboards, while Triana had a sack of ambrosia cakes and several bottles of nectar.

"If any of you have second thoughts," Pegasus said somberly, "now is the time to speak up. We are facing untold dangers—if you want to stay, it is understandable and there will be no recriminations."

Zephyr opened her mouth to speak, but then closed it again. "Nah, I'm fine."

"Can we just go?" Cylus said.

Pegasus nodded. "Good. Let us move away from the temple, and we can leave."

"Wait," Cylus said. "We need to get one more thing. Don't leave without us." The centaurs disappeared into the trees. They returned several minutes later with sacks tied around their waists.

Astraea crinkled her nose at the stink coming from the bags. She knew that smell: it was Mimic food. "Ugh, what are you bringing that for?"

Cylus explained, "Lergo waits for its food to die. These are dead animals. We can use these as bait to get that snake to follow us into the Solar Stream."

Astraea nodded, but plugged her nose. "Great idea, Cylus. I just hope we don't get sick with the smell."

"Indeed," Pegasus agreed. "Come, it is time to go."

They walked quietly into the trees and made their way back to the glass lake. On the shore was a large area that had been cleared by the Mimics. Tryn stepped forward and held up the ring. "Is everyone ready?"

When everyone nodded, Tryn said, "Take us to Zomos, daytime."

The Solar Stream burst open in a swirling vortex of light.

Tryn looked at everyone. "Here we go," he said, and stepped into the light.

# 10

JAKE SQUEEZED ANGIE'S HAND AS THE voices grew louder and closer. But mixed in with the voices was a soft whimper. Someone or something was suffering. They were both too frightened to say anything or move. But as they listened, the sounds slowly faded.

After so much violence, the silence was even more frightening. During the worst of it, Jake hadn't been aware of movement. But after, he realized that all the snakes were on the bunk with him and Angie. The snakes had been as frightened as they were.

"I think we're okay now." Jake's voice was little more than a hushed whisper.

"What was that?" Angie asked.

"I don't know," Jake said softly. "On this crazy world, it could be just about anything. And probably bad for us."

They fell silent and sat in the dark. Finally Angie moved back to her bunk and settled down again. When she did, all the snakes went with her. With nothing more to do until after sunset, Jake did the same, hoping that there wouldn't be a repeat of the horror.

It seemed an eternity that they'd been in the boat. Jake wondered how much of a time difference there was between here and Earth or Xanadu. With the endlessly long days and nights, the time difference must have been huge. As it was, it felt like his own body clock had shut completely down.

"Are you awake?" Angie called softly.

"Yep," Jake answered.

"Do you think the night is coming?"

"You're the one with the super vision. All I see is darkness."

"I can't tell from here, and I don't want to move too much," Angie said.

Nesso hissed briefly. After that, they heard a couple of snakes moving around. Before long she said, *"They have checked outsssside. It isss ssstill day."*

"It's still day," Jake repeated. "I was thinking, one day or night here must be like two or three at home."

"They are long," Angie said. She moved around and then touched his hand. "Here's some more ambrosia for you and Nesso."

"No thanks. We should save it for the snakes."

"I brought back plenty for all of us. You must eat to stay strong."

Jake laughed lightly. "Strong? Not even close. You're a lot younger than me, but you could break me in two if you wanted."

"I would never harm you!" Angie gasped.

"No, what I mean is that even though you are younger, you're really strong. All you Titans are. It's like you're made of steel or something."

"We are just as we are," Angie said. She yawned softly. "I am getting tired again."

"Me too," Jake agreed. "It's going to be a long night; let's try getting more sleep."

Despite the darkness of the boat, Jake still couldn't

sleep. He tried, but the more he tried, the harder it became. Counting sheep didn't work; thinking of floating on peaceful water didn't help. It was just so frustrating, being in the middle of a war, and yet he had to lie down and do nothing but wait.

Eventually a snake hissed, and Nesso said, *"The sssun isss going down and the Mimicsss are moving inssside."*

The sun was setting, but even that took forever. Like him, Angie hadn't slept again. Instead, they sat together, waiting for the dark.

*"It isss time,"* Nesso hissed.

"It's time to move," Jake repeated softly.

Angie left her bunk and crawled up to the hatch. She pushed it back carefully and peered out. She returned to Jake a moment later. "There's no one out there. Let me help you out."

Just like the previous night, Angie led Jake out of the boat, into the water, and back up onto land. As she guided him down the street, she started to slow down. "I see something on the ground."

"What is it?"

"I'm not sure." She bent down and peered closer.

"It's like Mimic goo, but not quite. Like something has been dragged and it was bleeding. . . ."

"Well, we did hear those strange sounds. Where does the trail go?"

"The same direction we're going. Toward the trees," Angie said.

Jake stopped. "The trees?"

"Uh-huh."

"Then I need you to keep a good close watch on everything. This could be a trap. Maybe they know about our visit last night."

Jake felt Angie tense as she stood up. She started leading him again. "This is where we enter the trees. Do we still go in?"

"I don't think we have much choice."

They continued off the pavement and onto the soft ground. Before long, Angie stopped. "Last night we went in this direction to find the others. The slime trail goes in a different one. What do you want to do?"

Jake knew he should say, *Go to the prison*. The others would be waiting. But the sounds from earlier haunted him. "Maybe we can follow the slime a bit longer. Just be careful."

After a few minutes, Angie stopped again. "There's a cage. It's much bigger than the one I was kept in."

"Is anyone inside it? Could it be Emily or Riza?"

Angie took them forward several more steps. "There is someone inside," Angie said softly. "But it's not a person. It's a—it's—a . . ."

Jake could feel her trembling. "What is it? Tell me, what are you seeing?"

"I—I think it's a Mimic. But it's large and shaped funny."

Jake's mind reeled with imagination. Why would they put a Mimic in a cage? "Take us closer."

Angie hesitated, but then started to walk.

"Tell me everything you see," Jake said.

"It's hard to tell what it is," Angie started as she took a hesitant step. "I can see a head, but it just doesn't look like a normal Mimic."

As they neared the cage, in the overwhelming silence, Jake heard soft whimpering.

"That's what we heard," Jake said. "Is it hurt?"

"Yes. There are deep cuts on its stomach, and one of its arms is almost falling off. And there's another cut on the side of its head."

As they neared the cage, the whimpering and moaning continued. "I think it's dying," Angie said.

Jake wasn't sure what he was feeling. He hated Mimics—all of them. And yet he felt stirrings of compassion for the strange Mimic-like thing in the cage. Perhaps he was moved by the pathetic sounds it was making.

When they took another step forward, Angie cried, "Jake, get back!" But it was too late. He felt a tendril wrap around his waist. The wounded Mimic was attacking him!

# 11

THE TENDRIL AROUND JAKE'S WAIST WAS tight, but not so tight that he couldn't breathe. And for some reason, he felt fine. No weakness, no passing out. What he did feel was a strange presence in his mind. He wasn't alone in his own head.

Jake heard Angie screaming, and he was able to tell her he was all right. But he couldn't say more as his mind was drawn into another consciousness. Soon it was as though he were sharing the thoughts and memories of someone else and could experience everything they felt. He couldn't see anything, but he could hear and he could feel.

*Within moments, he knew the presence was female*

*and that she was moving toward something very impor-
tant. She was completely surrounded by hundreds, perhaps thousands, of Mimics murmuring softly. There was
no aggression toward her. In fact, there was reverence.*

*Whoever she was, Jake could feel that she was pro-
foundly afraid. Not of the Mimics but of failure. The
presence had an overwhelming sense of trepidation and
obligation, as though something monumental was about
to happen that she wanted no part of.*

*Soon they arrived at a place of great significance, and
he felt her tremble.*

*Sharing the mind-link with the presence, Jake knew
she was here to fight but didn't want to. She had no
desire to harm anyone. All she wanted was peace. Yet she
was duty bound to fight.*

*As they proceeded, Jake heard a sound he'd heard
earlier that day. Harsh screeching and shrieking that
was filled with murderous rage. The presence he was
sharing a mind with held no rage and did not respond.*

*Soon a voice Jake could actually understand started
to speak to the presence and the screeching thing.*

*"Most reverent young queens," it started. "Your
mother, our beloved First Queen, has waited millen-*

*nia to find another Xan so she could finally spawn her special daughters. To give you the extra strength that makes you queens, she has absorbed the energy and power of the last two Xan, and passed it along to you. You carry all that we are, all we can be. Your future is our future. Your survival is our survival. Through you, we will spread even farther throughout the universe.*

"That which has not happened in countless generations must happen now. But you must earn your new colony. Only the strongest between you may take your place as a Risen Queen of a new world. Whichever one of you falls will die, nameless and shamed for all time."

The gathering of Mimics murmured even louder while the opposing queen continued to screech and threaten. The mind Jake shared offered no reaction. He could feel she still did not want to hurt anyone.

"Come forward, queens."

Jake felt the queen move forward without hesitation. Duty forced her. She had no choice. It had been her destiny from the moment she'd hatched.

But she didn't want to fight. It felt—wrong. She knew that to not fight was a betrayal of her royal *obligation, but she wanted nothing to do with this selection process. Even if it meant her death, she would not harm her sister.*

*Moments later a voice shouted "Go" and the two queens came together. Or rather, the opposing queen attacked Jake's queen while all she did was try to defend herself. She refused to fight, even as her sister tore at her and injured her greatly.*

*Jake could feel the deep wounds, but not the immense pain, as though he were being shielded from it. With each cut and bite, he cried out for her to fight back, but she refused.*

*He recalled how long the fight he and Angie had heard had lasted, and he wished he could tell his queen to run or get away. But this was a memory and he was just an observer.*

*Finally it was over. The opposing queen was too tired to continue. Somehow, Jake's queen had managed to survive. She was gravely wounded, collapsed to the ground and bleeding as pain tore through her.*

*Then the voice started again. "It is over. Our new queen has risen."*

*There were more murmurs and rumblings from all*

*the Mimics around them. But Jake couldn't hear them well, as the queen's pain was absolute.*

*"You," the voice spat. "You have dishonored yourself by surviving. We will not give you the release of a quick death. You will be removed from this place to die alone in your shame. You are fallen. You are nothing."*

*The Fallen Queen was shoved into a cage, and it was dragged away to where he and Angie had found her.*

The tendril around Jake's waist receded. Angie was beside him, calling his name.

"Whoa," Jake said, taking several steps back. "That was intense!"

Angie threw her arms around him. "You're alive! I was so scared that the thing was going to kill you. I just didn't know what to do."

Jake shook his head. "She wouldn't do that."

"How do you know?"

"Because when she touched me, she let me know who she is and what happened to her. She's a Mimic queen that was forced to fight her sister even though she didn't want to." He stroked Nesso. "Did you get that too?"

*"Yesss,"* Nesso said sadly. *"It wasss terrible."*

"I'm not a queen," the Mimic said softly. "I'm nothing. I'm fallen."

Angie gasped. "She can speak!"

Jake nodded. "She must have read my mind and learned when she let me into hers." He said to the queen, "Don't believe that guy. You're not nothing, and not fallen. You're brave for what you did."

Jake reached out for the cage bars.

"Jake, stop! She's a Mimic," Angie cried. "She'll kill us!"

"She won't," Jake said. "That's why she's hurt, because she doesn't want to kill anyone." He turned toward Angie and told her what he had experienced in the mind-link.

"Why did they make you fight?" Angie asked. "Couldn't you both be queens?"

There was a long, pain-filled sigh. "Only the most totally vicious will rise. If I'd won, I'd be a Risen Queen. Because I wouldn't fight, I'm dishonored and will die in my shame."

"No way," Jake said.

"Yes way," the queen said. "It's how it's always been done."

Jake was shaking his head. "We're going to save you."

"But, Jake," Angie said hesitantly. "She's really hurt. Maybe we should leave her here. The others are waiting for us."

"Yes, Jake," the queen said. "Go ahead and leave me. It won't be long anyway."

"No. We're getting you out of here," Jake said.

"It's impossible," Angie said. "Trust me, you haven't seen her."

"You don't understand," Jake insisted. "I felt and heard what happened to her. We gotta help her." Jake turned back toward the queen and wished he could show her that he knew she wasn't a failure, that to him, she was extra special. "That Mimic said you were young, but I didn't feel how young. How old are you?"

The queen whined, "I hatched four days ago."

"What?" Jake cried. "You're just a baby. Not even a week old, and they expected you to fight?"

"It was my duty," the queen said. "Just like it's my duty to die in this cage, frightened and alone."

"Nope," Jake said. "You are not alone and you're

not gonna die. We're going to save you."

Angie leaned closer and said softly to him, "I don't think you realize what you're saying."

"Angie, you didn't experience what I did. If you won't help me, fine. But you can't stop me."

"How can you want to help a Mimic when they want to destroy us?" Angie asked.

"You don't get it. They want to destroy her, too," Jake said. "There is a saying on Earth, 'The enemy of my enemy is my friend.' The Mimics wanted her dead, so if we help her, it will really bother them." He turned back to the cage. "How could you touch me and not hurt me?"

"I don't want to hurt you, Jake. I don't want to hurt anyone."

Jake frowned. "Does that mean the other Mimics can choose whether they are deadly to us or not? Like they can control it or something?"

"I dunno," the Fallen Queen responded. Then she moaned again. "Oh, this really hurts."

Jake leaned closer to Angie. "Watch this. . . ." He moved forward and touched the cage bars. Then he reached inside. "Please take my hand."

"Jake, no, don't." Angie caught his arm and pulled it away.

"Let go. I have to make you understand she's not like the others." He pulled his arm free and reached into the cage. "It's all right; please take my hand."

A moment later, he felt a cold wet hand take hold of him. There was no pain or drawing like with Mimics. It was definitely strange, but not harmful. He looked back toward Angie. "See what I mean? She's not dangerous. We gotta help her."

"Sorry, dude . . . ," the queen sighed. "It's too late for me."

"Dude?" Angie repeated. "Why does she talk like you?"

"Because she learned English from me," Jake said. "She's kinda like a California girl." He turned to the queen. "Do you really wanna die?"

"No," she said softly. "I am scared of what lies beyond. But the choice isn't mine."

"'Course it is," Jake said. "You just have to let us save you."

"Jake, we can't," Angie said. "It would take several Titans to move her."

"Then we'll go get some Titans. They're getting stronger."

"Jake, I know you wanna help me," the queen said. "But you can't. It's my duty to die."

"Stop saying that," Jake said. "You're just a baby; you shouldn't die. No babies should."

"My mother, the First Queen, says only winners can live. I'm a loser."

"What's your name?" Jake asked.

"Fallen."

"That's not a name."

"That's all there is for me."

Jake thought a moment and then said, "All right. So, you say you are a Fallen Queen that must die."

"Yes."

"I agree, as a Fallen Queen you should die—"

"*Jake, no,*" Nesso cried.

"What?" Angie said. "You said—"

"Wait, let me finish," Jake cut in. "The Fallen Queen can die. But this isn't a queen anymore; she lost the fight. So now she is reborn, and I give her the name Melissa. She is who we'll save."

"I don't understand," the Fallen Queen said.

"I saw Melissa in your mind. She's your boarding buddy."

"That's right. You've seen her, and Melissa is cool. So I'm going to call you Melissa because I think it's really awesome what you did earlier today. Even though your sister was tearing you apart, you refused to fight. I don't think I could have done that."

"I don't understand. Why would you want to save me?" the queen asked. "We both know what my kind are doing to your people. My mother is spawning. There will be many more queens. You can't stop them."

"Maybe not," Jake said. "But we're going to try. And you can help us. You owe your mother and the Mimics nothing. They hurt and betrayed you and wanted you to die. But I don't. Don't you get it? You're the first Mimic I've ever wanted to save because of who you are. You're amazing."

"I am nobody."

"No, you're not. You are Melissa," Jake said. "And that changes everything."

# 12

ASTRAEA AND THE OTHERS EMERGED
from the Solar Stream in the middle of the jungle.
She was once again struck by the heat of the world.
It was one thing to remember it being hot; it was
another to be back and feel the pressure on her chest.
Each breath was like inhaling fire.

There were calls of wildlife all around them, just
like on Xanadu. But unlike Xanadu, here most of
those came from creatures that wanted to eat them.
The sounds of scurrying and hunting filled the air.

Zephyr was nodding and snorting. "All right, I
remember now just how much I hate this place. This
was a bad idea. I think we should leave."

"Not yet," Cylus said. "Let's just find Lergo, and then we can go."

Astraea looked around, wondering if they were in the same area where they'd landed the first time they'd come. Zomos was a big world—what if they'd landed on the other side from where Lergo lived? It all looked the same. How were they to tell?

Tryn seemed to have the same thought and put his skateboard down on the ground. "I'm going up to see where we are and if there are any of those dinosaur things coming our way."

The centaurs' eyes were wide and searching as they held their bows high. Astraea kept a close watch on Cylus. He seemed to feel when danger was coming much sooner than the others.

Tryn was hovering above them and looking around. Finally he nodded and ordered his skateboard down again. "Well, the good news is, I can see the plateau. The bad news is, it's much farther away than last time. At least a day or two's walk from here."

"Or we could fly," Render offered hopefully. "I mean if Pegasus and Zephyr don't mind carrying us again."

"Fly?" Cylus gasped. "Not again!"

Zephyr snorted and shook her head. "Just when my legs were feeling better."

Pegasus considered a moment, then said, "Having heard what you all went through here and the dangers that lurk all around us, I agree that flying would be the best course of action."

Zephyr looked back at Astraea. "Now, how did I know he was going to say that?"

Astraea patted her friend. "It won't be a long flight."

Zephyr nickered. "If we're going to do this, let's do it now before I change my mind. Come on, Cylus, just like before."

"Feel free to change your mind," Cylus said. "I'm happier on the ground. It might be slower, but it's safer."

The words were just out of his mouth when a roar rose above all the other wild jungle sounds. It was close and sounded like it was getting closer.

"On the other hand," Cylus said, "the sooner we get out of here, the better."

While Triana climbed up onto Pegasus, Astraea

settled onto Zephyr's back and tucked her legs beneath Zephyr's wings as they prepared to fly.

Tryn ordered his skateboard into the air and looked down on Render. "Just like before. Grab on and don't let go."

Render grinned and reached up to hold on to the skateboard. "I love this!"

Cylus shot him a look but said nothing. Instead he stood behind Zephyr. "I'm ready when you are."

Zephyr flapped her wings hard and lifted off the ground. Astraea looked back and saw Cylus catch hold of her back legs.

"Go!" the centaur cried.

It was a repeat of the last time they were on this world, Zephyr flapping her wings hard to support the weight of the heavy centaur. Beside them, Pegasus was doing the same with Darek, though he appeared to be straining less than Zephyr.

"Lead us," Pegasus called to Tryn.

"And hurry!" Zephyr added. "It isn't any easier than before."

They climbed above the canopy of trees and saw the rise of the plateau in the distance. It was much farther away than last time, and Astraea worried whether Zephyr would be able to make it.

Her best friend was already straining under the weight of the centaur hanging from her back legs and the heat of the air. Above the trees, the merciless sun was pounding down on all of them.

"Keep going," Astraea coaxed. "You're doing great!"

"We weren't sup-supposed to be doing this again," Zephyr panted as she strained to fly. "Ju-just get in, get the snake, and go . . ."

"I don't like it either," Cylus complained.

Astraea gazed down on the centaur and saw that his eyes were shut tightly. Cylus's bow and quiver were over his shoulder, and the bag of smelly Mimic food was still tied around his torso where it joined his equine body. The poor centaur had to endure the stink of the food as well as the terrifying flight.

Ahead of them, Render was just the opposite. He was hanging beneath Tryn's skateboard and whooping and laughing with joy.

Each moment brought them closer to the plateau. Despite the heat, Astraea shivered at the memory of what had happened there. How they were badly sunburned and then nearly killed by Lergo. As it was, they still had no plan for how they would catch the deadly snake.

The sound of screeching brought Astraea instantly back. She looked around and gasped. Directly behind them and moving fast was a flock of large, bat-like birds. Their wingspan was wider than Zephyr's, and they were moving much faster. Their long beaks were open, revealing rows of sharp teeth.

"Zephyr . . . ," Astraea warned.

"Don't tell me; there are monsters coming toward us."

"There are monsters coming toward us," Astraea repeated. "Big ones!"

"Not again!" Cylus cried. "I hate this world!"

Astraea leaned forward on Zephyr and called to Pegasus and Tryn, "We're being hunted!" She looked back and screamed. A dark blue, leathery bird was snapping at Zephyr's tail. Another was moving down to go after Cylus.

"Zeph, they're right behind us!" Astraea cried. She pulled out her slingshot and loaded a stone. Clenching her legs tightly beneath Zephyr's wings, she turned back and aimed for the head of the nearest bird.

She let loose the stone, and it bounced off the bird's long beak. The creature squawked in protest but snapped at Zephyr again.

"Take us down!" Astraea cried. "Hurry!"

Zephyr tilted to go down into the canopy, but with the density of the trees, there was nowhere to land. "I can't!"

While Astraea loaded another rock to fire at the birds, Pegasus dipped down low into the canopy and ordered Darek to let go. The centaur released the stallion's legs and fell, screaming, into the trees.

"Take me down," Cylus called. "I'll go with Darek."

Before Zephyr could do anything, one of the birds flew faster and swooped down to Cylus. It caught hold of one of the centaur's front legs and started to pull.

"Cylus, hold on!" Astraea cried.

Astraea raised her slingshot again and fired at the predator. The rock struck the bird's wing, but it had no effect. The bird held fast to Cylus's legs.

Cylus screamed and tried to kick his leg free, but the bird's grip on him was solid and wouldn't budge. Despite his best efforts, one of Cylus's hands slipped away from Zephyr's back legs.

"It's going to get him!" Zephyr cried.

Everything started moving in slow motion as Astraea watched the blue bird trying to tear Cylus away. Farther back, Pegasus was in an aerial battle with two more birds as they snapped and nipped at the stallion's wings and legs. In a move Astraea never imagined possible, Pegasus did a flying circle in the sky until he was directly above one of the birds. He dipped down low and with his sharp hooves tore a large hole in the bird's wing.

The bird squawked in pain as it lost flight integrity and started to spin, spraying blue blood in the air. Within moments, the other birds attacking Pegasus gave up and started chasing the wounded bird. They caught it just above the canopy of trees and tore it to pieces.

Seeing that gave Astraea an idea.

"Zeph, stay close. I'm going to try to save Cylus."

"What are you going to do?" Zephyr cried.

"No time to tell you; just follow my lead!" Astraea pulled her legs up beneath her until she was crouching on Zephyr's back. She looked down at the large bird pulling Cylus by the leg. Drawing her dagger, she prepared to jump.

"Astraea, don't do it!" Zephyr cried. "It's too dangerous."

"I know!"

Astraea opened her tiny wings and leaped off Zephyr's back. She flew as best she could at the attacking bird. Her wings were not large enough to support her in flight, but they were big enough to slow her descent and direct her. She landed with a heavy thud on the bird's back, between its leathery wings.

Using her dagger, Astraea sliced into the skin of both wings the same way Pegasus had done. The bird released Cylus and screeched. It turned its head back and tried to bite her. But the more it tried, the more Astraea sliced into the leathery skin of the wings.

With its wings rendered useless, the bird lost control. It screeched and squawked, and started to spin in the sky.

"Astraea!" Zephyr shouted.

It was only then that Astraea realized her big mistake. Yes, Cylus was free, but she was now stuck on the back of a large bird that could no longer fly. The other predator birds saw the blood coming from the wounds and gave up their attack on Tryn and the others.

They squawked as they dove toward Astraea and the wounded bird.

# 13

"MELISSA," ANGIE REPEATED. "THAT'S A pretty name."

"It is," Jake agreed. "She's a really great skateboarder. She's fearless."

"I can't be Melissa," the queen said. "I'm not fearless; I'm afraid."

"Having to fight your sister would be very frightening, but you handled it great. We just have to figure out how to help you," Jake said, then turned to Angie. "What if we gave her ambrosia? That seems to heal everything."

"She's not a Titan."

"Neither am I, but it helps me. That guy in the

prison yard from Earth, Joel—it helped him, too. Maybe we should try some." He said to Melissa, "Do you need some of those flat, stinky animals that your kind eat?"

"Yuck, I don't eat dead things."

"Whoa," Jake said. "A vegetarian Mimic? No wonder they hate her."

"They hate me because I am fallen," Melissa said.

"Their loss will be our gain," Jake said. "I'm going to try ambrosia. So please hold on. We have to go for a while, but we'll be back."

"Please don't go," Melissa whined.

The pain in her voice tore at Jake's heart, and it surprised him how much he cared. Perhaps it was residue from the mind-link they'd shared. Did it bind them together just like Nesso's bite had?

"We have to go," he said. "But we won't be long, I promise. And when we come back, we'll bring something that might help you, so you won't hurt anymore."

Melissa made a sound that was like a whimper of pain and fear. "Don't forget me, Jake," she said softly.

"We won't," Jake promised.

Jake and Angie walked away from the cage and started back on the path to the prison yard.

"I'm not sure we should help her," Angie said. "She is still a Mimic."

Jake stopped. "Yes, she is. But you have to trust me, she isn't going to turn on us."

"I do trust you; it's the Mimics I don't like or trust. What if they heard what she said because they're all linked. What if they know about us?"

Jake stopped. "During our link, I didn't feel any other Mimics. Like she was completely alone in her mind. Maybe because she's a queen, she's different. We have to trust her."

"I don't think I can."

"Please try," Jake said. "Don't think of her as a Mimic or even a queen. Think of her as Melissa and that she's hurt. You wouldn't want to abandon anyone that's hurt, would you?"

In the dark, her long pause was telling. "Well?"

"All right, I'll try," Angie finally said.

"Thank you. Now, I wonder if she can eat ambrosia. I've never seen Mimics eat it, just those stinky animals."

"I guess we'll find out."

They made their way to the prison. Like the previous night, they could see the glow from the community yard. Once again, the prisoners were lying down or moving slowly around, looking half-dead. This time, Jake was sure it was a performance for the cameras, if indeed those boxes were cameras. This world was almost a twin to Earth. But did it have the same kind of technology?

"There are a lot of people in there," Jake said. "Is there enough ambrosia to feed them all once they escape?"

"There were a ton of containers in the cabin. I'm sure it will last a long time."

As they neared the cage, Jake looked around for any signs of change—anything to suggest that the Mimics knew they'd been there. But everything looked the same.

"I wonder why there aren't any Shadow Titans," Jake mused aloud. "You'd think they'd keep some posted here."

"I'm just glad there aren't any. They really scare me," Angie said.

"Me too," Jake agreed. But not seeing them

disturbed him almost as much as if there had been some posted. Was this a trap? Or were the Mimics arrogant enough to think the Shadow Titans weren't needed?

After making their way around the prison yard, they arrived back at the place where they were the previous night when they entered the bushes.

"Paelen, Joel, and Chiron are there," Angie said softly.

She started to move, but Jake caught her arm. "Stop. We don't know if it's really them or Mimics in disguise. We've been tricked before."

Angie gasped. "How can we tell? We don't want to be touched."

Jake stroked Nesso. "True, but here's our professional Mimic detector. She can smell them."

*"Jake, pleassse don't rely on me too much,"* Nesso said. *"Thisss whole area ssstinksss of Mimicsss."*

Jake reached up and stroked her. "Just try your best."

*"I will."*

As they had before, they darted over to the bushes. Crawling beside the cabin, they neared the cage.

"Well?" Jake whispered to Nesso.

*"I am sssure they are not Mimicsss."*

Jake looked back at Angie and whispered, "They're not Mimics."

Paelen raised his arms and stretched, then lay down, facing the bars. "You could have asked us if we were Mimics."

"You heard that?" Jake asked.

"Of course," Paelen replied.

"Yeah, well, I'm sorry to suspect you. But we have to be careful."

"That is wise of you," Chiron said. "We are glad you have returned."

"Us too," Jake said. "Did the Mimics notice the missing food?"

"The Mimics did not return today," Paelen said. "We have seen no one."

Jake looked at Angie and then said, "I think we know why." He explained about their day and the terrible sounds. Then they told of finding the Fallen Queen in the cage and Jake's mind-link with her.

"Do you believe you can trust her?" Chiron asked.

"Absolutely," Jake answered. "When she touched me, it was like I was her. I could share her memories and learn everything about her. She is peaceful. That's why she refused to fight. She could have killed both of us at any time with her tendrils, but she didn't."

Chiron looked at Angie. "Do you feel the same?"

Angie hesitated. "She didn't touch me, so I didn't experience what Jake did. But she sounds like she means it."

"But is it enough for us to risk our lives to save her?" Chiron said.

"Yes!" Jake said emphatically. "I promised, and I never go back on a promise."

"And she was hurt," Angie added. "She wasn't faking that."

*"You can trussst her,"* Nesso said.

"Nesso agrees with me that we can trust her," Jake said. "Please, Chiron, we have to help her."

"We will," Chiron said. "There may be much we can learn from her. We will take her with us tonight."

"We will?" Paelen gasped. "We are leaving tonight?"

"We must," Chiron insisted. "This is grave news that Jake and Angie bring to us. The Mimic queen has spawned and there is at least one new young queen.

There may be more. I have no doubt that soon they will be looking to move on to another world—perhaps Titus. We must not let that happen. This must end here. I had hoped for one more night of food and rest, but we dare not wait. We must move our plan forward."

"How can we get you out of this prison?" Jake asked.

"That is my job," Paelen said. "The cabin is connected to this prison yard by a large door. I will get out of here and go back inside to open the door."

*"Jake, what about the sssnakesss?"* Nesso asked. *"We can't leave them behind."*

"We won't," Jake said. "Even if it means we don't go with the others."

"What is it?" Joel asked.

"Nesso is asking about the snakes. They are still in our hiding spot."

"Those snakes are especially precious," Chiron said. "How many are there?"

"A lot," Angie said. "But we have containers now. If Paelen comes with us, we can get them and make it back here in no time."

"Better yet," Jake offered, "why don't some of you go for the snakes while the rest of us go back to

Melissa to take her out of her cage and get her some ambrosia? We can meet up there and then leave."

"That is a very good idea," Chiron said. "Let us move. The night is long, but we have much to do."

Jake and Angie crawled back as Paelen stretched out his body and slipped through the bars of the cage. Once free, he returned to his normal shape. It was still unnerving to Jake to watch him do it. He cringed with every pop of Paelen's bones.

They crawled to the front of the cabin and slipped in. Once again the stench of rotting flesh wrapped around them like a wet blanket and stole their breath away.

"Jake, stay here," Paelen warned. "I will open the outer doors. It will allow light in."

Angie stood with Jake as Paelen slipped through the room. They heard him fumble with some kind of lock, and a moment later, the double doors opened and light from the yard flooded in.

Angie had tried to describe to Jake the inside of the cabin, but her descriptions couldn't capture the true horror of what Jake was seeing. There were cages packed full of sad, unfortunate animals—but he couldn't recognize their species. Some of them looked like dogs, there were catlike animals, and even some that looked like monkeys. Others didn't look remotely familiar. The one thing they had in common was the terror on their faces as the Titans entered the cabin from the yard.

In the center of the room were tables. Jake didn't need to get closer to see what happened on those, as there were dark, wet stains on the surface. And at the end of the tables was a large press that must have flattened the animals. Drying racks were also set up around the room, stacked full of the flattened animals. Jake looked away, unable to conceive of what it must have been like to work in here. In that one moment, he realized he would never eat meat again.

"Jake," Angie said. "While they're gathering the ambrosia, would you help me with something, please?"

"Sure, what do you need?"

"I want to open the cages and free all the animals."

Jake had been considering doing the same thing. He approached Chiron. "Excuse me, Chiron. Are any of those animals in the cages dangerous?"

Chiron gazed back at the cages sadly. "No, they

are gentle and intelligent. I doubt any of us will ever forget the horrors we have had to do to them."

"Angie and I are going to open the cages and release them."

Chiron nodded, then called several filthy Titans over and pointed to the cages. "This ends for them as well. Help Jake and Angie open the locks. Set them all free."

"I'll help," Joel called.

Soon there was a group of Titans as well as the other species going through the cabin unlocking cage doors and freeing the animals. At first the poor creatures didn't understand what was happening and they shied back, but then Angie picked up a catlike creature and carried it to the front doors.

"Go on now, you're free. Go home."

The cat took a tentative step forward, looked back at Angie a final time, and darted off into the darkness. When the other creatures realized what was happening, they too started to run for the exit.

In a matter of minutes, all the cages were empty, and the prisoners had taken all the ambrosia. Everyone gathered outside the cabin. Those who were strong enough carried containers of ambrosia. Others helped the sick and weaker prisoners.

Chiron found Jake standing with Angie. "Jake, please climb onto my back; it will be faster. Angitia, will you tell the others where to go for the snakes? We must not waste a moment, as we have a lot to cover before dawn."

Angie helped Jake onto Chiron's back. He knew Astraea had ridden Render, but he'd never imagined that he himself would ever ride a centaur. He felt embarrassed by it.

"Um—sir," Jake said awkwardly. "Um—what do I hold on to?"

Chiron looked back at him and chuckled. "You may hold on to my arms, or my shoulders. Whatever makes you feel secure."

Jake reached up to Chiron's shoulders and felt better.

"Is everyone ready?" Chiron called.

There was an assortment of responses, but they all seemed to suggest, yes.

"Lead us, Angitia," Chiron said.

They started into the trees. Jake peered back, and before they lost the light completely, he saw just how many prisoners had been freed. He also heard heavy pounding. That was followed by loud creaking and then breaking. As he watched, the whole cabin collapsed in on itself.

Jake gasped. "We have to go. Why are they wasting time knocking the cabin down?"

Chiron paused. "You could not imagine the horrors we have endured in there. Yes, we must leave quickly, but tearing it down is the first step on the path to healing."

"Was that the Mimics' only food supply?" Jake asked.

"Unfortunately, no," Chiron said. "Occasional prisoners were taken from here and moved away, while others were delivered here. This was not the first camp I have been forced to work at. I have been at two others. I do not know why they keep moving us. Perhaps it has to do with keeping us from forming strong bonds of friendship that may lead to revolt. If that is the case, the Mimics have no understanding of Olympians or Titans. In fact, their cruel treatment has made us all closer."

They walked into the trees, and Jake was cast into complete darkness. After moving steadily forward for a while, Angie called, "There she is; that's Melissa."

There were gasps of shock from all around Jake.

"That is a Mimic queen?" Chiron said softly.

"A Fallen Queen," Angie said. "She lost the fight with her sister. She's supposed to die in there. Jake is hoping ambrosia will help her."

Jake heard all the gasps and reactions to Melissa and wondered what she looked like. Angie had said she was big and strange-looking. But what did that mean? A whale was big. So was an elephant, but they looked completely different.

"Melissa," Angie called softly. "We're back. We are going to get you out of this cage and take care of you."

"Angie," Melissa whined, "I'm so scared. There are strange sounds around me, and I can't see anything. Is Jake here?"

"I'm right here, Melissa," Jake said. "Don't be scared—and it's too dark for me too. But we're here to help you."

"We're not going to help that thing, are we?" The voice came up from behind Chiron. Jake could clearly hear the disgust it held.

"Yes, we are," Jake said back to him. "And if you don't like it, you can go right back to that prison yard and wait for the Mimics to find you."

"Who do you think you are, human?"

Jake heard Paelen's voice say, "This human is the one that saved us from that horror."

"Yes," Chiron agreed. "We owe Jake and Angitia more than we can ever repay. All they have asked is for us to help their friend. It is the least we can do after all they have done for us. Is that understood?"

The voice grumbled.

"Is that understood!" Chiron repeated.

"Yes, Chiron." The voice faded away.

Chiron turned back to Jake. "You must excuse him. He has been enslaved by the Mimics for a long time and has forgotten his manners."

"I don't care what they call me or think of me. I just don't want anyone trying to hurt or blame Melissa. She's as much a victim of the Mimics as we are."

"She will not be harmed. You have my word," Chiron said.

"And mine," a woman's voice called. "If any of you have a problem with us helping this Mimic, you will have to deal with me."

The strong, commanding voice sounded like someone Jake didn't want to mess with. He leaned forward on Chiron. "Who was that?"

"That is Diana, daughter of Jupiter. If she says she will protect Melissa, I assure you, she will."

With that settled, a group of volunteers came forward to go with Angie to collect the snakes. When they left, the strongest of the prisoners were called forward to help get Melissa out of the cage.

Jake stayed with Chiron, peering into the dark, unable to see anything as they worked. After a while, he heard the creaking of the door swinging open.

"Be calm," Diana coaxed softly. "Do not fear us. We will not harm you. I ask that you do not harm us."

"I don't want to harm anyone," Melissa whined. "But I hurt . . ."

"I can see your wounds," Diana said softly. "You are very brave. When we find a place to hide, we will take care of these."

"How bad is it?" Jake asked Chiron.

"Very bad," Chiron replied. "I am amazed that she is still alive. It must have been a vicious fight."

"It was," Jake answered. "Will someone please give her some ambrosia? I said it would help her."

"I'll get it," a man's voice called. "I'll get some for all of us."

They all settled down to eat and wait for the team going after the snakes. When they returned, everyone prepared to go.

Angie came up to Jake. "How is she?"

"Not good," Jake said. "She sounds so weak."

Diana called several others forward. "Look at that leg; she can't possibly walk. We'll have to carry her. Be gentle."

There were loud grumbles of protest until Diana raised her voice and threatened the others.

For as much as Jake blessed the darkness for keeping the Mimics away, he cursed it too because without starlight, he couldn't see a thing to help her.

Melissa whimpered and groaned as she was moved, and it tore at Jake. He had no idea why he felt so protective of her, but he was. Perhaps it was their link. Hearing her pain was like he was suffering too. "Please, be careful with her!"

"We are," Diana called softly. "We have her, Chiron. It is time to move."

# 14

ASTRAEA WAS CLINGING TO THE BIRD AS IT twirled out of control toward the treetops. The other birds chased after them and nipped at the wounded bird's wing tips.

"Astraea, no!" Zephyr howled as she tried to reach her friend, but the distance was too great.

"Astraea, we are coming!" Pegasus shouted. He sped toward her with Triana on his back. One of Triana's hands was gripping his mane, while the other reached forward.

"Astraea, get ready to jump!" Triana called.

Pegasus dove at her just as the bird's damaged wings gave way completely and it started to tumble.

Astraea took a deep breath and leaped off the bird's back. She was flapping her wings harder than she ever had in her life. It wasn't much, but her efforts helped her reach out for Triana's hand and catch hold of her.

Triana pulled hard and swung Astraea up to land on Pegasus's back behind her. When she was safe, Astraea put her arms around Tryn's sister and hugged her tightly. "Thank you!"

"Thank you for saving Cylus," Pegasus called.

Astraea looked back and saw all the large birds tearing at the wounded birds in the treetops. It was a terrible and violent sight, but at least Astraea and her team were safe for the moment.

Just ahead, Zephyr was still struggling to carry Cylus. The centaur had managed to get a better grip on her back legs, but he was still looking frightened. His front equine legs were cut and bleeding from the bird's sharp teeth.

"Zephyr, Tryn," Pegasus called. "Look ahead—there is a clearing. Try to reach it. We must land."

Pegasus flew past Zephyr and Tryn and led them down. They were soon over a clearing of broken and crushed trees. Astraea flashed back to the first time they were here and the two massive dinosaurs that had fought and brought down the trees. This looked like the same spot.

When they all touched down, Cylus's legs gave out on him and he collapsed to the ground. Astraea ran over to him and saw all the damage from the bird's sharp teeth. She knelt beside him.

Cylus threw his arms around her. "Thank you, thank you so much for saving my life!"

"It's all right," Astraea said. "We're a herd; we look out for each other."

As the others gathered around Cylus to treat his injuries, Pegasus looked back to the trees. "I'm going back for Darek."

Tryn put his skateboard down on the ground beside the stallion. "I'm coming with you. My skateboard will lead us."

"We will be back soon," Pegasus said. "Take cover; do not stay out here in the open. This world does indeed hold many dangers."

While Pegasus and Tryn went to find Darek, Astraea, Zephyr, Triana, and Render helped get Cylus into the cover of the trees.

"I can't believe how much I hate this world," Zephyr muttered. "We haven't been back long, and look what's happened. I should have kept my mouth shut about taking Lergo to Tremenz."

"Your idea is still a good one," Astraea said. "Lergo will be perfect to help with the Mimic problem. We just have to get it and us out of here in one piece."

"It's too late for that," Cylus said as he winced while touching his legs. "Look what that thing did to my hoof. It's going to scar."

"And you will wear it proudly," Render said. "We will speak of your bravery for many generations to come."

Cylus lowered his head. "I wasn't brave. Astraea was. She had to save me."

"No," Astraea said. "You would have saved yourself and all of us if you could have used your bow; we all know that. But you couldn't because you were hold-ing on to Zephyr. We're all in this together, Cylus, and we're all brave for coming here."

Cylus nodded, but Astraea knew it would be some time before he was himself again. He looked back in the direction that Pegasus and Tryn had gone. "I hope they find Darek."

"They will," Triana said. "Pegasus was really low to the ground when Darek let go. He'll be fine."

"He's going to be scratched to pieces from falling through the trees," Zephyr said.

"Yes, but we have ambrosia and nectar for him and you. . . ." Triana reached into her pack and pulled out ambrosia for Cylus. "Please eat; it will help."

Cylus started to shake his head, but when Astraea raised her eyebrows at him, he reluctantly accepted the piece.

They sat together under the cover of the jungle waiting for the others to return. Triana found a big leaf and started to fan herself. "It's very warm here, isn't it?" she said.

Astraea looked at her and burst into laughter. "Yes, it's warm to you and Tryn. But for the rest of us, it's really, *really* hot!"

"And it's full of bugs," Zephyr complained as her tail swished biting insects away. "Why does everything here want to eat us?"

"Guess we're fresh food," Render said. His own tail was constantly brushing insects away from his flanks.

Roars sounded from all around them, and despite his wounds, Cylus rose and loaded his bow. Render's bow was already at the ready. Astraea pulled out her dagger. It wouldn't be much good against bigger creatures, but it had helped with the birds.

After what seemed an age, they heard rustling in the trees. The sounds were getting louder and nearer. Astraea held up her dagger, Triana her slingshot, and the centaurs pointed their bows.

Tryn was the first to appear. His hands shot up in the air. "It's just us; don't shoot!"

"Are you crazy?" Cylus cried. "We could have fired on you. You should have said something!"

"If we raised our voices, we risked drawing predators," Pegasus said as he emerged.

Darek was trailing behind them. He was covered in scratches, and there were still leaves and branches caught in his short hair and equine tail. One of his eyes was swollen shut and going black, and he was cradling his left arm.

"Darek!" Astraea cried. She ran up to him. "Are you all right?"

"I'll live," the centaur said. "But I'm never flying

with Pegasus again!" He shot the stallion a dirty look. "When he told me to let go, I fell through all the trees until I hit the ground. I'm lucky to be alive!"

"I am gravely sorry," Pegasus said. "But I saw our height and knew you would survive the fall. It left me free to fight the birds that were attacking the others." He looked over to Astraea. "But Astraea took care of that herself." He turned to her. "That was a dangerous move, but it did work. Well done."

"Well done?" Zephyr cried. "Astraea, you nearly gave me a heart attack! I thought for sure you were going to be bird food!"

"I had to do it, Zeph; that thing was going to get Cylus." She walked over to Darek and brushed off the leaves and tried to wipe away the dirt covering him. "It could have been much worse."

Darek looked at Pegasus again, then said, "I guess, and I'm not really hurt *that* bad."

"Yes," Cylus said. "You might have been almost eaten like me!"

"They could have killed all of us," Triana said.

Tryn looked up at the sky. "It's over now and we're

all alive. We should keep moving if we hope to reach the plateau before dark."

Astraea looked over at Cylus. "Are you all right to walk?"

The centaur nodded. "Yes, the ambrosia helped. The sooner we move, the sooner we can leave this terrible place."

They agreed to stay on the ground after their aerial encounter. But walking through the jungle was slow, and the dense trees blocked their way. As the light started to dim, they approached a wide trail of knocked-over trees and crushed bushes.

They stepped onto the trail and looked around. "What made this?" Tryn asked.

Cylus nodded. "I know. And you all do too."

"Lergo . . . ," Astraea breathed.

Cylus nodded. "Look at the shape of the damage. It is round, just like the snake. I would imagine this is how it comes and goes to its cave." He bent down and winced in pain. "Look here, this is freshly broken. Lergo has been through here recently."

That comment made Astraea shiver despite the

intense heat. "Are you sure? Maybe it was from last night?"

Cylus shook his head. "No, there is still sap running from the branch." He rose again and looked around. "The question is, was Lergo leaving the cave to go hunting? Or did it return there?"

"That's a good question," Tryn said.

"So here's another one," Cylus continued. "Does anybody have any suggestions about how we're supposed to get that giant snake into the Solar Stream? I have the Mimic food, but I'm not sure how we can use it."

"Maybe we should go up to its cave, put the food down, and shoot the Solar Stream at it when it takes the bait," Darek offered.

Tryn shook his head. "I don't think that would work. We can't be sure Lergo is even up there. But even if the snake is there, can we shoot the Solar Stream at it, or does Lergo have to actually go into the Solar Stream?"

Pegasus looked around. "I have not seen this snake that you are talking about, but looking at this trail, it is massive. We may only get one chance, so we must make it count."

"Let's get closer to the mountain and maybe we can figure something out," Tryn said.

They followed Lergo's trail toward the plateau. All the damage to the area made the journey much easier. It wasn't long before they were gazing up the side of the rocky rise.

"It looks much higher from this angle," Zephyr said. "And look, the side is flat. How does Lergo get up there?"

"I don't know," Tryn said. "Unless it's that long. I never really saw it."

"Neither did we," Astraea admitted. "We were too busy hiding in water under some branches. We saw its front end, but not really how long it was."

Pegasus stepped up to the wall and gazed up. Then he looked back down the trail, and finally back up again.

"What is it?" Astraea asked.

"I have an idea," he said. "It will be dangerous, but it might work." Pegasus looked over at Tryn. "When we are ready, you will fly up to the cave entrance and place a couple of those dead animals that Cylus brought. Then return here quickly."

"Then what?" Zephyr said. "We just stand here watching it eat?"

Pegasus nickered in humor. "No, Zephyr. We lure it down here with the promise of more. And when it comes, I will have the dead animals on me for it to chase. You will all be positioned farther down this trail. When Lergo comes for me, you will open the Solar Stream and I will run into it with Lergo right behind me. Then you follow behind at a safer distance."

"What?" Cylus cried. "That thing will eat you in the Solar Stream!"

"Thank you for your concern, Cylus, but I have no intentions of being eaten. Moving within the Solar Stream is difficult, but not impossible. I have done it many times. But that snake will never have been in there before. I am confident it will not be able to catch me."

"You are gambling with your life, Pegasus," Tryn said.

"We are all risking our lives," the stallion said. "But I do not believe there is any other way of getting Lergo into the Solar Stream." He looked up again. "Though I do suggest we get moving. With that stinky food down here, I doubt we have long before

Lergo smells it. We must be prepared. While Tryn is taking a couple of the dead animals up to the cave, the rest of you will hang some from my flanks."

The moment Cylus opened the bags, the stench was overwhelming. Especially in the humid heat of Zomos.

Tryn pinched his nose with one hand and reached into the bag with the other. He pulled out two flattened animals. "Oh, that's bad," he cried. "Really, really bad!"

Astraea felt her throat constrict. "Pegasus, are you sure you want those things on you? Who knows how long it will take for the smell to go away?"

Pegasus shook his head. "I do not relish the thought of having them on me either, but to achieve our goal, I will gladly do it." He looked over to Tryn. "Get going. We will prepare down here."

Tryn nodded to everyone. "I'll go up and see if Lergo likes them. Everyone be ready; this could happen very fast." He looked at Astraea. "Are you ready with your ring?"

Astraea nodded. "You be careful. Move away from the entrance the moment you put the bait down."

"I will," Tryn promised as he ordered his skateboard to take him up.

While Tryn was rising in the sky, the others helped tie flattened animals together and drape them over Pegasus's back.

Zephyr was making gagging sounds and cried, "Render, come here and plug my nose for me."

"Plug your own nose," Render said as he kept one hand over his nose and mouth and tried to work with the other. "I swear I can taste them!"

Triana turned a dull gray as she picked up the flattened animals. "What do the Mimics do to these to make them smell so bad?"

"I don't know," Astraea answered. "And I don't want to know. Let's just hope this works." She split her attention between working to cover Pegasus in the smelly animals and looking up to check on Tryn.

"Tryn's in place." Astraea fought down the bile that rose in her mouth from the stink. "Are we ready?"

"I am," Pegasus said, though his voice was strained. "And I will say this now: Emily owes me a lot for going through this for her!"

"She'll owe all of us," Cylus agreed.

"Astraea," Zephyr said. "Would you and Triana get on my back? If that snake can move as fast as we think it can, I may have to fly out of here fast."

Astraea didn't argue with her best friend. She climbed onto Zephyr's back and then helped Triana up behind her. "Is everyone ready?" Astraea called.

Pegasus took a position in the center of Lergo's trail and nodded while the centaurs moved farther back.

"We're ready," Cylus called.

Astraea gave the signal to Tryn and watched him put the bait down at the entrance of the cave. Mere moments later, Tryn soared back with fear on his face and shouted, "Lergo's in there and has already taken the bait!"

Tryn started down the side of the rocky rise, with Lergo right behind him, moving fast.

Astraea was stunned at the snake. In the blazing-hot sunshine, it looked exactly like Belis or even Nesso, with colorful rings of red, blue, orange, and black. There was no question now. They were the same species and grew to enormous sizes.

"Get away, Tryn!" Triana cried. "It's right behind you!"

"Not yet," Tryn shouted. "It has to smell Pegasus first!"

Astraea held her breath as Lergo inched closer and closer to Tryn. At the last minute, Tryn soared away from the rocky side and back up in the air.

The immense snake paused its climb down the cliff just a few yards from the ground. Its head was suspended in air as its tongue darted in and out of its mouth.

Astraea gasped when she followed its long body up the side of the mountain. It continued into the cave. Lergo was so much bigger than they'd imagined.

"Look at the size of it," she cried. "It's too big. This was a terrible mistake!"

"It is too late to stop; get ready," Pegasus called.

Almost as though the snake heard him, its head shot downward, toward Pegasus. It started moving again.

"It's coming!" Render shouted.

"Open the Solar Stream!" Pegasus ordered.

Astraea held the ring above Zephyr's head. "Take us to Tremenz, nighttime!"

The Solar Stream burst to life from her ring, and

a swirling vortex of light appeared along the trail. Pegasus was already charging forward but stopped just before the blazing entrance. He looked back at the snake.

"Pegasus, go!" Triana shouted.

"Go!" Astraea cried.

But Pegasus just stood there, waiting.

When Astraea looked at the snake, she understood. Lergo was several lengths behind the stallion, but it had stopped. Its tongue continued to flash in and out of its mouth, but its tilted head suggested it was wary of the vortex.

"It's not working!" Astraea cried. "Lergo won't go in!"

"Cylus, no!" Darek called from their hiding place behind the snake.

"Stop!" Render cried.

Cylus sprang from the hiding place and charged along the length of Lergo's body. He had the bag holding the remaining dead animals in his hands and was reaching inside. "Come on, you stupid beast," he cried. "Eat!"

When he neared Lergo's head, he threw several

pieces of dead animals before it. The snake's tongue dipped out and caught the first one and pulled it back. Then it went for the second one and took it also.

"You want more?" Cylus cried, throwing another piece right at the snake. "Come and get me!"

Lergo ate everything Cylus threw at it and started to chase him toward the Solar Stream.

"Cylus, get away!" Pegasus shouted.

But the centaur kept running and throwing flattened animals to the snake. Lergo's head snapped at Cylus several times, missing him by a heartbeat as it increased its speed.

"Pegasus, go!" Cylus cried.

With the snake now bearing down on both Cylus and Pegasus, the stallion had no option but to run.

Pegasus was the first through the Solar Stream, followed by Cylus, who, right up to the last minute, continued to throw the Mimic food at the snake.

Astraea and the others watched in horror as the snake moved even closer to the centaur. Without pausing, it slithered right into the Solar Stream and vanished.

# 15

ONCE THE WHOLE SNAKE WAS THROUGH the vortex, Astraea called the others together. Tryn soared down on his skateboard, and the two remaining centaurs charged forward. They all entered the Solar Stream together.

Seated on Zephyr's back, Astraea felt Triana's arms slip around her waist as they traveled through the blazing light. With the brightness coming from all around, she couldn't see Pegasus or Cylus ahead of them. What she could see was the back end of the snake. She realized that when they left the Solar Stream, they would be directly behind it.

Time seemed to stop as the long journey lay before

them. Astraea found herself dozing off several times. She felt the pressure of Triana's head against her folded wings and knew that Tryn's sister was asleep.

Tryn was beside her, leaning against Zephyr and sleeping soundly. Beside him, Darek and Render kept their bows at the ready and were showing no signs of fatigue.

Darek felt her eyes on him and turned. He nodded to her, and she nodded back. Of all the changes in her life from the first day at Arcadia to now, the biggest had come in her friendship with the centaurs. If anyone had ever told her back then that they would be close, she would have called them crazy. Cylus was a bully and his whole herd were mean and unapproachable, bordering on dangerous.

But since then, everything had changed—the centaurs had changed, and she had too. She was now part of their herd and they had learned to be considerate of others and more generous than she'd expected. Astraea couldn't have asked for more loyal friends. When this nightmare finally ended, she knew they had forged a deep friendship that would last the ages.

Her mind also went back to Jake. That strange,

funny friend she missed so much. He was nothing like she'd expected a human to be. He was fun, caring, and showed a true wonder at everything around him. She just hoped he was still alive. But she couldn't put aside her fear that the Mimics had done something terrible to him and Nesso and all the others they'd taken.

Her brothers were also missing. She had tried to suppress her fear for them because the feelings were just too overwhelming. But after all their searching, her brothers still hadn't been found.

Were they with Jake? Were they safe? Or were they somewhere locked away beyond her reach? Within the whirling lights and colors of the Solar Stream, there were no distractions to take her away from her fears.

Astraea hadn't been aware of the tears streaming down her cheeks. But when she felt Zephyr's wings tighten on her legs, Astraea looked up to see her best friend watching her.

"Are you all right?" Zephyr whinnied loudly.

Astraea wiped her tears and nodded. "I'm fine. I'm just worried about my brothers."

"Your mother's fine," Zephyr shouted. "She's with your father!"

"Not my mother, my brothers!" Astraea shouted back.

"The others will be all right too!" Zephyr called.

"No, my brothers!"

"Who do you want to smother?" Zephyr asked. Then she winked at Astraea and tightened her wings again. "Gotcha!"

Astraea smiled and shook her head. She stroked Zephyr's fine mane. "Thank you."

Zephyr neighed in humor and faced forward again.

For as long as the journey from Titus to Xanadu normally took, the trip from Zomos to Tremenz was so much longer. But finally they emerged into darkness.

And then insanity.

Lergo was just ahead of them and thrashing around the area as its long tail whipped back and forth in the air.

"Everyone, move!" Tryn shouted as he took off on his skateboard.

From being at a full stop in the Solar Stream, Zephyr had to launch into the air to get away from the enraged snake, while the centaurs ran in the opposite direction.

The ground beneath them was paved and looked like roads. There were houses and other buildings all around. Some had lights on. Soon doors opened and Mimics were seen on doorsteps. They saw the massive snake and slammed their doors shut again.

"This is the place!" Zephyr called.

"Where's Cylus and Pegasus?" Astraea cried as she searched the area.

"Over there!" Triana called. She was pointing into the sky across from them. "Cylus is holding on to Pegasus."

Astraea followed Triana's finger and saw the stallion rising higher in the sky with Cylus clinging to his rear legs. Lergo was following close behind them, raising his head high and snapping at Cylus.

"It smells the animals on Pegasus!" Astraea called.

"I'll get them!" Tryn shouted as he whooshed past on his skateboard and flew toward Pegasus and Cylus.

When he caught up with Pegasus, he was able to

pull the stinky animals off the stallion's rump. As each animal fell, Lergo caught it in its mouth. Soon all the dead animals were gone, but still Lergo continued to pursue Pegasus and Cylus.

The massive snake's movements were erratic and unpredictable. Its head thrashed from side to side, and its tail whipped the air, smashing holes in the buildings around them. Watching it, Astraea realized something was wrong. Traveling through the Solar Stream must have completely disorientated the snake.

"They have to get higher or Lergo will catch them!" Astraea called.

"Astraea, Triana, hold on!" Zephyr called. "I have an idea!"

Zephyr put on more speed and flew closer to Pegasus while avoiding the deadly snake's snapping mouth.

"Tryn, move with me!" Zephyr shouted. "We have to help carry Cylus's weight so Pegasus can gain more height!"

Tryn nodded and zipped over to the other side of Pegasus. Then he moved closer to Cylus and called back to Zephyr, "I'll take his front hooves; you guys get his back ones!"

Zephyr dipped lower and was soon positioned beneath the dangling centaur.

"Careful, Zeph!" Astraea cried as she looked back and saw the wide, gaping mouth of the snake snapping just beneath them. Despite its erratic movement, it was still chasing them. "Lergo's getting closer!"

"Cylus," Zephyr shouted. "We're coming under you for support. Don't let go of Pegasus but let us help!"

Cylus looked down. "Hurry, my hands are slipping!"

Astraea looked back at Triana. "I'll take one of his back hooves, you take the other, then we lift."

With no time to waste, Zephyr flew as close to Cylus as she dared. Astraea reached up and caught hold of the centaur's back left leg while Triana took the right. Tryn took a position in front and draped Cylus's front hooves over his shoulders.

"We got him!" Astraea called. "Pegasus, go!"

With the centaur's weight evenly distributed between all of them, Pegasus was able to gain more height and rise beyond the enraged snake. Giving up, Lergo started to slither through the narrow streets, snapping at buildings and knocking things over.

There was little time to celebrate, as Cylus was still in danger. Pegasus turned slowly in the sky, and the others supported the centaur as he did.

"Pegasus," Astraea shouted, "you have to get into water. You still smell of the animals. Lergo will track you!"

"I will, the moment we find somewhere to hide." They looked around for a place to land, but they were in a built-up area. Over to their left were tall buildings, not unlike the ones they'd seen on Earth in Detroit. To their right there were other, shorter buildings, and then farther away, homes. There was no sign of water anywhere.

"My hands are slipping!" Cylus cried. "Please, take me down, take me down!"

They worked as one and flew lower and lower in the sky. Finally Pegasus glided along a street. Without speaking, Astraea and Triana released Cylus's back legs while Tryn flew free of his front end.

Once they were away from the stallion, Pegasus

flapped his wings hard and started to hover, lowering Cylus gently to the ground.

When they were all safely down, Astraea realized she was shaking. Not from Cylus's weight, but from fear for the centaur.

Cylus looked at all of them, and his mouth went tight with emotion. "Thank you," he finally managed. He patted Pegasus's neck. "I owe you everything."

"You owe me nothing, Cylus," Pegasus said. "That was a foolish and dangerous thing you did back there. But it worked. We are now on the same world as my Emily." His voice choked. "I can feel her. She lives."

"Where is she?" Astraea asked as she balled her hands into fists to calm the shaking.

Pegasus turned in a circle. "Something is very wrong. . . . She suffers greatly." Pegasus threw his head back and whinnied in pain.

Astraea walked up to the stallion and put her arms around his neck. "We'll find her, Pegasus. I promise, we'll find her."

Pegasus laid his head low on Astraea's shoulders. "We must. There is no life for me without her."

"First we find Darek and Render," Cylus said. "They were stuck on the ground. Did anyone see where they went?" Cylus was shaking, and though he would never openly admit it, Astraea knew he'd been terrified. They'd all been.

"They were with us when we arrived," Triana said. "But then we flew and they ran. I don't know where they could be."

They all stood in the center of the street. There were lights shining out the windows. But no Mimics ventured outside.

"I think we should get moving before they send the Shadow Titans," Tryn said.

"With that snake here, they've got bigger problems," Astraea said.

Pegasus looked at the centaur. "Cylus, can you run?"

"I can run faster than you!" he retorted. Then he said, "I'm sorry, I'm still a little shaken up. Yes, I can run."

"Then we had better get moving," Pegasus said. "We have to find somewhere safe and then go after Darek and Render. After that, we will make our plans."

They started running down the long street. But soon they felt a heavy pressure slowing them down, and they moved into a trot. When they reached a crossroads, they changed direction and kept moving. While they moved, they listened for signs of Lergo tearing through the city. At one point, they heard tremendous crashing and what might have been a building collapse, but it was far in the distance.

After a time, they found an area of squat buildings with no lights on. They slowed to a walk and looked around.

"This looks very much like Earth," Pegasus commented softly. "It is not what I would have expected of the Mimics."

"Me neither," Astraea agreed. "But you know what? How do the Mimics get around? I haven't seen anything like a chariot or a car or anything. We know they can't fly. So what do they do?"

The group stopped and gazed around at the empty street. There were no vehicles around them at all.

"You're right," Tryn said. "Maybe they don't like to travel. Or, this is the only place they live. But if there are other cities, they might just stay there. From everything we've seen of them, the Mimics don't seem interested in anything other than taking over other worlds."

"That could prove helpful for us," Pegasus commented.

"Yes, for those of us that can fly," Zephyr said. "What about the centaurs? They're as grounded as the Mimics."

"But we can run faster than Mimics," Cylus said.

"True," Pegasus agreed.

They reached the end of another street and were faced with a four-way intersection. They all looked at each other questioningly. "Now where?" Zephyr asked.

"We're moving farther and farther away from Darek and Render," Cylus said. "We have to find them."

"He's right," Astraea said. She looked up at the dark windows around them. "This area looks deserted, but we have no way of knowing. We may have to go farther to avoid the Mimics." She looked at Tryn. "If you go while it's still dark out, with their poor vision, the Mimics might not see you in the sky."

"I agree," Pegasus said. "Tryn, use your board to find Darek and Render and bring them here. I am going to fly around and see if I can get a better sense of the area, and check on our large friend."

When Tryn and Pegasus left, Zephyr carried Astraea and Triana closer to one of the buildings. "I think we should get off the street."

Cylus was holding his bow at the ready. "There's a doorway there; let's get in so we only have to defend one side."

They moved into the doorway. Astraea slid off Zephyr's back and tried the door. It was unlocked. She pushed it open a fraction and peered inside.

"Are you trying to get us caught?" Zephyr asked. "What if there are Mimics in there?"

"I don't think there are," Astraea responded. "There's a thick layer of dust on the floor. It runs the whole length of the corridor. We all know the Mimics can't stand mess. I don't think anyone has been here in a very long time."

Cylus looked inside. "Why would the Mimics build this and then not use it?"

Astraea shrugged. "Your guess is as good as mine."

They closed the door and stood in the darkness waiting for Tryn to bring Render and Darek back.

It seemed to take ages. Astraea would occasionally look up to see if Pegasus was returning, but there was no sign of the stallion either. "You don't think he's gone to find Emily by himself, do you?"

Zephyr snorted. "He's not that stupid. . . ." Then she paused. "But then again, it is Pegasus, and we all know how he feels about her. . . ."

"He was very emotional," Triana said. "Especially when he could feel her. I hope he doesn't try it alone."

They fell into an uncomfortable silence as they waited. Astraea started to worry. What if dawn arrived before the others? What if Pegasus didn't come back? What if Lergo tracked them down?

The harder her imagination worked, the more anxious she became. Each sound had her jumping out of her skin. She hated staying still, but now they were forced to wait for the others.

Finally they heard clopping. Astraea peered out of the doorway and looked down the street. "It's them!" she cried. "It's Tryn with Darek and Render!"

Cylus ran out and down to the others. He embraced

the centaurs and slapped Tryn on the back affection-
ately.

"We were so worried," Astraea said as they all met
up in the doorway. She hugged each of them tightly.

"Us too!" Render said with wild, excited eyes.
"That snake went crazy. It's tearing the place apart.
When you flew away, it smashed down on the ground
and just started biting anything, including buildings.
We had to hide—there's no way we could outrun it."

"Where is it now?" Zephyr asked.

"Across the town," Tryn answered. "I think we're
safe here for the moment."

Pegasus returned and clopped up to the doorway.
"Lergo is moving farther away from us. Also, I have
not seen any lights in this area and do not believe the
Mimics use it. This might be the best place for us to
hide as we make our plans."

Astraea tried not to let it show, but Pegasus still
stank of the dead animals. "Did you, um, see any
water?"

Pegasus snorted. "I am aware that I still stink,
Astraea. I did try looking for a river or even a pond,
but there are none in this immediate area. We are

definitely in a city. I can feel Emily; she is here with us. Somewhere."

Tryn walked closer to Astraea. "Jake is still alive too!"

Astraea gasped, "How do you know?"

"My skateboard," Tryn said. "Before I found Darek and Render, I told it to find him, and it was taking me away. It wouldn't have done that if he was dead."

"Do you have any idea how far he is?" Astraea asked.

Tryn shook his head. "But I'm thinking it's quite far, considering the board was taking me high up."

Pegasus nodded. "If it was taking you up, then yes, Jake is far from here. The higher you go, the shorter the journey."

Cylus frowned. "How does that work?"

"It has to do with planetary rotation," Tryn said.

Cylus looked at the other centaurs. "Nope, still doesn't make sense."

Astraea looked at Pegasus and Tryn and pointed back to the building. "It doesn't look like anyone's been inside there for ages. We could use this as our base."

"Let's go in, then," Darek said.

"Wait," Astraea said. "Not this way. I think we should go in from above."

"What?" Cylus cried. "Why?"

Pegasus nodded. "Very good, Astraea. I agree. We can carry the centaurs up."

"Wait, what am I missing?" Cylus said. "Why can't we use the door?"

"You've seen it. There are no footprints in the dust in there," Astraea explained. "If we go in through the door, we'll make some. Then if the Mimics come, they'll see them and know we're here. But if we go in from the roof . . ."

"Then they won't see our trail," Cylus said, nodding. "That's really smart."

Tryn looked up to the roof. "Let me try up there first to see if there's a way in and if it's safe. This isn't Earth. There may not be a door."

Tryn walked back out into the street and used his skateboard to fly up to the roof. He was gone for some time. But when he returned, he was excited and carrying something in his hand.

"Guess what? This isn't the Mimic's home world. They stole it from others just like they're trying to take Titus and Xanadu!"

"How do you know?" Astraea asked.

Tryn handed over the item he was carrying. "These are empty homes. Like apartments. I got into one and found this. It's a kind of photograph. There were loads on the walls too. None showing Mimics, just these people that were once here. Look, they weren't too different from us. I mean, they do have three eyes, but that's not too different."

Astraea looked at the picture and saw what looked like a family. There were two very tall, odd-looking adults, with three smaller ones. They had flat faces, three eyes, and appeared to be smiling.

"If what you are suggesting is true," Pegasus mused, "the Mimics take worlds. But what do they do with the people?"

"I hate to think," Triana said. "But they do eat smelly animals."

"Ugh," Render cried. "Are you saying the Mimics ate the inhabitants and want to eat us, too?"

"We must not get ahead of ourselves," Pegasus said. "We do not know what they do. Tryn, can we all get in from above?"

Tryn nodded. "Yes. Whoever they were, these people were much taller than us. Wider too. There are stairs, but they should be easy for you all."

"Easy, he says," Zephyr said. "Sure, I love stairs, can't get enough of them."

"Would you rather stay out here?" Pegasus teased.

"No," Zephyr insisted. "But just once, I would like ramps. What is wrong with ramps? Two-legged Titans can use them. Titans with hooves can use them. They'd be perfect."

"If we ever find the designer, I will tell them," Pegasus said. "For now, we must get inside."

Pegasus, Zephyr, and Tryn helped carry the three centaurs up to the roof. They found the stairs down into the building, and Tryn led them to the apartment he'd investigated. The whole building was eerily silent and covered in undisturbed dust.

Once they were settled inside the spacious apartment, Tryn, Astraea, and Triana carefully went through the whole building to check if there was anyone else around. But after a thorough search, they found nothing.

"This is so strange," Astraea said, returning to their apartment. "It's like the people all just walked away from their lives. There's no damage or signs of a fight anywhere."

"I imagine a lot of homes on Titus look exactly the same right now," Pegasus said. "It is how the Mimics take over—they use stealth until it is too late."

"I hope it's not too late for us," Render said.

"It won't be," Cylus responded. "We're going to stop the queen, and then we're going to take Titus back. The fight with the Mimics ends here."

"Indeed," Pegasus agreed. "Once we find Emily and Riza, they can help us in this struggle."

Astraea walked over to one of the windows and peered out. "Is it just me, or has it been dark for a really long time? Maybe there is no sun on this world."

"It has been a long night," Tryn agreed. "But since the Mimics can't see well in the dark, I'm sure they wouldn't choose a dark world for their home base."

"So what do we do now?" Cylus said. "We can't just stay here and do nothing."

"We're not going to," Tryn said. "Now that we have a hiding place, while it's still dark out, I will use my skateboard to find Emily and Riza. Once we know where they are, we can start to plan how to get them out."

"I am coming with you, Trynulus," Pegasus insisted.

"I thought you might," Tryn said. "After we find them, we'll look for Jake."

"We want to come too," Astraea said.

"We do?" Zephyr cried.

Astraea nodded. "Of course. But if you're tired, you can stay here with the others. I'll go with Pegasus."

Zephyr snorted. "Now, why did you have to go and say that?"

"Zeph, it's okay. Stay here. We won't be long," Astraea teased.

"You know, Astraea, you are not a nice person!" Zephyr walked back to the door. "Come on, let's go."

# 16

BEFORE LEAVING THEIR APARTMENT, ASTRAEA gave her Solar Stream ring to Cylus "just in case." The centaur wasn't happy to receive it, but in the end he accepted it.

The search party climbed up to the roof and looked around. There was no sign of Lergo anywhere near their building. Nor was there any sign of the dawn.

"Trynulus, please, lead us," Pegasus said. The stallion pawed the roof with a sharp hoof, and his tail whipped around anxiously.

Tryn stepped onto his skateboard. "Take us to Emily Jacobs. . . ."

The tiny wings on the skateboard appeared from the wheels and started to flap. Tryn was lifted off the building, over to the side of the roof, and into the open air.

Pegasus was close behind him.

"You're sure about this?" Zephyr asked.

Astraea felt nerves bunch up in her stomach. They were actually going to look for Emily Jacobs. "You bet! Let's go."

Zephyr took off right behind Pegasus. They followed Tryn across the rooftops and well away from their area.

Astraea sat up higher on Zephyr and looked down to memorize the route, to ensure they could find their way back to the centaurs and Triana. She also kept a sharp eye out for Lergo but couldn't see the snake anywhere. She felt a tinge of guilt for bringing it here. Not for the Mimics, but for Lergo. The snake was used to the jungle; now all it had was buildings and concrete. Despite its size, it must have been frightened.

The journey was longer than Astraea expected. When Pegasus said he could feel Emily, Astraea had thought she must be close. But that was far from the truth. Yet despite the length of time it took to travel, the sky remained dark.

Finally Tryn started to descend.

Astraea looked around. Again there were buildings surrounding them. But in this area, they were bigger and looked more like Jupiter's palace than the buildings of Earth. She also saw a few trees and a park, which were the first she'd seen since they'd arrived.

The skateboard took them down to ground level and slowed, but kept moving. Some of the buildings had lights on, but as Astraea studied the windows, she didn't see any movement.

She was surprised that there weren't any fences, gates, or guards, especially if there were Xan being held here. "Why isn't there any security?" she called to the others.

Tryn looked back at her and shrugged. "Maybe the Mimics think they're unstoppable."

"They are unstoppable," Zephyr said.

"Not anymore," Pegasus said darkly.

They continued at ground level a bit farther and then approached a set of steps leading up to one of the biggest buildings. "It's taking us in there," Tryn said as they neared the entrance.

Pegasus snorted. "I feel her. She is close but still suffering."

They climbed the steps and approached a line of doors going into the building. If anything, it reminded Astraea of Arcadia One back on Titus.

Tryn reached for the handle and pulled. The door swung open easily. He held it open for Pegasus and Zephyr. Astraea remained on Zephyr's back and had to duck down to get through the doorway. Once inside, she loaded her slingshot and made sure her dagger was within easy reach. As a final precaution, she opened the flap on her special bracelet and whispered to the two snakes hidden inside, "We're going into a Mimic building. We might need you."

The two snakes raised their tiny heads and hissed. Then they settled down again.

"How are they?" Tryn asked.

Astraea nodded. "Ready, just like us."

Tryn also loaded his slingshot and held it up as the skateboard continued to lead them to Emily Jacobs.

Before they'd gone halfway down the corridor,

their noses were assaulted by the worst stink Astraea had ever encountered. It wasn't the smell of the Mimic food; it was something else. Something much worse.

The skateboard led them to a set of stairs. But instead of taking them up, it carried Tryn down.

Astraea tightened her grip on Zephyr as she took the stairs one at a time. Pegasus was also cautious on the steep stairs. When they reached the bottom, they were met with a nightmare.

The building structure had been changed by the Mimics. Walls had been crudely knocked out, and instead of there being a corridor with rooms, there was a large, dimly lit chamber. In the center of the chamber was an unimaginable sight.

Astraea gasped and Tryn's eyes were huge as they beheld a Mimic nursery. The floor was covered in thick slime, and small, maggot-like developing Mimics writhed and wriggled in it. Among the maggot Mimics were about ten adults tending to the babies. Some were turning the maggots over, while others were moving them around. Along the back wall were crates of what looked like eggs. One Mimic was carrying an egg and placing it in the goo. Another was pulling away the empty shells of a hatchling.

When they heard Astraea gasp, the nursery attendants looked up and started to scream and charge forward.

There was no time to think, only react. Astraea fired her slingshot at the approaching Mimics. Her pebble shot through the first two before getting lodged in the third. Moments later, they started to melt.

Tryn also fired at the charging Mimics and brought more down.

Without weapons of his own, all Pegasus could do was dart away from the tendrils that the Mimics shot at him.

Astraea wasn't sure how many rocks she fired, but just as quickly as it had started, the fight ended, and all the adult Mimics were rendered into puddles that melted into the goo on the nursery floor.

"We have to move quickly," Tryn said. "They have a form of silent communication; others may come with Shadow Titans."

Tryn looked back at Astraea. "Stay here; we don't know what that stuff is. It might be just as deadly as melted Mimics. I'll go search the room for Emily." He commanded his skateboard to find her.

As Tryn rose above the maggots and started to cross the room, Pegasus stood back with Zephyr and Astraea, pacing impatiently. His tail swished and his ears were pricked forward. "Hurry!"

When Tryn neared the back of the chamber, he stopped. He was looking down and shaking. A moment later, he flew back. His face was gray.

"What is it?" Pegasus demanded. "Emily is there; I can feel her."

"Yes, she is," Tryn said. "But there are two extra-large baby Mimics lying across her. If I reach for her, I might touch one and pass out."

"We cannot leave my Emily there," Pegasus cried. "We must get her! I will try."

"Pegasus, stop," Astraea said. "I'll go on Tryn's board with him."

"Astraea, you can't!" Zephyr cried. "You're not immune to those things. If you fall in, it could kill you."

"I know, but if Tryn holds on to me, and I lift Emily away from the Mimics, even if I pass out, Tryn should be able to carry the both of us back here."

"It's too dangerous," Zephyr protested.

"We're not leaving Emily there," Astraea said. She looked at Pegasus. "Emily is still alive, right?"

"Yes," Pegasus moaned. "She is alive and in such pain."

"Then I'm going!" Astraea looked at Tryn. "Let's go."

Tryn hesitated for a moment but then nodded. "All right. Get on my board and kneel at the back. I'll take us over there and see if we can find a clear way to grab Emily. I'll hold on to you; you won't fall. But keep your feet up and don't let them drop."

Astraea followed Tryn's instructions and knelt at the back of his skateboard.

"Be careful," Zephyr warned.

"We will," Astraea promised.

When Tryn commanded his skateboard to move, Astraea looked at all the baby Mimics. There was nothing cute about them. They were like horrible insects. Their heads were still tucked into their bodies, with only eyes and mewing mouths showing. There were only the tiniest traces of hands and feet starting to develop from the torso.

Worst of all was the smell. Astraea had to fight back the bile that rose, bitter, in her mouth. Looking over the moving mass beneath her, this was a sight that would haunt her for the rest of her life.

"We're almost there," Tryn warned.

Astraea nodded. "Take us down close."

The mewing sounds from the floor and the writhing in the goo was sickening. But even that wasn't as bad as the sight that came next. Two large, swollen pink-and-gray Mimic maggots were lying across Emily and holding her down. Emily's hair was matted with slime as she lay in the mess.

"Are they eating her?" Tryn asked.

Astraea could see their mouths. "No, they're not. They're just touching her. Probably draining all her life force like the Mimics do when they touch us. But why are these two so big?"

Tryn groaned. "I don't know. They're so different from the others. Arious said there was a spawning coming. These might be the next generation of queens that will spread across the universe."

"Didn't Arious say that the queen would use a Xan to spawn?"

"Arious only speculated," Tryn said. "Remember, no one knows exactly how they spawn."

Astraea rose higher on the skateboard and looked around. "I can't see Riza in here."

Tryn joined her in looking around. "I don't think she's here."

Astraea looked back at Emily. "We have to stop them. I'm going to use my dagger to kill them."

"No, don't," Tryn warned. "If they melt, it will go all over Emily. We don't know how much more dangerous dead baby Mimics can be. We have to get her out without killing them."

Astraea looked at him for a moment and wondered if that was really his concern. Or was it his peaceful nature that couldn't bear the thought of hurting any other living being? She turned back to the two babies, searching for the best way to reach Emily. "All right, I won't kill them. Circle around the area. I need to get a better look."

Tryn moved the skateboard in a circle. "Stop!" Astraea called. "Look, I can see Emily's hand. It's raised and not lying in the goo. If you can get me closer, I can reach for it."

Tryn hovered lower. "Be careful," he said nervously. "Those things are moving."

Astraea looked at the two babies and gasped. "Tryn, they don't have eyes. They're blind. But all the others have eyes. They're so different, they must be queens."

"Being blind doesn't mean they're not dangerous," Tryn warned.

Astraea balanced more firmly on her section of the board. She wrapped one arm around Tryn's steady leg and started to reach down beside one of the mewing queens.

"Just a bit more," Astraea coaxed. "I've almost got her."

The board dipped lower. Astraea stretched out her hand and wrapped her fingers around Emily's wrist. "Got her! Pull us up."

Tryn ordered his board to rise slowly. Inch by inch, Emily's arm rose.

The weight of the two Mimic queens was more than Astraea had expected, and she needed to strain to pull. Moment by moment, Emily was raised into a seated position. "That's it, Emily," Astraea said. "Just a bit more and we'll be free of that second queen."

Tryn reached down and caught hold of Emily's

hand above Astraea. They worked together to pry Emily away. But just as Emily was pulled free of the second queen, a thin tendril shot out of it and latched on to Astraea's arm.

Astraea gasped as the sickening weakness started. But it was much worse than a normal Mimic touch. She felt a painful drawing, as though the Mimic were sucking the life force right out of her.

Unable to move, scream, or even breathe, Astraea's world went black.

# 17

NOTHING MORE WAS SAID AGAINST MELISSA as the mass of escapees moved through the long night. The pace was brisk and confident as they headed deeper into the woods.

Jake stayed on Chiron's back as they walked beside the ex-prisoners carrying the Fallen Queen. Occasionally Melissa would cry out, and Jake would reassure her that she was safe. At his gentle and kind words, Melissa would settle.

In the darkness, he still had no idea what she looked like, and by the shocked reactions around him, it had to be bad. But he didn't care. Something had happened during their mind-link. It connected him, Nesso, and Melissa tightly together. To not help her would be as impossible as it would be to abandon a family member.

The long night dragged on and on. If the Titans and Olympians were growing tired, they gave no clue. They just kept moving. Finally Jake could see the tiniest hint of light.

"Nesso, is that dawn, or are my eyes playing tricks on me?"

*"It isss dawn,"* Nesso hissed. *"We mussst find cover sssoon."*

"I'm sure they realize that," Jake said.

"Realize what?" Chiron asked.

"Nesso said that we should find some cover soon."

"Your little friend is correct," Chiron said. "Two hunters know of a series of caves that we might hide in and defend. They found it ages ago when they were out checking the animal traps. They had the opportunity to escape, but their Olympian loyalty brought them back to us despite the chance at freedom."

"Cool," Jake said. He didn't mention the story of Lergo living in a cave or concerns for what else could be in there.

The dawn was just as slow as always. Fatigue was setting in and Jake was getting sleepy, but he forced himself to stay awake.

"Are you getting tired?" Jake asked Chiron. "It's almost light enough for me to see by. I can walk if it would help."

"Thank you for your consideration," Chiron said. "But you are safer where you are. I am very tired, but it has nothing to do with you. We have all been starved a long time. It will take more than a few meals for all of us to recover."

"Just as long as I'm not too heavy for you."

Chiron turned back to him, and in the rising light, Jake saw the warmth in the centaur's eyes. He smiled. "You are not too heavy at all."

They continued in a comfortable silence. Part of Jake wanted to look over at Melissa. But another part was frightened. Everyone was so shocked by her appearance. What if he was horrified?

Each minute, Jake fought the urge to look. But with the sunrise, the temptation became too great. He turned and got his first sight of her.

He gasped.

Melissa was one of the strangest-looking creatures he'd ever seen, even after all the Titans he'd met. At any other time in his life, he'd have been terrified of her. But somehow, he wasn't. She was just—Melissa.

There was no denying that she was immense. She had to be at least twice the size of an elephant, with a huge bulbous head and a long, wide fleshy body. She did have two arms like Mimics, and two legs. But she was bright pink, with a big gray head.

Jake had almost expected her to look like a queen bee. But she didn't. If anything, she looked more like a maggot with arms and legs. In the growing light, he could see the injuries she'd sustained during the fight with her sister. There were deep cuts across her body, and as Angie had said, one of her arms looked like it might fall off. Her face was covered in bites as well. He realized that during their link she really had shielded him from experiencing the horrific pain she was suffering.

When he looked back at her head, he also realized why he hadn't seen anything in her memories. Melissa didn't have any eyes—she was completely blind. He now understood why there had been so many Mimics around her before the fight; they'd had to lead her.

Looking down to her mouth, he saw how her sister could inflict such injuries. Melissa had a wide mouth that revealed rows of sharp teeth every time she winced in pain.

The Titans and Olympians were stooped over as they carried her on their backs, but it was difficult because she was soft, and if they moved wrong, their hands and arms would push into her body and she would whimper. Everyone was straining to keep her up.

When Jake had insisted the Titans help her, he'd had no idea what he was asking of the exhausted, starved prisoners. Seeing them struggle to move her, he felt guilty for asking. But not guilty for wanting to help her.

Melissa hadn't whined or whimpered for some time. Her silence worried Jake. "Are you all right, Melissa?"

"It hurts, Jake. Please, make it stop," she whimpered through her wide, gray mouth.

Jake wasn't sure what hurt on the poor creature.

All her wounds, or the way the Titans had to carry her. "We're almost there; just hold on for a few more minutes."

"All right," she said softly.

If Jake closed his eyes, he heard the voice he recognized. But when he looked at her, he couldn't imagine that small frightened voice coming from such an enormous, terrifying creature.

Gazing past Melissa, Jake also got his first clear look at all the prisoners that had escaped the cage. There had to be almost a hundred of them. Maybe more. Their clothes were in tatters and their faces gaunt and exhausted. But even now, after the long trek through the night, he could see fierce determination rising in their eyes.

Among the Titans and Olympians, Jake also spotted other beings. Several were like the figure from the statue, with three eyes and tall bodies. Their skin color was pale blue. Other beings, he simply couldn't recognize. There was also a group of three tall, willowy beings that moved so gracefully, they almost glided. Their bald, downcast heads were pale and looked almost like pearls as they struggled to walk.

Each one of the bald people had a Titan beside them, supporting them as they moved.

Jake was instantly reminded of some of the stories he'd studied in history class about forced marches, where people were half-dead but kept moving. This wasn't a forced march, it was an escape, but the people looked just as bad as from the history books.

"Everyone looks so sick," Jake said to Chiron.

"We will recover," Chiron said. "In time."

"Do you know everyone here?" Jake asked. When Chiron nodded, Jake continued. "Who are those three really tall people with the bald heads?"

Chiron sighed heavily and remained silent for some time. Finally he looked back at Jake. "Those are three Xan who were taken millennia ago. They survived but are shells of their former selves. Their powers are gone, and they have no memory of who they are or where they came from. I fear it will take more than Arious to heal them."

"They're Xan?" Jake cried. He looked back at the three. One raised its head as though it felt him looking. Their elliptical eyes were like pearls. Despite the filth, there was such beauty there that he actually choked.

"They are perhaps the most beautiful creatures in existence," Chiron said. "It tears at me to see what the Mimics have done to such magnificent beings and what they might be doing to Riza and Emily."

"Tryn says that Riza and Emily are really powerful. Maybe if we can free them, they can help these Xan."

"I would hope so," Chiron said. "But first we must save ourselves. Look. . . ." The centaur pointed forward. "I believe that is our destination."

Jake looked past Chiron's finger and through the trees; he saw two scouts in the distance, pointing at a tall mountain.

"We are near our sanctuary!" Chiron called to everyone behind them.

There were actual cheers of relief from the mass gathering. Jake looked back and saw the three Xan looking up. Their beauty brought tears to his eyes. "I—I don't understand," he said. "They're just people, but I can hardly look at them because they are so beautiful."

"You will get used to them. They will always be beautiful, but after a time you will see more of their inner beauty and not just what lies on the outside."

Jake looked back at the Xan and nodded to them. When they nodded back, he caught his breath and wondered what a healthy, fully powered Xan looked like.

The mountain was farther away than it looked, and it took an age to get there. But just as the sun was high over their heads, they finally reached the base. Melissa was lowered to the ground, and everyone sat or lay down to rest.

Jake slid off Chiron's back. "Thank you again, Chiron; I appreciate that."

"It was my pleasure," Chiron said. "After we have rested and had something to eat, we will start to go through the caves."

While a container of ambrosia was opened and distributed among everyone, Jake looked for Angie. He found her with all the snakes. They were out of the ambrosia containers and scattered around on the ground. She was handing them pieces of ambrosia.

"How are they?"

"Fine," Angie said. "I'm sure they're glad to be out of those cramped containers."

Nesso hissed. *"They are. And they are ready to give more venom."*

"That is good news," Jake said. "I'll get one of the bottles and we can start."

As Jake went to collect the venom bottle, he saw Melissa lying down beneath a tree. She was all alone, and the people around her looked at her with a mix of fear and resentment.

"Hey, Melissa," he said gently.

Her large, bulbous head turned at the sound. "Jake, where are we?"

"I don't really know," Jake said. "But it's far from the Mimics. You'll be safe here."

"They don't like me," Melissa said sadly.

"They don't know you yet. Give them time."

"They don't like me because of what the others have done to them. Do you like me?"

Jake approached the strange-looking Fallen Queen. He reached out and patted her good arm where it lay on the ground. "You know I do."

"I like you and Nesso too," Melissa said weakly. "You're cool."

*"Thank you, Melisssa,"* Nesso hissed.

"You're welcome," Melissa said.

Jake gasped. "Can you understand Nesso?"

"Uh-huh," Melissa said. "Just like you. Jake, am I going to die?"

"Not if I can help it," Jake said. "Stay here. I'll get you some more ambrosia. That will help."

Jake went to one of the containers and pulled out a large chunk of ambrosia cake. He took a bite and then handed a small piece up to Nesso.

*"Sssome of the otherss were watching what you were doing with Melisssa. They ssstill do not like her."*

"I don't care if they like her or not. Just as long as they leave her alone."

*"They will be essspecially angry if they sssee you giving her ambrosssia."*

Nesso was right. Some of the resting Titans and Olympians were watching him suspiciously. He sought out Diana in the large gathering. She was seated with two men. One looked very similar to her, and Jake realized it must be her twin, Apollo. But he didn't recognize the other.

"Diana, I need your help, please," Jake said lightly.

Diana rose slowly to her feet. She stood taller

than him and had electric-blue eyes and striking black hair. Apollo also had blue eyes and dark hair. He stayed on the ground. The other man rose and smiled at him.

"Jake, is it?" he asked. "I'm Steve Jacobs. I'm from Earth too. Thank you for getting us out of there."

"Jacobs?" Jake repeated. "Are you Emily's father?"

He nodded, and a shadow passed over his face. "I'm desperate to know what those monsters are doing to her and Riza. My sister is missing too. I fear she's at another work camp."

"I'm sorry, sir, I don't know where anyone is," Jake said. "But I do know Pegasus is anxious to get back to her. I'm sure they'll be here soon."

"We are so relieved to hear that he lives," Diana said.

Steve added, "We thought for sure they'd killed him."

"Almost, but he's fine now." Jake looked up at Diana. "Would you come with me, please? I want to give Melissa some more ambrosia, but people are looking at me funny. I don't want any trouble."

"Of course," Diana said.

Jake, Diana, and Steve carried ambrosia over to Melissa. "We're back," he said to the Fallen Queen. "Are you hungry?"

"I hurt," Melissa whimpered.

Jake looked over at the mess that was her arm. It had been shredded. He had no idea what Melissa's sister hand done to it, but whatever it was, it was bad. "Maybe if you eat some more, you'll feel better."

Melissa raised her good hand to receive the ambrosia. The moment she did, a couple of Titans stood and walked closer. "You're not feeding that thing again. We need all that ambrosia. That is ours; we have earned it."

"Her name is Melissa, and I helped get that food," Jake said. "So I'll give her my share."

"I do not care what its name is," one Titan said angrily. "That ambrosia is for us."

"It is for everyone," Diana said sharply. "She will be fed as we all have been."

When two more Titans rose, Apollo approached, followed by Chiron.

"Are we going to have a problem?" Apollo challenged.

The Titans stood their ground for a moment, looked at Diana, Apollo, and Chiron, but then backed down. "It is not fair, Apollo; she is one of them."

"She was betrayed by them," Apollo said. "Wounded and abandoned by her kind." Apollo raised his head and addressed everyone. "I will make this very clear. This human, Jake, freed us. If he wants to give ambrosia to this Mimic, he may, and I will challenge anyone who tries to stop him."

There were grumbles of protest, but they faded away.

"This could be a problem," Steve said.

"There will be no problem," Diana said. "I will not tolerate anyone going against our orders." Diana turned her fierce eyes on Jake. "You may take care of your friend."

"Here, Melissa, eat," Jake said.

Melissa turned her head toward him. "Why do they hate me?"

"They don't understand," Steve said softly. "Just give them time."

Jake placed the large piece of ambrosia cake in Melissa's hand. She ate it in one big bite. "Thank you," she said softly.

"Would you like more?" Jake offered.

"No, I'm cool."

"Then just lie back and relax."

As Melissa settled back, Jake nodded to Diana, Steve, and Apollo. "Thank you."

"You are welcome," Diana said. She leaned closer to Jake. "I just hope your faith in her is not misguided."

"It isn't," Jake said. "I know it."

While everyone else settled down to rest, Jake found Angie with the snakes. He retrieved the venom bottle, and together they started to gather more from the snakes. After they finished, Jake stood up and looked around.

They were in a fully wooded area. The trees were so much like Earth, Jake could almost convince himself he was home. Then he saw the centaurs, satyrs, and Xan resting among the other strange camp survivors, and those thoughts vanished.

"Are you all right?" Angie asked him.

Jake nodded. "This just looks like home," he said.

"You'll get back there soon," Angie said lightly. "We all will."

After everyone had rested and eaten again, groups were formed. Some were sent out to seek another source of food and water, while others were organized to be security patrols and defense. A third group started to work to clear out two caves that were selected to hold the large group.

Jake stood with Steve, Joel, and Angie. "I'm not sure what I should be doing. I'm not as strong as everyone else, and I don't know this world."

"I know what you mean," Joel said. "Paelen's out there working like a machine. I do have this arm that's strong, but the gravity here is so heavy, I get tired quickly."

"Me too," Jake agreed.

"Joel, you've been hurt and are lucky to be alive," Steve said. He turned to Jake. "And you already have a job. You have to look after Melissa and show Joel and me how to milk those precious snakes."

"We will," Angie said proudly. "They're really sweet."

As they chatted, the three tall Xan approached. Once again, Jake's eyes were locked on the strange, entrancing beings. They were almost identical in appearance, and yet Jake knew they were women. "Thank you for freeing us," one of them said softly.

"Yes, thank you," another said. "We are in your debt."

Their voices were as beautiful as they were. All they needed were wings, and Jake would have been convinced he was talking to angels.

"Um, it—it was nothing," Jake stammered.

"No, child, it was everything," the first one said. "We have been in that cage for an eternity." The Xan bowed her head and offered her hand. "I am Ezmi." She pointed to the others beside her. "This is Mila, and Jili. We no longer recall our home or our people, but we will be joyous to return there."

"Xanadu is really cool," Jake said.

The three Xan smiled at Jake's comment. "Then we shall be grateful to return and see how *cool* it is."

They nodded again and drifted away.

To Jake it looked like they were floating. He turned to Joel and Steve. "Are you guys sure they're not angels? Tryn told me they were beautiful, but I mean, wow!"

"I know," Steve said. "It takes a while to get used

to them. Riza is the same, but with a wicked sense of humor." He sighed heavily. "I just pray we can free Riza and Emily before their memories are wiped like those three."

Jake saw the pain in their eyes. Tryn had told him that Joel and Emily were especially close. Not knowing what the Mimics were doing to them must have been agony.

As the seemingly endless day passed, two caves were prepared to house the escapees. Jake went into one of them and marveled at the change. Somehow, the workers had managed to make rough beds. There was a cooking area with a way for the woodsmoke to be vented, and even a store of water that had been put in some of the emptied ambrosia containers. There was also a small area to house the snakes.

"This reminds me of *Robinson Crusoe*," Jake said to Steve as they walked in together. "Like we're stranded on an island or something."

"It sure does," Steve agreed. "I just hope the others come from Titus or Xanadu so we don't have to wait here too long. Those Mimics are going to be furious when they discover we've gone. They may come after us."

"And we shall be ready if they do." Diana approached carrying two long spears. She handed one to Steve. "We have started to prepare weapons using the venom," she said. "We can only hope it works."

"It does," Jake said. He looked around the cave. "So where does Melissa sleep?"

Diana inhaled. "Unfortunately, the others refuse to share the caves with her. She must remain outside."

"But they carried her here. How can they be so mean now?" Jake cried.

"They carried her because Chiron and I ordered them to and because of what you did for us. But there is only so far you can push an Olympian or a Titan. Sharing the cave is asking too much."

"But that's not fair!" Jake protested. "She's hurt—we have to protect her."

"I am sorry, Jake," Diana said. "But there is nothing more I can do. To be honest, I do not trust her and would not feel comfortable with her in here either."

"Fine," Jake spat. "If you don't believe me when I say she's safe, then you don't trust me either!" He stormed out of the cave.

Jake couldn't believe these Titans and Olympians.

If Astraea and Tryn had been there, they would have done anything they could to protect Melissa if he asked them to. He walked across the clearing and over to the Fallen Queen, questioning his high opinion of the Titans. They were behaving just like everyone else on Earth with their own prejudices. It seemed like nothing he could say would ever change their opinion.

When he reached Melissa, she appeared to be asleep and was whining softly with each breath.

*"They don't undersssstand our connection to her,"* Nesso said. *"We will help her even if they won't. Jake, Melisssa is important. We must protect her."*

Jake reached up and stroked Nesso's smooth scales. "They're so stupid. She hasn't done anything to them, but they hate her. They probably don't even like the snakes and are just using them for the venom." He looked angrily back at the caves. "We're not spending one night in there with them."

*"If I am with you, that isss all I need,"* Nesso said.

Her calm voice soothed Jake's anger. "Thanks, Nesso. So we'll just find our own cave." He searched the area for Angie and found her sitting beneath a tree surrounded by the snakes. There was a large group of them settled in her lap. He sat down near her. "We have a problem. The Titans won't allow Melissa in either of the caves. She has to stay outside."

Angie looked over at Melissa and said nothing.

Jake stood up quickly. "You're just like them, aren't you? You don't trust her either. I thought you under-stood. Fine, I'll help her on my own!"

"Jake, wait!" Angie rose and ran after him. She caught him by the arm and turned him around. "Please don't be mad at me." Tears rose in her eyes. "I'm sorry, it's just that I'm scared of her."

Seeing Angie's tears, Jake lowered his head and pulled her into an embrace. "I'm not mad at you, Angie. It's just, well, I'd hoped you'd understand that she's not like the other Mimics. I know she's big and scary-looking, but she's a kid, just like you and me. And she's in pain. If you'd experienced what Nesso and I had, you'd see she's as gentle as those Xan."

Angie looked over at Melissa. "You're sure she's safe?"

"She's as safe as me and Nesso," Jake said. "I don't

care about everyone else, but it really matters to me that you believe me."

"I do believe you, and I want to help. Please, let me come with you."

Jake pulled her closer. "Of course. We're a team, you and me."

*"And me,"* Nesso added.

Jake chuckled softly. "Always you, Nesso."

Before they left, Jake and Angie settled the snakes into their nest of soft tree boughs in the cave. Every time they started to walk away, the snakes followed.

Angie bent down and stroked several of them. "I'm going with Jake for a while. You all need to stay here to be safe. I promise we'll be back."

All the snakes looked up at them as their tiny tongues flicked in and out of their mouths.

*"They will ssstay,"* Nesso said.

Jake and Angie walked back to Melissa. "I think she's asleep," he said softly.

"No, I'm not," Melissa said. "I heard what you said, Angie. Please, don't be scared of me. You, Jake, and Nesso are my only friends. It hurts me that you don't like me."

"I'm sorry, Melissa," Angie said softly. "I didn't mean to." For the first time, Angie reached out and actually touched Melissa's good hand. "We are friends, always."

Melissa sighed heavily. "Thank you."

"Melissa . . . ," Jake started.

Melissa cut in, "I know they don't want me with them and that you are leaving to find us a new home."

"Wow, you've got really good hearing," Jake said.

"I hear everything," Melissa said.

"So you know that Nesso and I are going to stay with you."

"And me," Angie added.

"No," Melissa wept. "I don't want you to leave the others. You belong here. I should have died. Why did you save me?"

"Don't talk that way," Jake said. He took her large hand in both of his. "You survived the fight because you are stronger than you know. I don't want you to die. Neither does Nesso or Angie. And you won't. We're going to find a quiet place, just for us. Then you can recover."

"This isn't right. Jake, I'm just a big loser with a capital *L*. I shouldn't be alive. I'm a Fallen Queen."

"Stop saying that. I told you, you're Melissa and you're our friend. We're not going to let you die. So just stay here and rest. We'll come back, and then we'll all go together."

Before Melissa could say more, Jake and Angie walked away from the makeshift camp and started to search along the base of the tall mountain. There were enormous trees that shot way up into the sky, and bushes with colorful berries. But remembering what Tryn had said about alien worlds, Jake didn't eat anything.

"What about over there?" Angie said.

"Where?" Jake asked.

"There." Angie pointed. "Look."

Jake couldn't see what Angie meant until she ran ahead and disappeared behind a large boulder. She reappeared again. "It's big enough for Melissa. Come and see."

Jake reached the cave and saw it was well concealed behind the boulders. Inside, the ceiling was high, and the walls were wide. There was plenty of space for Melissa.

"This is perfect!" Jake said excitedly. Then his mood dropped. "But how do we get her here?"

"The ambrosia has healed most of her cuts—it's just her arm that's still a mess. She might be able to walk."

"How?" Jake asked. "You've seen her. Her body is *really* long and round. How is she supposed to move? And please don't say we can roll her like a bowling ball."

"A what?" Angie asked.

"Never mind." Jake rubbed his chin and went back out of the cave and looked around. "Well, the terrain isn't that rough; maybe she could walk, if we help her."

"We will," Angie agreed.

It was a short trip back to camp. So their cave wasn't so far from the other two caves and a source of food. But they'd be far enough away that they wouldn't have to worry about the Titans turning on Melissa.

"We're back," Angie said lightly as they approached the large Fallen Queen. "And we've found the perfect place for all of us to stay."

"It isn't far," Jake said. "Do you think you can walk?"

"If it means leaving here, I will try." Melissa leaned forward and cried out as she moved. But with a lot of straining, she made it to her feet. The Titans and Olympians around them stared in stunned silence as Melissa rose to her full height. Jake gazed up at her and realized she had to be at least four times his height. Her torso looked even pinker than it had earlier. Whether that was a good thing or a bad, he couldn't tell.

"Wow, you're really tall," he said to her.

"Am I?" Melissa said.

"You betcha," Jake said. He reached out and touched her lower abdomen. "This is where I am."

"I'm not tall; you're short," Melissa teased.

Jake gasped at the first humor from the Mimic. Then he laughed. "I'm not short; Angie is."

"No, I'm not," Angie cried. Then she laughed as well. She looked up at Melissa. "I think you're beautiful."

Jake looked at her, searching for lies, considering what she'd said earlier. But he saw no trace of deceit or fear in her face.

Melissa's wounded arm hung limply at her side, but she reached down with her good arm and offered her hand. "Where do we go?"

Jake reached up and took it. "I'll lead you; it isn't far, and the walk should be easy for you."

Melissa's steps were uncertain as she moved her bulky body. But when Angie stood on her other side and placed her hand on the Fallen Queen's stubby leg, Melissa's steps became a little more confident.

"That's it," Angie coaxed. "You're doing fine."

As the others watched them moving away from the camp, Paelen and Joel approached.

"Where are you going?" Joel asked.

"Away from here!" Jake said angrily. "I thought the Titans and Olympians were tolerant of others, but I was wrong. But then again, they didn't like my friend Tryn because he's silver, and me because I'm human, so I guess I should have expected this."

"It's not their fault," Melissa said softly. "I am their enemy."

"No, you're not," Joel said. "You haven't done anything."

"Thanks, dude, but to them I have," Melissa answered.

Joel stopped and repeated softly, "Dude?"

Jake explained about the mind-link and the California connection. "So we've found a cave where we'll stay. At least until Melissa is well enough to go farther."

"Let me help you," Joel said.

Jake noticed Paelen staring up at Melissa with a strange expression on his face. "What?" Jake challenged.

Paelen looked at him. "Her back is moving."

"Yeah, like we're walking . . . ," Jake said.

"No, I mean it's moving," Paelen repeated. He pointed up. "Look."

Jake and Angie looked up at Melissa's back. Paelen was right, there was rippling beneath the pink skin.

"Melissa, are you all right?" Jake asked.

"It hurts," Melissa said.

It looked as though something were alive beneath the skin and trying to get out. "We'd better get her to the cave," Jake said quickly.

Much to his surprise, Joel and Paelen stayed with them and helped clear a path for Melissa to walk. Each step was uncertain and hesitant, and Jake realized that this was what he must have looked like each night when Angie helped him move around in the dark.

The trip was slow, and on two occasions Melissa had to stop to rest. Jake was amazed she could move at all, as her short legs had to bear the weight of all the bulk.

"We're almost there," Angie coaxed. "Just a bit farther."

Melissa's whining grew more intense as they neared the cave. "It really hurts," she wept.

"Is it your arm?" Jake asked.

"It's everywhere."

It was then Jake realized that Melissa wasn't getting any better. The ambrosia might have helped with some of the external injuries, but she was looking worse. Her skin was dry and going waxy, and it appeared she was swelling even more.

He realized there must have been an infection starting, that no amount of ambrosia could cure. When they reached the cave and Melissa settled down inside, Jake feared that the Fallen Queen was much sicker than they'd imagined.

Joel and Paelen stayed with Jake and Angie, helping to make Melissa as comfortable as possible. She could no longer sit and had to lie down. Jake inspected her wounded arm and found that it was withering away. There didn't seem to be anything he could do to save Melissa.

"Would you like some water?" he offered.

"No, thanks," Melissa whimpered softly. "Just don't leave me alone."

Jake stroked her strange, bulbous head. Even that seemed swollen. It was now a dark gray bordering on black and appeared to be drawing into her body. Whatever was happening to her, it was happening fast. "I won't, I promise. But I do have to go outside the cave for a bit to get more branches for you to lie on. But I won't go far."

"I'll stay with you," Angie said softly, stroking Melissa's hand. "You're not alone."

Melissa responded with a soft moan.

Jake joined Paelen and Joel outside the cave. They had already gathered a large supply of soft pine boughs.

"She doesn't look good," Joel said.

Jake felt this throat constrict. "I think her sister did more damage to her than we knew. It could be an infection."

"I am sorry," Paelen said. "I know you care about her."

"I do," Jake said. He nodded back toward the Titan camp. "But they don't. She used up whatever energy she had left to get here. I'm sure they'll be glad if she dies."

"Don't be too hard on them," Joel said. "We've come through something really terrible. All they see is Mimic when they look at her. They can't imagine that there could be a Mimic unlike the others. To them, they're all the same."

"Then they're stupid," Jake said. "She's nothing like the others."

They worked together to select only the softest boughs and then carried them into the cave. As Paelen and Angie lifted Melissa's heavy head, Jake and Joel placed the boughs like a pillow beneath it.

"Is that better?" Jake asked.

"Yes," Melissa said softly. She reached her swollen hand up and took his. "Thank you, Jake; thank you, Nesso; and thank you, Angie. Thank you for being my friends. I—I really love you. . . ." Her voice trailed away as she lay back and slipped into unconsciousness.

Tears sparkled in Jake's eyes as he leaned forward and kissed Melissa's swollen face. "We love you too. Sleep well; we'll be right here. . . ." He sniffed, making no attempt to hide his tears.

The four walked outside the cave again. Jake had his arm around Angie as she started to weep.

"I'm sorry," Joel said. "I don't think she's going to make it."

Jake nodded and wiped his eyes. "We're not leaving her. Not until . . ."

Joel nodded. "We'll bring you some ambrosia and water. We should also let Diana and Chiron know what's happening."

Jake was too emotional to speak. Instead he nodded as he and Angie returned to the cave to stay with Melissa until she died.

# 18

TRUE TO THEIR WORD, JOEL AND PAELEN
returned several times during the day with ambrosia
and water. When the sun started to set, they had to
go back to their camp but promised to return in the
morning.

Melissa hadn't moved a muscle and looked like she
was barely breathing. The swelling was worsening as
her features became unrecognizable. Her stubby legs
were soon sucked up into the swelling.

Jake knew it wouldn't be long, but he said nothing
to Angie.

"*At leassst ssshe'sss not in pain anymore,*" Nesso
hissed.

"True," Jake agreed as tears streamed down his cheeks. He sniffed. "I just wish she could have had some happiness in her life."

"*Ssshe did,*" Nesso said. "*Ssshe had usss, and didn't die alone in that cage.*"

Angie and Jake sat side by side, leaning against the wall on the opposite side of the cave. When the light was gone, Jake was back to being completely blind. He considered trying to make a campfire but decided against it. He didn't want to watch the end of the Fallen Queen.

After a while, they curled up on the floor of the cave and slept. Just like on the boat, the nights were longer than their body clocks, so they awoke several times.

Each time, Jake asked if Melissa was still breathing. Each time Angie said yes, but she was still swelling and was now unrecognizable. When the light of dawn finally started to creep into the cave, Jake woke to the sound of weeping. He didn't need to ask to know that Melissa was gone.

Jake sat in silence, grieving Melissa's death. He couldn't help but be resentful that the Titans hadn't tried to help her more. Maybe they could have saved her. Or at least made her feel welcome so that when the end came, she knew she was cared for.

Instead it was just him, Nesso, and Angie.

"Has she melted like all the other Mimics?" Jake finally asked.

*"No,"* Nesso hissed softly. *"Ssshe'sss like a big boulder with no projectionsss. Her armsss and legsss are gone."*

Jake wasn't sure what to say.

Angie finally said, "Jake, she knew how much you cared for her. I'm sure that meant a lot."

As the dawn broke brighter in the sky, Jake could make out the lump that was Melissa. Nesso was right, she had changed completely. In death, she was just a shapeless dark hulk. He got up and touched her to see if there was a chance she might be alive. But Melissa's remains were hard and cold like a rock.

When the light was higher, Joel and Paelen returned.

"She's gone," Jake said softly.

"Whoa, what happened to her?" Joel asked.

Jake shrugged. "We expected her to melt like the other Mimics; instead she just turned to stone."

"I am sorry," Paelen said softly.

Jake nodded. "As Nesso said, at least she's not in pain anymore."

Angie was standing next to Melissa. "Do you think we should bury her?"

Jake shook his head. "No, let's let her rest in peace here. We'll cover her up with branches and leave her. The others don't know where this cave is, so she'll be left alone."

They worked in silence to cover Melissa. Before leaving the cave, Jake patted the Fallen Queen's remains. "I'm so sorry we couldn't save you. But at least you were free at the end."

Angie started to weep again. "Good-bye, Melissa. . . ."

Jake put his arm around her as they walked out of the cave. They made their way back to the Titan camp. Guards with spears were posted around it and nodded at them when they returned.

Jake didn't return the nod. He was still too angry.

"I'm going to check on the snakes," Angie said.

"I'll come with you," Jake offered.

They headed over to the cave where the nest had

been made for the snakes. As they neared it, Diana and Steve approached.

"How is she?" Steve asked.

Jake felt his anger rise again. "You'll all be relieved to know she's dead."

"I am sorry," Diana said.

"No, you're not," Jake spat. "You're happy. I've only come back here for them." He pointed at the snakes that were slithering out of the cave to greet them. "If I could be anywhere else, believe me, I would be!" Without waiting for their response, he stormed into the cave.

Jake and Angie sat down in the nest as all the snakes gathered around them, hissing excitedly.

*"Try not to be too angry with them,"* Nesso said softly. *"They didn't know her the way we did."*

"They didn't even try," Jake said. "I know they brought her here for me, and I'm grateful for that. But why go through all of that and then treat her like they did?"

*"I do not know,"* Nesso said. *"But often I don't underssstand a lot of what you big thingsss do."*

Jake chuckled softly. Nesso still insisted on calling

him and all the others "big things." "I don't understand them either," he said.

"Me neither," Angie agreed.

They sat together playing with the snakes. After
a time, Jake reached for the venom jar and noticed
that at least half the venom had been used to coat
weapons. It seemed the Titans hadn't believed him
when he'd said Melissa was safe, but they did believe
his claims that the snake venom would kill Mimics. Somehow, their picking and choosing what they
believed from him made him even angrier.

Once all the snakes were fed, he and Angie gathered more venom.

They spent the better part of the morning in the
cave. Others came and went, but Jake refused to
speak with them. Eventually, he and Angie got up
to stretch and go for a walk. It didn't surprise them
when all the snakes followed.

"Seems like they're bored too," Jake commented.

*"They like you and Angie,"* Nesso said. *"They want
to ssstay with you."*

Activity around them was high. Everyone was
busy. Some gathered large branches and put them in

a pile. Others were peeling off the smaller branches and leaves and shaping the shafts into spears. A final group used jagged rocks to sharpen the ends.

When Jake saw Joel and Paelen with a bunch of spears, he approached them. "What's going on?"

Joel said, "Scouts have returned. Last night they went into the city you told us about to look for Emily and Riza." His head dropped. "They didn't find them. But they did rescue Vulcan and Pluto."

"They're here?" Jake cried.

"Yes," Paelen answered. "They are in the other cave sleeping. They have been treated badly and have not been fed. They are both very weak."

Joel looked up. "More scouts are going out at dark to continue the search."

Paelen added, "We have all decided it is time we fought back. We cannot wait for Jupiter and the others to rescue us. Diana, Apollo, and Chiron are hoping to find the queen and stop her from spawning again."

Despite his anger, Jake was relieved to hear this, that the prisoners were doing something instead of just waiting around. "Have there been any signs of Mimics tracking us?"

"Not yet," Paelen answered. "Perhaps they do not care."

"You don't really believe that, do you?" Joel said.

Paelen grinned. "No, but I thought I would say it anyway."

Joel gave him a friendly shove.

"What can we do to help?" Angie asked.

Paelen shrugged. "You have to ask Chiron. He is organizing tasks."

Jake shook his head. "No, thanks. I'd rather not talk to any of them right now. Maybe we could help you."

"Sure," Joel said. "But, Jake, you're going to have to get over your anger. This is a small camp and we need to work together."

"Yeah, well, Melissa was on our side, and look how they treated her. If I wasn't useful to them, I'm sure they'd do the same to me."

"I didn't say they were always right. But we do have to help each other," Joel said. "So how about you two helping us gather more spears."

They spent the day working closely together. Going into the forest, Paelen and Angie climbed trees and used their Titan strength to pull off straight branches that could be turned into spears.

Jake and Joel remained on the ground and sorted what Angie and Paelen tossed down.

While they worked, Jake and Joel talked about their lives before and after they got involved with the Titans and Olympians. Jake marveled at all the stories Joel told, but the one he liked best was how Joel had first met Emily in New York City, when Pegasus had crashed on her apartment roof and broken his wing.

Joel paused, leaning against a branch. "I was sitting on my brownstone steps and was so close to telling Emily to get lost. I mean, she came to me with this crazy story of how Pegasus had been hurt and how she knew I liked him because of the doodles I drew on my schoolbooks. . . ."

"But you went with her anyway to help him?"

Joel shrugged. "I figured, why not? There was a blackout in New York, and nothing was happening. I hated my foster family anyway, so I went with her. I've never looked back and never regretted a single thing."

"Don't you want to go back to Earth?" Jake asked.

Joel shook his head. "No way. My life is with Emily, Paelen, and the others. There's nothing for me back there."

Jake thought of how much his life had changed. A big part of him wanted to go home to see his family. But another part didn't want to leave. Yes, he loved his family more than anything. But could he be happy back in Los Angles, just riding his skateboard after everything he'd been through and all the places he'd seen? He just didn't know.

"It's addicting," Joel said lightly.

"What is?"

"Life with the Olympians. There's just something special about them. I couldn't leave even if Emily hadn't turned into a Xan and was still an ordinary girl."

"I know what you mean," Jake agreed. "Astraea and Zephyr are really special. Tryn, too."

"I like Tryn a lot," Joel said. "And his sister, Triana, is crazy."

Jake grinned. "Yes, she is. I really like her."

"Oh really . . . ," Joel teased. "You and Triana?"

Jake felt his cheeks going hot. "I mean . . ."

"I know, she's cute," Joel said.

As the long day passed, they carried their loads back into camp to be added to the pile that was being turned into spears.

Chiron approached them and said to Jake, "Diana told me what happened. I am sorry to hear about Melissa. Diana says you are very angry at us."

Jake turned away. "It's better if I don't say anything. Excuse me, I have to go." He started to walk away, but Chiron trotted after him.

"Jake, wait, please." Chiron caught him by the arm. The grip was firm but not painful. But it was enough to let him know that the centaur wasn't about to let go. "We cannot allow anger to fester, especially considering the danger we are all in."

Jake turned to him. "I know you've all been through a rotten time. I get that. But you didn't have to take it out on Melissa. None of this was her fault. She was just a child, and she was hurt—by her own kind! All I asked for was a bit of help. But you all wanted her to die. Well, you got your wish. She's dead!"

"And that is unfortunate," Chiron said. "But perhaps for the best."

Hearing that, Jake tried to wrench his arm free. But Chiron held him tightly. "Listen to me, Jake. Melissa was a queen. Yes, in her world, a Fallen Queen, but she was still a *Mimic queen*. We cannot know what she would have grown into. There are some creatures, even on Earth, that are sweet and friendly when they are young. But when they grow up, that changes. They can become deadly. Can you be absolutely certain that Melissa wouldn't have been the same?"

"Yes!" Jake insisted. "Melissa could have hurt me or Angie anytime, but she didn't want to. She didn't even want to eat those flattened animals when she hatched. She went into that fight starving. Even if she had eaten, she still wouldn't have fought. It went against everything she believed."

Chiron considered for a moment. "After everything we have been through, it is difficult to conceive of a peaceful Mimic."

"That's because you never gave her a chance. Believe me, she was peaceful. A lot more peaceful than me!"

Chiron nodded. "Then we might have made a grave mistake."

"Duh!" Jake said angrily. "Now, if you don't mind, I have work to do."

The centaur still refused to release him. "Jake, you are suffering, and I am truly sorry that we contributed to that. But we need you. You have done so much for us already, but I must ask more of you. You have greater insight into these Mimics than we do— even though we slaved for them for so long."

"What do you expect me to do?"

"You can put aside your anger and help us defeat them before the new queens leave this world to start their own colonies. Will you do that, Jake? Will you help us?"

Jake looked over at Joel and Paelen, who had been watching but turned away quickly when he caught them. Then he looked at Angie and the snakes. Even if the others didn't need him, Angie and the snakes did. Angie was so much like Molly; he couldn't turn his back on her.

Finally he looked back at Chiron. "All right. I'll help all I can. But I won't forget what happened with

Melissa, and don't expect me to forgive. That's asking way too much."

"I understand," Chiron said. "Now, will you please come back to camp and tell me everything you know about these Mimics and their Shadow Titan controllers?"

Jake looked over to Angie, who was nodding. He was still just as angry, but Chiron was right. They were in a war. He couldn't afford to stay angry and bitter. Finally he said, "Yes, I'll tell you all I know about the Mimics."

# 19

THE FIRST THING ASTRAEA BECAME AWARE of was the intense pounding in her head. It felt like someone was locked inside and trying to get out. There was the sound of moaning that was making her head throb even more. She wished whoever was doing it would stop.

"It's all right," Zephyr said softly. "You're safe."

"Zeph," Astraea said, "whoever's whining, it's too loud. Please tell them to stop."

"I can't," Zephyr said softly. "Because it's you."

"Wha—what?"

"How is she?" The sound of Pegasus's voice hit like an explosion in her brain.

"Please stop shouting," she begged.

"I think Astraea has a bit of a headache," Zephyr whispered.

"I am sorry, Astraea," Pegasus said softly.

Astraea felt a warm muzzle and soft whiskers press against her cheek. She couldn't open her eyes to see who it was, but then Pegasus whispered, "Thank you, Astraea. Thank you for giving me back my Emily. Sleep and heal, my dear friend."

Astraea wanted to ask more about what had happened. How was Emily? Where were they? But the pounding was getting worse. She felt dizzy and sick, and then she felt nothing.

When Astraea awoke again, it was to pressure on her lips. She tasted sweet nectar and drank gratefully.

"That's it, keep drinking," Triana said softly. "This will help you get better."

Astraea opened her eyes and saw the concerned face of Triana leaning over her and pulling back the cup. Behind her were Zephyr and the three centaurs.

"Finally," Cylus said, but not too loudly. "We didn't think you were ever going to wake up again."

Her head was still pounding, but it was much easier than before. She could barely remember waking and the explosion of pain. "How is Emily?"

"Not great," Render said softly. "We can't get her to wake up. Pegasus is frantic."

Astraea closed her eyes again. "That queen only touched me for a moment, and it knocked me down. But there were two lying on top of her. . . ."

"Tryn told us," Render said.

Astraea opened her eyes and frowned. "Where is Tryn?"

Zephyr snorted. "The idiot's gone to find Jake. We told him to wait, but he said after what he saw in the cavern, he just couldn't wait if it was happening to Jake, too. We tried to stop him. . . ."

"You can't stop Tryn," Triana said. "Not when he sets his mind on something."

Astraea started to sit up but felt weaker than she ever had in her life. Even weaker than when they'd gone ages without ambrosia on Zomos. "I can't remember anything after the queen touched me. What happened?"

Zephyr looked over at the others, then back at

Astraea. "Well, now, there's quite a story. . . ."

Cylus chuckled. "I wish I could have seen it."

"Seen what?" Astraea said.

"When Tryn carried you and Emily away from the queens, the moment Pegasus saw what they'd done to her and you, he became enraged. Who would have thought he had such a ferocious temper?" Zephyr said.

"And?" Astraea coaxed.

"Then more Mimics came—" Zephyr started.

"What?" Astraea cried. She winced at the pain it caused.

"Yep," Zephyr said. "They kinda had us surrounded and blocked the stairs leading out. So, you know how Pegasus has this power to draw water out of the ground? Well, he was so angry, he slammed his hooves down and the floor cracked. Then he showed me how to do it. It was amazing, the place practically exploded with water. We all got soaked!"

Cylus started to smile. "Guess what? Mimics hate water!"

"They sure do," Zephyr said. "The moment they were touched by the water, they became paralyzed and started to float on the surface like leaves on a river. They couldn't even shoot their tendrils. We had to race out of there because the water was coming in so fast."

"And," Cylus said excitedly, "they flooded the whole area. The water is still rising over there right now."

"At least it washed the goo off Emily and the smell off Pegasus," Darek said.

Astraea could hardly believe what she was hearing. She remembered the pond Pegasus had created on Xanadu after his fight with Jupiter, but this sounded much bigger.

"So can you do it now?" she asked Zephyr.

If Zephyr could have grinned, she would have. "Oh yeah . . ."

Astraea frowned again. "But—what about Riza? Was she in there?"

"No," Render said. "Tryn used his skateboard in the nursery, and she wasn't there. After they brought you back, he tried again. The skateboard was taking him in the same direction as Jake, so he left. We'd hoped he'd be back by now."

Astraea looked at the bright sunshine pouring through the bedroom window. "It hasn't been that long. Maybe he's waiting until tonight."

Zephyr shook her head. "You've been asleep since the first night we arrived here, and that was two nights ago—believe me, these days and nights are really long."

"Two nights?" Astraea cried, then winced at the pain. "Tryn should have waited for me. I could have helped."

"Tryn promised to just look," Triana said. "He's not going to do anything stupid. Once he finds Jake and Riza, he'll come back for us and we'll all go to free them."

"Even so," Astraea mused. "He should have waited."

"Astraea, you can't even hold a cup right now, let alone take on more queens," Zephyr said. "So just lie back and rest. We can't do anything while it's light."

Astraea lay back but didn't think she could sleep anymore. The centaurs and Triana left the room. Alone with Zephyr, Astraea looked around. "This isn't too different from my bedroom," she observed. "The bed's a lot longer, but it's still a normal bed."

"This whole place is a lot like Titus. Or, Titus mixed with Earth," Zephyr said. "Tryn and Triana explored the building and found more pictures of the people who once lived here. They really aren't that different from Titans, apart from the three eyes. But then again, we have Cyclopes, and they only have one eye. Pegasus thinks the Mimics might have killed the original people."

"A whole planet of people?"

Zephyr nodded.

Astraea felt bad for those who used to live there. "I wonder how long the Mimics have been here."

"A long time, by the age of everything," Zephyr said. "The covers on your bed are clean but rotten with age. Everything is rotting."

Astraea looked over to the window. "Have you seen any signs of Mimics out there?"

Zephyr nodded. "They are looking for us. Patrols have been checking the area. They came up our street, but before they reached our building, Lergo came through and got them all. I think that snake likes the taste of Mimics. It's hunting them more than we expected."

"Lergo is on this side of town?"

"Lergo is everywhere," Zephyr said. "Pegasus and I go out at night and check. That snake is really wrecking the place. It's permanently black now, and it is eating anything. I've seen it devour a whole bunch of Shadow Titans in one gulp."

"I wonder if it's starving," Astraea said. "The Mimics are just goo—there won't be any substance to them."

"I thought that too," Zephyr said. "But at least it's doing what we hoped and keeping them distracted."

They spent the better part of the day just being friends and talking about the things they were going to do once this was over.

"First thing for me is a long soak in a lake," Zephyr offered. "I stink, my legs ache from carrying Cylus, and I'm always looking out for Mimics. Just to stop and relax would be wonderful."

Astraea nodded. "For me, the first thing will be going back to Arcadia. . . ."

Zephyr whinnied, "What? You want to go back to school?"

Astraea started to laugh. "No, silly. I just want a

big family dinner with all of us together. We could invite Jake, Tryn, Triana, and their family, and the centaurs. It will be a big celebration."

"Yes, that would be nice. But I'm not so sure about Jake. You really don't want a human in your house; you'd never get the smell out again. . . ." Zephyr stopped and winked at Astraea.

They laughed and talked like they used to, and for a short while forgot where they were and what they were up against. Finally Astraea threw back the covers.

"I need to stretch my legs. Would you help me? I'd like to see Emily."

With Astraea holding on to Zephyr's wing, they left the bedroom and walked down the hall to the main lounge. A bed had been carried out of one of the other bedrooms and was now set up in the center of the room.

Pegasus stood beside the bed like a statue. The three centaurs were lounging on the floor not far away and nodded at Astraea as she approached.

"How is she?" Astraea asked softly.

"She sleeps," Pegasus said. "Much like you, but

deeper. I try not to let myself fear that she will not awaken."

Astraea looked at the pale girl with the dark hair, lying motionless in the bed. Her chest rose and fell evenly, but she was so thin, and the dark rings around her eyes told of the ordeal she'd been through. Her arms were burned and blistered from where the queens had lain.

Approaching the bed, Astraea reached out and stroked Emily's forehead. "Come back to us, Emily," she said softly. "We're all waiting for you."

Stealing a look at the stallion beside her, she could see tears sparkling in his eyes and trailing down his face. Pegasus was crying.

# 20

ASTRAEA DIDN'T RETURN TO HER ROOM. She settled down in the lounge with everyone else, watching and waiting for Emily to awaken. As she lay in the bed, Emily looked like an ordinary girl and not the great and powerful Xan she had turned into. How long would it take for her to regain her strength? What might Riza look like once they found her?

Several times throughout the day, Triana poured tiny amounts of nectar into Emily's mouth, but Emily didn't move or react. As time passed, Pegasus's despair grew.

"He's really scared," Zephyr whispered to Astraea. "I hate to see him like this."

Astraea was stunned by Zephyr's comment. For so long Zephyr had hated the stallion and the constant comparisons to him that she went through. Now, after working and fighting together, they were becoming close. She now considered the comparisons a compliment. So to see him so frightened for Emily, she was really feeling for him.

"I know," Astraea agreed. "I wish there were more we could do."

As they sat in the bright room, Astraea understood what the others meant about the days and nights being long. She was sure the sun should have set before now, but peering out the window, it was barely overhead. There was a long way to go before dark.

Her bracelet was open, and she was stroking the two snakes. Feeling their cool, smooth scales helped to calm her unsettled mind. She fed them tiny pieces of ambrosia and smiled at the comments Zephyr made about them.

When the sun did move to the horizon and start to set, the pain in Astraea's head finally faded and she was almost back to herself. Though, she did notice the new scar on her arm from the Mimic queen's tendril. The surface was bumpy, red, and raised. Something told her it would be permanent.

Throughout the long day, they heard Lergo tearing through the city. This was often followed by crashing and the sounds of collapse. The immense snake was still on the rampage.

When the sun was down, Cylus, Darek, and Render drew out their bows and moved for the door.

"What are you doing?" Astraea asked.

"We're going to start searching the city for more Titans," Cylus said. "There were a lot taken; they've got to be here somewhere."

"You can't go out; you'll disturb the dust at the front door, and if the Mimics come, they'll notice."

Cylus shook his head. "They haven't been back here since that snake got the last group. Astraea, we didn't come all this way just to sit here. We need to find our people and free them, then find the queen and kill her before she spawns any more!"

Pegasus looked up from his vigil beside Emily. "Cylus, I appreciate your feelings. You are anxious. So am I—our people, our family, are here somewhere—but sometimes, the best action is no action, just for a while."

"What are we waiting for?" Cylus demanded. "We're warriors; we should be fighting, not hiding."

"True, but you will risk your lives searching. Lergo is out there. As you must stay on the ground, you could not outrun it if it tracks you. It is unfortunate that Tryn chose not to remain. But he is not foolish. I have every confidence he will return, and when he does, that precious flying board of his will lead us to the others."

"So we just sit here and wait for Tryn?" Cylus cried. "What if he doesn't come back? What if he's been killed or something?"

Triana gasped. "No . . ."

"Cylus, stop!" Astraea said. "You're upsetting Triana. We don't know that anything has happened to Tryn. Maybe he found Jake and they're together. He'll be back. I know he will. Until then, we must wait."

Astraea said words she had no faith in. Since waking, she'd had the same fear. What if Tryn had been captured by the Mimics, or worse, hunted and killed by Lergo? She felt just as helpless and frustrated at the centaurs. She wanted to go out and tear this city apart looking for the others. They were in a war, and sitting and waiting wasn't what she'd expected to do.

"I can't do it," Cylus said. "I can't just sit here."

"I understand," Astraea agreed. "How about this? You all stay here and protect Emily. Zephyr and I will go out. We'll stay up high and we will fly around looking for any signs of our people."

"Astraea," Pegasus warned.

"She's right, Pegasus," Zephyr said. "We'll fly higher than Lergo can reach, and we'll look for any signs of Titans or Tryn."

"I will not try to stop you," Pegasus said. "I owe you more than I could ever repay. . . ." He looked down on Emily. "But I will ask you this. If you insist on going out, and should you find our people, come back here and get us. We will go and free them together."

Astraea nodded. "Agreed." She turned to Cylus. "Is that all right with you? If we find anything, we'll come back and get you."

Cylus didn't look happy, but he nodded. "Is that a promise?"

"Absolutely," Zephyr said. "Believe me, I don't want to play hero alone."

* * *

When the sun was fully set, Astraea and Zephyr prepared to go out on a search mission. Astraea packed up her slingshot and accepted extra pebbles from Triana and the centaurs.

Cylus walked with them up to the roof, complaining all the way. "We should be going with you. You need us."

"I know," Astraea said. "But we don't need you being hurt, maybe even killed, because you had to stay on the ground. You know we'll come right back if we find anyone. For now, please take care of the others. You can see how distracted Pegasus is; it's up to you to keep everyone safe."

Cylus nodded. "You're right," he said seriously. "I'll watch over them." He helped Astraea up onto Zephyr.

"Thank you, Cylus," Astraea said. "We'll be back soon."

"See you later," Zephyr called as she opened her wings, trotted to the edge of the roof, and then jumped into the air.

Zephyr circled back over the apartment to make sure they knew where they were, then started to fly in ever-increasing circles over the city.

"Wow," Zephyr said as they glided over fresh ruins. "That is one angry snake."

There were whole areas that had been reduced to rubble. Mixed among the ruins were pieces of Shadow Titans.

"There's nothing here that we can see," Zephyr said. "Let's try even farther out."

They both kept watchful eyes as they passed over the sprawling city. After a time, they started to see greenery at the edge.

"At least this world isn't all built over," Zephyr said.

"Let's try that way," Astraea advised. "Toward the trees."

Zephyr flew out over the woods, and the fragrance of sweet pine filled the air. "This is much better."

"Let's look for some water," Astraea suggested. "We can't keep drinking nectar; we have to save it."

They continued far out over the trees, but saw no signs of rivers, lakes, or ponds.

"How is this possible?" Astraea asked. "There are so many trees. Where are they getting their water from?"

"It's probably underground," Zephyr said. "I have an idea." She turned back and headed toward the city again.

Astraea frowned. "What are you planning?"

Zephyr landed on a street. There were lights on in the buildings, but no activity on the ground.

"Zeph, we can't stay here. It's too dangerous; there are Mimics here."

"Yes, there are," Zephyr said. "But look around. Wouldn't this be the perfect spot for a nice large pond?"

Astraea gasped. "What? You're not thinking what I think you're thinking."

"Oh yeah," Zephyr said. "We need water, and Pegasus showed me how to get some."

"Yeah, but I don't want to drink water that has Mimics floating in it!"

"Then I'll just have to do it again. Hold on!"

Astraea gripped Zephyr's mane and tightened her legs against her. She could feel a kind of vibration emanating from her best friend.

"Zeph, what's happening?"

"Watch and be amazed!"

Just as Pegasus had done, Zephyr reared up high and then came crashing back down to the ground with ferocious pressure.

After three strikes, the ground started to rumble. Astraea looked down and saw a large crack forming in the pavement. Then a trickle of water started to swell in the area near Zephyr's hooves.

Two strikes later, and the water was coming faster. With a final strike, water shot high in the air like a fountain with too much pressure. "That should do it!" Zephyr whinnied over the sounds of roaring water.

She flapped her powerful wings and took off into the sky. Instead of heading back to the apartment, they circled the area, watching the water rise. It soon poured into the buildings and flowed along neighboring streets.

More lights in the buildings came on as the Mimics inside felt the vibrations of the water. They peered out the windows and watched the fountain. There was no sign of it slowing.

"Um, Zeph," Astraea said as they watched. "Did Pegasus teach you how to turn it off? Like when there is enough water?"

"Not exactly," Zephyr said. "He didn't even tell me where the water came from. Just that we could draw it up."

"So you don't actually know when it's going to stop."

"Uh—no," Zephyr said. "But how much water can there be?"

"Do you think it could reach our hiding place?"

"Good question," Zephyr answered.

As the water rose, they heard crashing starting several streets away. Zephyr flew toward it. "Looks like we have company."

Lergo was tearing through the streets. The massive snake stopped near the water flow, and it's tongue dipped in and out of its mouth as it started to drink deeply.

"Wow," Zephyr said. "I guess it was thirsty."

"I didn't think about that," Astraea said. "Lergo needs water just like we do." She followed the length of the snake's body and saw just how large it was. "It's unbelievable—I never imagined a snake could grow so large."

"Why would it want to eat me?" Zephyr said, referring to when Lergo had nearly killed her. "I wouldn't have been more than a treat."

"Well, we do eat grapes, and they're small."

"Oh great," Zephyr said. "Now you're calling me a grape."

"Well," Astraea teased. "If the fruit fits . . ."

They hovered, watching the snake drink. After a while, Lergo paused and looked up.

"Uh-oh," Zephyr said.

Without warning, the massive snake rose and launched itself at them with its mouth wide open. Missing them by a breath, it slithered up the side of a building to chase them.

"Zeph, fly!" Astraea cried.

Zephyr flapped her powerful wings hard to get away, but Lergo was fast. Very fast. It used the building as a launchpad and threw itself into the air to catch them. Using all her strength, Zephyr climbed high in the sky and screamed when she felt the tip of the snake's snout graze her hooves as its mouth tried and failed to bite her.

Lergo crashed back down onto the rooftop and collapsed it with its weight. They didn't stay to watch the whole collapse, but they heard it.

"I hate that snake, I hate that snake, I hate that snake . . . ," Zephyr screamed as she tore out of the area and headed back to their apartment.

They landed on the roof of their building and were still shaking. Astraea slid off Zephyr's back, and her knees nearly gave out beneath her. Holding on to Zephyr's wing for support, she leaned against her best friend.

"No more night excursions, okay?"

"Agreed," Zephyr panted. "I don't think we should tell the others what happened."

"I won't if you won't," Astraea said. "Let's just calm down a bit before we go in."

# 21

JAKE WAS SLOWLY GETTING OVER HIS ANGER with the Titans as he heard more stories of the cruelty and abuse they'd suffered at the hands of the Mimics. The day after he and Angie returned to camp after the death of Melissa, a winged Titan approached him.

"Jake," he said. "I am Vulturnus. I have been told that you know my parents and sister?"

He was tall with shaggy long blond hair. His face was gaunt and his arms were like twigs. Jake had noticed him before and saw that he had no feathers on his wings. It was only now that Jake realized the likeness. "Are you Astraea's brother?"

Vulturnus nodded. "I am here with my brother Aquilo. If you had not found us when you did, I am certain he would have died. He was hurt in that cabin by the animal press. The Mimics would not allow us to treat him or give him more ambrosia. All I could do was give him my portion. I am so grateful to you and Angitia."

"Is he all right?"

Vulturnus nodded. "With thanks to you. He is still very weak, but I am certain he will recover."

"That is such a relief," Jake said. "I know Astraea's going nuts worrying about you."

"As my brother and I have been about her."

Jake knew it would be rude to ask, but he did anyway. "Did the Mimics do that to your wings?"

Vulturnus opened a wing and looked at the devastation. There was only pale bare skin with open pores where feathers had once been. He nodded. "They plucked us to keep me and my brother grounded. The feathers will grow back, but it will take time. Please, will you tell me how my family is?"

The winged Titan looked so frail and delicate that Jake didn't have the heart to tell him that the last time he'd seen Aurora was in Detroit and she had been thrown off the back of a taxi when she and Pegasus had tried to help him.

"They're great," he said. "I really like Astraea and Zephyr. We met on Titus when the Mimics brought me there." Jake briefly told him the adventures he'd been through with Astraea and how they'd first met. "They are all on Xanadu with Jupiter and the others."

Instantly it looked like a great weight had been lifted from Vulturnus's shoulders. "That is such a relief. Now if we could just find my other brothers . . ."

"We will," Jake promised. "Soon."

Vulturnus nodded, but he still looked exhausted. "I can only hope. Thank you again for everything."

"No problem," Jake said. "No offense, but I think you should lie down. You look like you're ready to collapse."

Vulturnus smiled, and it was just like Astraea's smile. "I must say I do not feel particularly well. Perhaps I will." He walked back toward the cave.

Very soon a strange kind of routine settled in the camp. Each afternoon, just before sunset, teams headed out to venture into the city to search for Emily, Riza, and any other prisoners of the Mimics.

Despite their searches, they had yet to find anyone else. Several times the searchers entered buildings and encountered Mimics working. These were quickly dealt with, proving the precious value of the snakes and their venom. After that, respect for Jake and Angie grew even greater in the camp.

Those that didn't go on the city search teams did what they could to keep the camp going. With ambrosia supplies dwindling, another search party left the camp looking for food. They returned with fruit that they'd found in a wild orchard. It was the same they'd been fed at the camp. It wouldn't replace ambrosia, but it could help extend it.

A large group was just returning from a fruit run when their scouts charged into the camp. "Mimics and Shadow Titans! They are advancing on us. Prepare for battle!"

"Everyone, gather the weapons," Chiron cried. "The time has come to fight!"

Jake ran over to the wall of spears that had been prepared. But when he reached for one and started to follow the fighters, Diana stopped him. "No, Jake, you are too important to fight. You and Nesso are the only communication we have with the snakes. Please stay here and keep them and Angie safe. They are our only defense."

Jake was about to protest, but then he saw the fear on Angie's face. They had never discussed what the Mimics had done to her when she'd been their prisoner in the lab, but now that they were coming to the camp, she was terrified.

Jake nodded and grabbed a second spear. He handed one to Angie. "You probably won't need this, but it's good to have. Let's go keep an eye on the snakes."

When they made it back to the cave, they weren't alone. The three Xan—Mila, Ezmi, and Jili—were seated among the snakes. Their faces were impassive, but the trembling of their hands revealed their fear. Jake knew they were a peaceful people, but if it came down to it, he wondered if they would fight. Tryn had, even though it went against everything he believed.

"We will defend the snakes," Jili said.

Jake had become accustomed to their incredible beauty, but the fear hidden in their eyes tore at his soul. "We'll help," he said. "Angie, you stay here with the Xan. I'll take the cave entrance."

Despite his instructions, Angie took a place at the entrance beside him. Jake wanted to tell her to go back, but he welcomed her presence.

"You okay?" he asked.

Angie nodded, but it was obvious she wasn't.

"I won't let them take you again," he promised. "We'll stop them."

They stood, side by side at the entrance of the cave. Outside was teeming with activity as Titans, Olympians, and the original people of this world gathered weapons and prepared to engage the Mimics and their Shadow Titans.

Not far in the distance were the sounds of screaming and breaking branches. The fighting was getting close. He gripped his spear tighter.

Paelen and Joel arrived at the cave and took a position beside them.

"Remember," Jake said. "The Shadow Titans are controlled by the Mimics. Get the silver controller away from the Mimics, and the Shadows become ours to command. Just don't touch the goo."

"How many have you killed?" Joel asked.

"A few," Jake said. "It ain't pretty, and it's messy."

They stood together with their spears raised. When the scout said the Mimics were coming, Jake never imagined how many there could be. He gasped when a wide, solid wall of Shadow Titans marched into the camp.

"We are so toast," Jake said softly.

"Not yet," Joel said. "There are a lot of us here, and none of us want to go back into one of those camps."

As the Mimic Shadow Titans advanced into the camp, defenders, weak and strong, rose against them. But they only had sharpened sticks and were nothing against Shadow Titans with swords and brute strength.

Jake and the others in the cave watched in horror as the Titans fought bravely but were being cut down by the Shadows.

What followed was even worse, as Mimics marched in behind them, shooting tendrils at the defenders.

"There are too many!" Paelen cried.

Joel shook his head. "We can't win." He looked over at Paelen and Jake. "It's been great knowing you."

Jake nodded. "You too."

Jake turned to Angie. "Go to the back with the Xan. It will be over quickly, I promise."

Angie shook her head. "I'm staying with you."

Jake smiled at her and was once again reminded of his sister. As he raised his spear and prepared to enter a futile battle, he thought of his mother, so far away. She would never know what happened to him. How he died on an alien world trying to stop a race of monsters that were planning to invade Earth after they finished with Titus and Xanadu.

She would never know how much he'd grown up and realized just how important family was. And he would never get to see his new little brother or tell Molly that he loved her more than anything. It would all be gone in a heartbeat.

Taking a deep breath, Jake and Angie joined Paelen and Joel charging forward into the fight.

# 22

JAKE HAD GONE ONLY A FEW PACES WHEN a loud screeching rose above the sounds of battle. He looked up and saw what he could only describe as a giant praying mantis–like creature swooping down from the sky. It was massive, with a dark pink body and clear cellophane wings that came out from beneath hard, dark wing covers on its back. It had a large, gray triangular head with giant, purple insect eyes. The black slit pupils panned the area carefully.

Like a mantis, it had two upper raptorial forelegs, with spikes on the femur and tibia that looked sharp enough to cut someone in half if they were unfortunate enough to end up in the monster's grip. There were four other thicker back legs that supported the distended body of the creature.

One of the forelegs looked badly damaged and couldn't open properly. But that didn't stop the creature from charging into the fight.

But it wasn't attacking the Titans or Olympians. The mantis-like creature only went after the Shadow Titans. It knocked them over with its powerful forelegs or bent down and bit them with its strange mouth and threw them away.

Jake was paralyzed on the spot as he stared up at the creature. Every movie he'd ever seen with insect monsters flashed before his eyes. But here and now, this was the very worst of them all, as the mantis stormed through the camp, cutting down Shadow Titans and tearing them to pieces.

When more Mimics emerged from the trees and saw the mantis, they stopped and started to make clicking sounds.

The mantis screeched again, and when it did, the Mimics called into their controllers. All the Shadow Titans stopped fighting and stood, stone-still.

From the frantic insanity of the battle, the sudden cessation of fighting and the ensuing silence was overwhelming. Jake looked around, unable to believe what he was witnessing.

The Mimics were still and clicking softly at the mantis.

Jake took a step and frowned. The mantis was a terrifying sight, yet somehow, as it stood before them, he felt something. A drawing to it, as though he knew it and realized it was there to help.

Jake gasped and ran out. "It's Melissa!"

"Jake, get away from there!" Steve Jacobs called. He ran forward with a spear in his hand.

"No, it's Melissa!" Jake repeated. He ran up to the mantis's leg, which rose high over his head, and hugged it tightly. "You're alive!"

The mantis hissed at Steve, "Back off, dude!" Then her triangular head came down to Jake's level. "Well, duh, of course I'm alive, silly." Then she laughed. "So that's what you look like. You really are short!"

Jake didn't know whether to laugh or cry. "No, you're just really tall!" He reached up to stroke her head.

Melissa's head moved closer. "Hello, Nesso. Aren't you pretty!"

Nesso hissed, *"You are beautiful!"*

"Melissa!" Angie cried as she ran up. "I'm so glad to see you."

"You too, chickpea!" Melissa said.

The mantis rose to her full height. "You lied to me, Jake. You said you wouldn't leave me. But you did. I was in that cave all alone. . . ."

Jake was stunned by how much older she seemed. She had the same pout in her voice that Molly always got. He realized that Melissa wasn't so much a needy child anymore. In a short time, she had grown into a moody young teen. "I'm—I'm so sorry, Melissa. We really thought you were dead. I swear we wouldn't have left you if we'd known."

"I wasn't dead; I was changing."

"We didn't know that. You were hurting so much that when you turned to stone, we thought it was over." Jake looked way up to her head. "Boy oh boy, that is some change!"

"Awesome, isn't it? Look, I've got wings!" She turned and opened the wing covers to reveal her insect wings. When she turned back, she looked around at the destroyed Shadow Titans and then to the Mimics that were still clicking at her. "They were going to hurt you, but not now. Now they'll obey me." She tilted her head at Jake and winked a large, purple eye. "Watch this!" She made a loud screech, and all the Mimics lay down on the ground. Then she clicked and they raised their legs in the air and started to kick.

She laughed at Jake. "Is that cool or what? What do you want them to do? Tell me, and I'll tell them to do it."

"I just don't want them to kill us."

"Oh, they won't." After another screech, the Mimics threw their silver controllers to Jake. Melissa laughed through her strange insectoid mouth. "This is so great!"

Jake looked from Melissa to the Mimics and back to Melissa again. "That's totally rad! They're really obeying you."

"That's because she's a queen," Steve called.

Melissa looked at him. "No way. I'm not even, like, a Fallen Queen." She looked over to Jake and Angie. "I'm Melissa, aren't I?"

"You bet you are!" Jake said. He looked back at

the Mimics standing before her. They didn't move or speak. They just watched her. "They really are yours."

"You can keep them. I don't want them," Melissa said bitterly.

Chiron and several fighters arrived from their battle in the trees. They all stopped and stared up at Melissa.

"It's all right, Chiron," Jake called. "It's Melissa. She didn't die. Look, she controls the Mimics."

Chiron looked around at the Mimics, who stood stone-still, gazing up at Melissa. He approached the mantis. "Melissa, do you remember me?"

"Yes," Melissa said. "You and the others carried me here when I hurt. But then you made me go away."

Chiron nodded. "And that was a grave mistake. I am so sorry. I sincerely hope you can forgive me."

Melissa looked at Jake. "Do you think I should forgive him?"

Jake looked at Chiron and then said, "Yeah . . . he's cool. They kinda all are."

When Diana approached, Melissa lowered her head. "You won't try to send me away again, will you?"

"No one will," Jake answered firmly. He shot a warning look at Diana and the others. "I won't let them."

"Neither will I," Angie agreed.

"You are welcome among us, Melissa," Diana said formally.

The Mimics around them continued to click and stare up at the mantis.

Paelen and Joel came closer. "So, what do we do with those things? We can use the Shadow Titans, but what about the Mimics?"

"They don't live very long," Jake said. "If we do nothing, in a short while they'll just melt."

"I really don't like them," Melissa said. "I might just tell them to get lost."

"Works for me," Jake said. "But before you do, can we ask one a few questions?"

"Go ahead," Melissa said. She screeched, and a Mimic came closer.

Jake held up his hand. "That's close enough."

The Mimic looked at him, and its bulbous brows drew together in a frown. "What are you doing with this queen, spawn?"

Jake looked over at Paelen and Joel. "The Mimics call us 'spawn' because we're young." He focused on the Mimic again. "Where is the First Queen? This queen's mother?"

The Mimic snorted. "I don't have to answer you. You are nothing."

Melissa screeched and lowered her head close to the Mimic. "Tell him what he wants to know, or I'll slap you really hard!"

The Mimic bowed its head. "The First Queen is far from here. We brought the two grubs here for their Trial of Worthiness. Other pairs of grubs will be sent in other directions for their Trials of Worthiness. We must keep them apart or they will kill each other and no queens will rise."

"Trial of Worthiness?" Chiron repeated.

"I think they mean the fight that Melissa got hurt in," Jake offered. "It's a fight to the death so the winner becomes a Risen Queen." Jake turned his attention to the Mimic again. "How many new queens will there be?"

The Mimic spat, "There will be many, and you will all be defeated!"

Melissa moved faster than Jake could follow. Her upper limb swooped down and struck the Mimic. It flew across the camp and smashed into a tree. "Oops," Melissa said. "I didn't mean to do that. . . ."

Everyone in the camp gasped at the speed and strength of the mantis.

"Jake . . . ," Steve warned.

Jake turned back to him. "She's fine. She's just young and doesn't know her strength."

Melissa looked back at Steve. "I really didn't want to do that. I said I'd slap him. It just got away from me. But"—she looked back at the Mimics—"if any of them try to hurt any of you, I can't say what I'll do." She called another Mimic forward.

Before asking the same question, Jake frowned and looked back at Melissa. "Say, can you feel your mother? Do you know where she is?"

Melissa rose to her full height and closed her eyes as her head rotated around. After a moment, she came back down. "Sorry, I can't feel a thing. I know she's out there, but I don't know where."

"Thanks for trying," Jake said. He focused on the Mimic and repeated his question. "Where is the First

Queen? Is she in the city near where you kept the prisoners?"

"No," the Mimic answered. "She is far. She is safe. You will not defeat us!"

"Stop being so rotten!" Melissa shoved the Mimic back with her head and commanded another to come forward.

The Mimic looked up at the queen.

"Go on, answer him," she commanded.

"She is three days away," the Mimic said.

"Which direction?" Diana asked.

The Mimic turned and pointed. "She is that way. But you will not reach her. She will stop you. We all will."

A pebble was shot through the Mimic, and it started to melt. Jake looked back and saw Diana lowering her arm. "He had a bad attitude."

It took the better part of the day and multiple Mimics to get the details they needed to find the First Queen. Even though the Mimics bowed to Melissa, they were belligerent and uncooperative with the Titans and sometimes refused to answer. That never ended well for them, with Diana's temper.

The remaining Mimics were ordered to stay just outside the camp. Jake was amazed that they obeyed, considering they back-talked the Titans. But every command Melissa gave was followed.

When Jake questioned her about it, she answered that she didn't know how it worked—it just did. Steve heard the question and suggested, "It could be pheromones. Queen bees give them off to send messages through the hive. You've said these Mimics are like a hive. I imagine it's the same. They smell her and know she's a queen."

"Ew," Melissa said. "You're saying I smell?"

Steve chuckled. "We all have smells and scents, Melissa. Not just you. But yours can really help us with the Mimics."

"Oh, that's okay, then," the tall mantis said.

In a while, the captured Shadow Titans were posted around the camp, completely encircling it. The battle had been brief but brutal, and several of the planet's original inhabitants had fallen, while multiple Titans and Olympians had been badly wounded.

When all the injured were treated as best they could be, everyone gathered in the middle of the camp. Jake,

Angie, Paelen, and Joel were off to the side with Melissa. The Fallen Queen was quite happy to be included in the discussions and stood proudly among them.

"Three days to get to the queen the way Mimics travel should be one and a half or two for us, if we run," Diana was saying. "We can mount an assault against her before she spawns again."

"It will be very dangerous," Apollo said. "Many of us will fall. But we must do this."

Melissa leaned down to Jake and whispered, "You don't think they'll want me to go, do you?" she asked softly. "She is my mother. I'm not sure I could fight her. You know how I feel about violence."

"I do," Jake said. "But what happens if she or one of your sisters tries to kill you? Please tell me you'll defend yourself. I don't want to see you hurt again."

*"You may not have a choiccce, Melisssa,"* Nesso said. *"The First Queen may sssee you asss a rival or a threat to her planss of ssspreading through the ssstarsss."*

"Rival?" Melissa repeated. "I'm not a rival. I don't want to be a queen and I don't want anything to do with the Mimics." She paused. "But if they try to hurt you, I will defend you."

"And we'll defend you, too," Angie said.

The discussions continued until it was dark. A large bonfire was lit, and everyone stayed around it. They all felt a bit safer now that the camp was protected by Melissa and the Shadow Titans. When the discussions ended, they retired to their caves.

With Melissa too big to go into the cave, Jake and Angie settled down outside to stay with her. They had only just started to doze off when a familiar voice called from above.

"Hey, Jake! Jake!"

Jake woke and looked up and screamed. Tryn was on his skateboard gliding down into camp. When he touched down, they embraced like long-lost brothers.

"You found us!" Jake cried. He checked the sky behind Tryn. "Where is everyone? I thought Astraea, Zephyr, and Triana would be with you."

"They're safe." Tryn looked around the camp. "I can't believe you found the missing Titans. Is Riza here?"

"No," Jake said. "I don't know where she is. These people were locked in a prison and forced to kill animals to make Mimic food. It was awful. Chiron is here, and he said that there are more camps. But we did find two of Astraea's brothers. Her other two are still missing."

"She'll be thrilled," Tryn said. "We'll use our boards to find the others."

When Tryn reached into his backpack, he pulled out Jake's skateboard.

Jake clutched it gratefully. "I thought this was gone forever!"

"No, we kept it for you," Tryn said.

Melissa came up. "Jake, who is this?"

Tryn's eyes opened wide at the sight of the massive mantis. "Um . . . Jake?"

"Tryn, this is Melissa," Jake said lightly. He turned back to the mantis. "Didn't you see him in my mind? He's, like, my best friend."

"Oh, yeah, now I remember. Howdy, Tryn," Melissa said as her large head came down to Tryn's level.

"Hello," Tryn said nervously.

Jake patted Melissa's tall insectoid leg. "Angie and I found Melissa when she was a grub. She'd been hurt by her sister in a fight. The Mimics wanted her to die, but she lived, and now look at her. Isn't she magnificent!"

"She sure is," Tryn said. He looked at the mantis. "Why were you fighting with your sister?"

"It was a challenge to see who would rise to be a queen. I wouldn't fight, so I am fallen," Melissa answered.

"You're a queen in our eyes," Jake said proudly.

"Aw, thanks," Melissa said coyly.

"This is a Mimic queen?" Tryn gasped.

Jake nodded. "Not what I expected either."

"You're not like Jake, or the others," Melissa said to Tryn. "You smell and look different."

"I am from a different world. But we are good friends."

"That's totally awesome. Can I be your friend too?" Melissa asked.

Tryn nodded and looked at Jake with raised eyebrows. "Totally awesome?"

Jake whispered, "It's complicated, but we shared a connection through a tendril. I experienced her life and she did mine. Now she sometimes talks like a Californian."

Vulcan charged forward. "Tryn!" He scooped him up in a bear hug. "It is wonderful to see you!"

Soon everyone was gathered around and stories were shared. Jake told Tryn everything he and Angie had been through, and Tryn shared the events leading to this moment.

Joel threw his arms around Paelen and lifted him into the air. "Em's alive! Did you hear that? Em is alive!"

"Joel, stop. You are crushing me!" Paelen cried.

"She's safe," Tryn said. "They're in another city, far from here. It's taken me two days and nights to fly here. After we rescued Emily, Zephyr and Pegasus managed to drown two young queens."

Tryn realized what he'd said and looked at Melissa. "I'm so sorry. I didn't mean to tell you like that. They were your sisters."

"We aren't a close family," Melissa spat. "If I saw them, I wouldn't even speak to them!"

Steve approached Tryn. "I've got to get back to Emily. Please, Tryn, take me on that board of yours and let's go."

Diana shook her head. "Steve, I know you want to

see Emily again. So do I. But we cannot. She is with Pegasus and is safe; that is enough for now. We dare not waste precious time going to see her when we should be going after the First Queen. We must stop her from spawning and sending out new queens to take over more worlds. You are strong and a valuable fighter."

Jake could see the fatherly conflict in Steve. He needed to see his daughter. But Diana was right, they had to go after the First Queen before she spawned again. "Steve, please go with everyone." Jake looked back at Tryn. "We'll go get the others and join you."

Tryn took off his ring and handed it to Diana. "Here, it's a Solar Stream ring. You can use it to send the injured members of your group back to Xanadu to recover."

"Thank you, Tryn," Diana said. "We will."

"What about me?" Melissa asked. "You're not going to leave me here?"

"No way," Jake said. "You're coming with us too."

"Cool," Melissa said.

Tryn looked at the Fallen Queen. "It will be dangerous for her to come with us. Lergo is rampaging through the streets. It may smell her."

"She can fly; she'll be fine," Jake said. "But we're not leaving her."

"I wasn't saying leave her," Tryn said. "Maybe she should go with the others."

Melissa shook her triangular head. "No way. I'm staying with Jake, Nesso, and Angie."

"Fine," Tryn said. "But we have to get moving."

"Wait." Astraea's brother Vulturnus rushed forward. "Please, take me with you. My brother and I have been frantic about Astraea. Aquilo is too weak to move and must go to Xanadu. I am not strong enough yet to fight with the others. But I am recovering. Please, let me see my sister."

Jake looked at Steve, knowing he'd been told he couldn't go to see Emily. Was it fair to take Vulturnus?

"It's all right," Steve said. "Take Vulturnus to his sister. I will see Emily soon."

Jake nodded. "All right, climb onto my board. But we must go now. Each moment we waste, more grubs will be hatched, and more queens will rise."

"Go," Chiron called. "We will meet you on the way to the First Queen."

# 23

THREE DAYS HAD PASSED SINCE TRYN HAD left. Astraea was frantic with worry that something terrible had happened to him. Considering how Lergo nearly got her and Zephyr, she was frightened that the snake had caught him.

In the front room of the apartment, Pegasus was inconsolable as Emily remained unmoving in the bed.

"I cannot wait any longer," Pegasus said. "I must take Emily back to Arious. She helped Emily once before; she may do so again."

"We can't leave," Astraea said. "We have to wait for Tryn."

"I know," Pegasus said. "That is why I am going to take her to Arious alone and then return."

"You're leaving?" Cylus said as he and the centaurs entered the room carrying a plate of ambrosia cakes.

"I must," Pegasus said. "You have seen her. Emily is not recovering. Her only hope now is on Xanadu. Then, if anyone is left there, I will bring them back to help find the others."

Astraea hated the thought of Pegasus and Emily leaving, but the stallion was right. Despite their care, Emily wasn't recovering. "When do you want to go?"

"Right now," Pegasus said. "There is no point waiting. The sooner I go, the sooner I can return. While I am gone, I am asking you, please do not leave here. This is where I will return to."

"Of course," Astraea said. "We'll be here."

Pegasus looked at the centaurs. "Will you lift Emily onto my back?" Then he turned to Astraea and Triana. "We are going to need to tie her on. Would you find something that could work?"

Within a few minutes, Emily was on Pegasus's back. Her hands were tied beneath his neck and her legs were tied together going under his stomach. Cylus stepped back and inspected his work.

"As long as you don't try anything too fancy, she should stay there."

Pegasus nodded. "I will be especially careful." He paused and looked at each of them. "There are no words that could convey my gratitude to you all for helping me find my Emily. . . ."

"Don't go getting all mushy on us, Pegasus," Cylus said uncomfortably.

Pegasus nickered in humor. "All right, I will not. Instead I will simply say thank you." He walked forward to the wall. "Astraea, would you use your ring, please? It will be faster than me flying up into the Solar Stream."

"Of course." Astraea followed him over to the wide lounge wall. She hugged his neck. "See you soon."

Pegasus rested his head against her. "Yes, I will be back shortly." He raised his head and looked over to Zephyr. "You behave yourself, young lady."

Zephyr looked around. "What? Why's he looking at me like that?"

They all smiled as Astraea held up the ring. "Take

Pegasus to Xanadu, inside the Temple of Arious to the corridor outside her chamber."

The Solar Stream burst to life. Pegasus took a step forward and then looked back at everyone. "I promise you all, I will be back, and then we can end this."

They called their good-byes as he walked into the blazing light. When he was gone, Astraea closed the portal. The room suddenly sounded painfully quiet.

"So now what?" Cylus said. "We just sit here and wait?"

"We promised Pegasus we would stay here," Astraea said. "Besides, we don't know where Tryn is, and I don't think we can find the queen on our own."

"Why not?" Render asked. "You have the Solar Stream ring; use it."

"To go where?" Astraea said. "Even if we wanted to leave, we need the name of our destination. I doubt saying 'Take us to the queen' will work."

"Well . . . well . . . ," Cylus said. "Well, we can't just sit here."

Astraea started counting off on her fingers. "So our choices are, we stay and wait a bit longer, or we use the Solar Stream and go back to Xanadu or Titus."

"I'm not leaving without my brother!" Triana insisted. "I'm staying."

"So am I," Astraea said.

"Well, I haven't anything important to do on Xanadu," Zephyr said. "Guess I'll stay too."

Astraea looked over to the centaurs. "If you want to go, I understand."

"No way," Cylus said. "We're not leaving you here. I just hate waiting around." He looked at Darek and Render. "We could go out tonight and try to find some trees to make more arrows and spears."

"That's a great idea," Render agreed. "As long as we have something to do other than sit around."

"We did see trees," Zephyr said, "but they are a long, long way from here, and with Lergo in the area, well, you know." Zephyr looked at Astraea in quiet understanding of what had happened to them with the snake.

"That doesn't mean we can't look in this building," Astraea suggested. "We could even break through to the building next door. There's lots of stuff here we could use, like doorframes and the doors themselves!"

"Or the floor," Zephyr offered. "This is wood. So is most of the furniture."

Cylus looked around and considered. "You're right, there's lots right here we could use. While we get started, would you draw more venom from your two snakes?"

"Sure," Astraea agreed. "Let's get to work."

They spent the whole day going through the apartment building, looking for anything to convert into weapons. By nightfall, they had pieces of broken doors and furniture that they were trimming down to points using knives that they took from several kitchens. While the centaurs did their best to make arrows, Astraea and Triana sharpened the ends of planks to make into spears.

As fatigue set in, the centaurs settled down in the lounge to rest. Triana retired to her bedroom while Astraea and Zephyr returned to theirs. They slept, woke, and then slept again. When Astraea woke again, she peered over to the window. It was still dark out, but she knew she wouldn't get back to sleep. She wondered if Pegasus had made it to Xanadu yet, and if Arious had told him what her parents had said when they'd found out where she, Zephyr, and the others had gone.

"You awake?" Zephyr said softly.

"Yep," Astraea said. "How about you?"

"No, I'm fast asleep!"

The two giggled like they used to before the word "Mimic" had entered their lives. Astraea reached out and stroked Zephyr's neck. "Do you think Tryn is dead?"

"Aren't you a little ray of sunshine," Zephyr said. "No, he's not dead. He's too strong and clever to be caught by Lergo or the Mimics. He's probably found Jake, and that crazy human has taken him on an adventure without us."

Astraea so wished it were true. But as the days had passed, she'd started to fear the worst. Becoming restless, she rose, and together she and Zephyr made their way into the kitchen for a snack.

Astraea saw the two snakes from her bracelet waiting on the cushion she'd given them, set up in the middle of the counter.

"Hi, Frick and Frack," she said, greeting them.

Zephyr snorted. "You know, I thought 'Belis' was a dumb name, but really? 'Frick and Frack'?"

"I think they're cute names, just like the snakes." Astraea pulled pieces of ambrosia cake out of the container and offered some to them. Then she gave a larger piece to Zephyr and took one for herself. They ate in silence, gazing out the kitchen window into the darkness.

Before long, the centaurs rose and joined them. They still had a good supply of ambrosia because they were being careful. But it wouldn't last forever.

Darek glanced at the window. "This is what I hate most about this world," he said. "The endless days and nights."

"Me too," Triana agreed as she entered the kitchen. She yawned and reached for a small piece of ambrosia.

"I wonder how long we've been gone from Xanadu," Cylus said. "And how the battle for Titus has gone."

"What really bothers me," Astraea said, "is that we told Arious what we were planning. She would have told Jupiter. I thought for sure some of them would have followed us."

"I know," Cylus said. "I was sure my mom would come for me."

"Maybe they couldn't," Triana said. "Perhaps the Mimics attacked the temple again. Maybe they had to stay and fight."

"Who's fighting without us?" Tryn called.

Astraea gasped and turned around to see Tryn and Jake standing in the doorway of the kitchen.

"Tryn!" Triana squealed as she ran to her brother.

"Jake!" Astraea embraced him tightly. "We thought you were dead!"

"As if," Jake said as he hugged Astraea again. "Boy, have I missed you guys! What took you so long?"

"We came as soon as we could," Astraea said. While Tryn and his sister were still hugging, Astraea reached over and slapped Tryn lightly. "Why did you leave without me?"

"I had to find Jake and the others. I knew you were safe here with everyone. We couldn't waste time." He reached over and grabbed the container of ambrosia. "I'm starved. Come on upstairs to the roof; we have a surprise for you." He looked at the small snakes. "Bring your two friends; they should hear this too."

"Yeah," Jake laughed excitedly. "You're gonna love it!"

Astraea shouted in joy when she saw her brother standing at the top of the stairs to the roof. They embraced tightly, and both had tears in their eyes. "I was so scared," Astraea cried. "When you weren't in the prison on Titus, I thought for sure I'd never see you again."

"It was only fear for you that kept me and Aquilo going in that terrible camp."

"Hey," Zephyr called. "It's my turn!"

Astraea sniffed and laughed as Zephyr greeted her brother. Ever since they'd been young, Zephyr and Vulturnus had had a special friendship. He was always giving her treats and apples every time he saw her.

"I am all right," he said softly, stroking her neck. "I am sorry I do not have any apples for you."

"You can owe me," Zephyr sniffed.

They walked farther onto the roof and stopped suddenly as they spied the immense creature standing with Angitia.

"Astraea!" Angie cried as she ran and threw her arms around Astraea. "Come here, you have to meet Melissa!" Angie took Astraea's hand and drew her over to the mantis. "Melissa, this is . . ."

"Astraea," Melissa said warmly. "It's fab to meet you. I know all about you from Jake." She then turned to Triana. "You look and smell just like Tryn. You must be Triana."

Triana grinned. "I am."

Melissa lowered her head closer and winked. "Jake really, really likes you. You know what I mean?"

Astraea laughed as Triana's cheeks turned dark silver and she looked back at Jake.

"Thanks, Melissa," he said awkwardly.

"Anytime," Melissa responded.

The three centaurs reached the roof and gasped when they saw Melissa. "What is that thing?" Cylus cried.

"Thing?" Melissa responded. "You're the thing. What are you? Part horse, part boy? Make up your mind!"

"Hey, I'm no horse," Cylus shot. "I'm a centaur!"

"Yeah, and I'm a Melissa!" the mantis responded.

Jake stepped cautiously forward, unable to see in

the dark. "Hey, everyone, calm down. We're all friends here." He turned toward the sound of the centaurs. "Cylus, Render, Darek, this is Melissa."

Tryn added, "She's a Mimic queen and can control the Mimics."

"Fallen Queen," Melissa corrected.

"No, you are a wonderful queen," Tryn said.

Melissa tilted her head to the side. "Ah, that's so nice. I can deal with that."

"A Mimic queen," Cylus gasped. "We're going up against that?"

"Not me, silly," Melissa said. "My mother."

"Oh, I feel so much better," Cylus said, rolling his eyes.

After the introductions, the remaining ambrosia was brought up to the roof and handed out. While they ate, Jake repeated the story of his time on Tremenz, starting with the lab, finding Angie, and then freeing the prisoners and finding Melissa when she was still a grub. He finished with, "Some of the injured have gone back to Xanadu, while Diana, Chiron, and the others are headed to the queen. We're going to meet them on the way."

Astraea was seated beside Zephyr and was watching Jake and the others talking. Angie was right beside him and laughing at everything he said. Astraea was thrilled that the two had found each other, and by the looks of it, they were already very close. She worried about how hard it would be when the time came for Jake to go home.

"So now what?" Cylus asked.

"Now we get a bit of rest," Tryn said. "Then we can head out and find the others to join the assault against the queen—"

The sound of shattering glass interrupted Tryn's comment. Everyone rose as Astraea approached the edge of the roof and peered down. She screamed, "Lergo is climbing the building! Run!"

Astraea barely had time to take two steps toward Zephyr before the massive snake rose high above her and its head came smashing down onto the roof. Broken timbers and debris filled the air as the roof collapsed from Lergo's weight.

There was no time to fly, no time to run as the roof broke apart. Astraea heard Zephyr screaming, but it was far away as they tumbled through the destruction.

# 24

ASTRAEA AWOKE WITH A POUNDING HEAD
and intense pressure on her chest. She tried to move
but discovered that she was pinned down by a large
beam. The air was thick and acrid from the dust and
debris. At first disoriented, she soon remembered.
Lergo. It had attacked and destroyed their building.

She opened her eyes but saw only the plumes of
dust from the old broken beams. She tried to call
out to the others, but rubble pressed down on her so
hard, she couldn't take in a deep breath to scream.

Astraea wasn't sure how long she had been unconscious, but by the sounds of groaning beams and
a strange rainfall of debris, some time had to have

passed since the attack. As her eyes adjusted, she saw sunlight spattering through the mess. It was daylight!

"Zephyr!" she struggled to call. "Vulturnus? Tryn, Jake, anyone, can you hear me?"

"Astraea," Tryn responded softly. "Where are you?"

"I don't know," Astraea said. "But I think I'm beneath you. I'm trapped. I can't move because there's a heavy beam across my chest."

"I can't move either," Tryn said. "Triana is here, but she's unconscious. I can hear her breathing, but I don't know how badly she's been hurt."

"Zeph!" Astraea called as loudly as the beam and her breath would allow. "Zeph, answer me!"

"Jake!" Tryn called. "Angie? Is anyone out there? Cylus? Render? Darek?"

Astraea and Tryn fell silent as they listened for the sounds of others. But there was only the creaking of beams and rubble still falling.

"Can you dig yourself out?" Astraea called to Tryn.

"I'm trying. But my legs are caught."

Astraea tried to push away the beam across her, but it was supported by other timber. "If I move, the beam on my chest shifts and I can't breathe. I'm lying on my wings and they really hurt."

"Do not move, Astraea," Vulturnus warned. "It could crush you. Just stay still."

He sounded closer than Tryn. "Vulturnus, where are you?"

"I am directly beneath you," he said. "I can see your foot."

Astraea felt her brother touching her foot. She tried to move her head but found she couldn't. "Can anyone see Zephyr?"

"No," Vulturnus answered. "I cannot see anything but dust and your foot. I am on my wings too and fear they are broken. But I cannot move to check."

"Zeph! Zeph!" Astraea called. But there was no response.

Astraea was growing close to panic. Had Lergo gotten Zephyr and the others? Had they been eaten, or were they lying buried somewhere in the collapsed building?

With only one hand that could move, Astraea tried to pull debris away from herself. But each time she moved, it destabilized the beam, and more of its weight dropped onto her chest.

She could hear Tryn above her, and Vulturnus beneath her trying to dig themselves out, but it was difficult. They were all well and truly stuck.

As Astraea followed a small pinprick of sunlight drifting over the heavy beam, she realized the day was passing. When it faded from her view, she became aware of the sounds of digging and movement.

"Vulturnus, is that you?"

"No," he answered. "Tryn, are you moving?"

"It's not me . . . ," Tryn said softly. "It's coming from above us. Maybe it's Zephyr or the centaurs."

"Zeph!" Astraea called again. "Cylus, Render, Darek, is that you?"

"No," Melissa called. "It's me. I've brought help. We'll get you all out of there in no time."

"Help from who?" Tryn called. "Is Jake with you?"

"Yes," Melissa said. "He's safe on another building."

"Where is Lergo?" Astraea called. "Did it get Zephyr?"

"No, she is buried here as well." Then Melissa's voice dropped. "Lergo took Render and Angie. I tried to stop it, but it was bigger than me and tried to eat me."

Astraea gasped. Render and Angitia were gone . . . ? She felt her throat constrict. Deep sobs soon started, but they caused the beam to shift. It creaked, and then there was another collapse as the debris supporting the beam gave way. Its full weight came crashing down onto Astraea's chest.

"Can't . . . can't breathe," she choked.

"Astraea!" Vulturnus called. "Astraea!"

Astraea fought to take a breath, but the pressure on her chest was too great. She started to panic and thrash, but it only made things worse as more of the building collapsed around her. In the past, she and Zephyr used to play a game of who could hold their breath the longest. Zephyr always won. But Astraea wasn't too far behind her. She tried to calm herself and remember the game. She couldn't allow herself to panic, as she'd use up what little air she had. But as the minutes passed, her strength was ebbing.

With the sound of blood rushing in her ears and her heart pounding like thunder, the need to breathe became unbearable. Astraea couldn't hear the tearing around her. She wasn't aware of more debris raining down. All she knew was she couldn't breathe.

Then, she could.

Astraea gulped air gratefully and coughed out the thick dust that had settled in her throat. After several deep breaths, she looked up and saw Tryn's frightened face above her. His hair was white with dust and his skin was dull gray. His wonderful, speckled eyes sparkled with concern.

"Try . . ."

"Don't speak," Tryn said. "Just breathe."

Astraea focused on each breath. She could hear Vulturnus calling and Tryn responding, saying he'd reached her and that she was breathing again.

As she calmed, she noticed that Tryn's hands were bleeding and there was a deep cut on his face. His shirt was torn, and he was breathing hard because he was bending down at an awkward angle from above. Somehow he had managed to shift the big beam and all the debris off her from that twisted, bent position.

Just how strong was he?

"Thank you, Tryn," Astraea said softly. "I thought it was over."

"Not quite," Tryn said. He smiled at her. "But I'd sure appreciate it if you'd stop getting into trouble."

Astraea smiled back at him. "I'll try. I can't make any promises."

"Astraea, talk to me. Are you all right?" Vulturnus called.

"I am now," Astraea responded. "Tryn saved me." She looked up at Tryn again. "Do you think you could help me get out of this?"

He shook his head. "There's no way up from here yet; they've got to get us from above. Not to mention, that beam that nearly killed you is all that's stopping this whole area from collapsing. I'll go and see if I can find out where Melissa and the others are."

Tryn kissed Astraea lightly on the forehead. "Don't go anywhere. . . ." Then he disappeared back up the way he'd come.

A few minutes later, they heard him scream.

"Tryn," Astraea shouted. "Tryn, are you all right?"

"He is," Triana called. "He was just frightened."

"I wasn't frightened," Tryn responded. "I was surprised."

"What's happening?" Vulturnus called.

Triana called, "When Melissa said she got us help,

she meant it. She's brought Shadow Titans with torches. They're here digging us free."

"Shadow Titans!" Astraea cried.

"Yes," Tryn said. "They're like ants; they're swarming all over the place."

Astraea gasped. "If there are Shadow Titans, that means there are . . ."

"Mimics, yes," Melissa said. "They're down on the street. I made them come to rescue you. I thought, with all the trouble they've caused us, they should be the ones to help."

Astraea settled back to wait for the rescue teams. She was still in a lot of discomfort, but at least she could breathe. But nothing could compare to the pain of losing Render and Angitia to Lergo. Angitia was so young and filled with life. And Render, sweet Render, was alive with curiosity and dreamed of flying. That dream was gone. He didn't deserve this. They both didn't.

They'd all known this was a dangerous mission, but somehow Astraea had hoped that they would all make it home alive.

Zephyr was still missing, and Astraea was terrified.

Where was Zephyr? Was she badly hurt? After what seemed half the night, Astraea heard a scream, and it brought pure joy to her grieving heart. Zephyr was whinnying in fear.

"Zeph, can you hear me?" Astraea shouted.

"Yes! There are Shadow Titans here!"

"I know, they're helping us—calm down. You're safe!"

"But they're Shadow Titans!"

"They are controlled by Melissa," Tryn called. "Don't fight them."

Astraea could do nothing to dig herself out of the rubble. Every time she moved, more debris rained down on her. Considering what had happened earlier, she knew she would have to be patient and wait for the Shadow Titans to free her.

It finally happened sometime during the long night. The Shadows said nothing as they carefully picked away the pieces of roof and supporting beams. Tryn was with them, directing them. But the Shadows did all the work.

When the large beam was finally supported higher above her, Tryn was able to crawl down and pull

Astraea free. She threw her arms around him tightly.

"It's all right," Tryn reassured. "You're safe now. Go with this turtle Shadow Titan; it will help you get above."

Astraea shook her head. "Vulturnus is down here, and I'm going to help get him free."

"Astraea, go," her brother called.

"We'll go together," Astraea said. "That's final."

It seemed to take an age to reach Vulturnus. He wasn't that far beneath her, but he was buried in a spider's web of old pipework and roof debris. His legs were locked under large pieces of roof beams, and his wings were open and twisted at odd angles beneath him. When he was finally free, they found that his wings weren't broken, but they were badly sprained.

With the help of the Shadow Titans, he, Tryn, and Astraea were assisted to the top of the rubble. Astraea hadn't realized it, but she and her brother had fallen through three floors and been trapped in the middle of the remains of the building. There was nothing left of their hiding place. It had all been destroyed by Lergo.

Standing at the top of the destruction, Astraea saw

that Zephyr and the others had found refuge on the roof of the building directly across the street. Even in the dark, Astraea could see that her best friend was a mess. Zephyr was filthy, but more than that, there were cuts and gouges all over her body that were still bleeding.

Cylus and Darek were also on the opposite roof. Like Zephyr, they were covered in cuts and bruises, but they were alive.

Jake flew over on his skateboard. In the torch-light she could see the trails of his tears in the dirt on his face. Losing Angie was hardest on him, and his chin was still quivering. He reached his hand out to Astraea. "I'll fly you over to Zephyr."

Astraea accepted his hand and climbed up onto his skateboard. When they arrived on the opposite roof, Astraea put her arms around him and held him tight. "I am so sorry, Jake."

He was shaking as the sobs started again. "Angie— she—I mean, I, I really liked her. She—she was like a sister to me."

*"Ssshe wasss very ssspecial,"* Nesso hissed softly.

"She was . . ." Jake wept.

Astraea reached up and stroked the small snake. "At least you are safe," she said softly as her own tears started. "But Angitia and Render . . . it's just awful."

"It's my fault," Zephyr moaned as her head hung low. "I killed them because I said to bring Lergo here. . . ."

"No you didn't," Astraea said. "None of us could have known that would happen."

"We should have," Zephyr said. "We knew how dangerous it was. Look what happened to us a few days ago. How could I have thought this would work? That snake is just as wild and deadly to us as the Mimics. Now . . . now it's killed Render and Angitia."

Astraea limped over to Zephyr and put her arms around her neck. They held on to each other, saying nothing as they were overwhelmed with grief.

Jake returned to the rubble to collect Vulturnus. After a bit of searching, Tryn found his own board and joined them on the opposite roof.

Standing all together on the edge of the roof, they looked at the destroyed building. No one spoke; there was no need. They all knew the worst had happened. Two of their team were dead.

# 25

TIME PASSED, BUT STILL NO ONE MOVED.

Their mission had seemed so simple. Get in and stop the Mimic queen. But as Astraea looked at the remains of the building and the others around her covered in cuts and bruises, she realized they were fooling themselves. They were just kids. Not heroes. How could they imagine that they could stop the queen of a race of beings that were destroying worlds? What did they think they could possibly do that millions of others before them couldn't?

She looked at everyone. "I'm so sorry; we shouldn't be here. I really thought we could do this, but we can't. The camps, Lergo, the queen, it's just too much.

Now we've lost Render and Angie. I can't bear to lose any more of you. We have to go back to Xanadu."

"What are you talking about?" Cylus said. "You want to give up?"

Astraea walked over to the centaur. "What choice do we have? We can't do this anymore. You and Darek have lost your bows and arrows. I've lost my slingshot. All I've got left is my dagger. We can't win, not against the Mimics. Even if we manage to find the queen . . ." She looked at Melissa. "If that's what we're up against, there's no way we could beat her, let alone all the Mimics that are going to be around her."

Anger crossed Cylus's face, but then it softened. "We can't give up, Astraea, not now. If we do, Render and Angitia will have died for nothing. We all knew that this would be dangerous and that some of us might not make it back. But we came anyway and stayed when we could have gone back with Pegasus. We have to stop the queen from destroying our people and the people of other worlds."

Tryn stepped up to Astraea. "He's right. If we go back now, all is lost. The queen will spawn again and there will be more new queens to go out and take other worlds. Right here and right now is where it must stop."

Astraea looked at Tryn. He was limping and both his shins were badly injured, as silver blood trailed down his legs. He'd hurt himself saving her but was still prepared to fight on. "You want to go after the queen?"

"We must," Tryn said. "And yes, I realize that any one of us could be killed. Maybe all of us. But what's the alternative? Titus and Xanadu are already defeated. Jupiter is trying to fight back, but it won't mean much if more queens rise to take Titus and Xanadu."

"Astraea," her brother said. "I have been one of their slaves. I would rather die right now than go back into one of those camps. Being trapped in there is a kind of living death. There is no hope, only despair and pain. Right now, while we're here on this roof debating what to do, others are out there suffering with no hope, believing everyone has forgotten about them. But we haven't forgotten about them. We must be their hope."

"Earth will be next," Jake added softly. "My family is there. They have no idea what's coming or what the

Mimics are. I can't go back to Xanadu; it will only prolong the inevitable. The Mimics will take it and we will all be slaves. But that doesn't have to happen if we can stop the queen. We're not alone, Astraea. Out there somewhere, Chiron, Diana, Steve Jacobs, and so many others are marching on the queen. They are expecting us. We can't let them down."

Astraea looked around the roof. Tryn and Triana were nodding, and so were the centaurs. She looked at her best friend. "What do you say, Zeph. What do you want to do?"

"What I want isn't the real question," Zephyr said somberly. "I want to go back to the Titus I knew. The Titus before the Mimics, when all you and I complained about was having to go to school, or getting mad because someone compared me to Pegasus. The same Titus where we played and had pillow fights, never knowing that Mimics existed. That's what I want. But that life doesn't exist anymore. That Titus is gone. So I say we stay here on this roof for a while longer, gather our strength, and do what we came to do and stop that queen."

"I agree!" Melissa said. "I don't want them to hurt

anyone else. The First Queen is my mother, and if I have to fight her to protect you all, you can bet I will."

"Thank you, Melissa," Jake said. He patted her leg. "That really means a lot."

"See, Astraea," Cylus said finally. "Going back to Xanadu isn't a choice for any of us. Yes, we're just kids and we may never be heroes and we might all die. But if we don't try to stop the queen now, everything we've ever loved will be lost."

Astraea looked around again. "So we fight?"

When everyone nodded, Zephyr whinnied. "Yes, we fight."


Sunrise was still a long time away, but they remained on the roof, trying to rest. It had been a terrible night and they needed time to recover.

Astraea was sitting beside Zephyr and leaning against her best friend. She opened the secret compartment on her arm bracelet and checked on Frick and Frack. The two snakes were banged up, but alive.

"We still do have these two," she said, holding them up.

*"And me,"* Nesso said.

"And that means venom," Tryn said. He stood up. "I'm going down into this building to see if I can find a container to store it in."

"I'll come with you," Jake offered. "Maybe we can find something to make new weapons out of."

"Wait for me," Vulturnus said as he climbed to his feet. "There must be things we can use down there."

While they were gone, Astraea, Zephyr, and the others waited on the roof, watching Melissa doing a strange kind of crouch and flexing her one working foreleg.

"Melissa?" Astraea asked. "What happened to your other upper leg?"

The mantis stopped and looked at her mangled foreleg. "My sister did this to me when I was still a grub. She bit my arm and damaged it so badly, when I changed, it didn't grow back."

"It must have been terrible," Triana said.

"It was," Melissa agreed. "But I survived. Then the Mimics put me in a cage so I would suffer and die. When Jake and Angie found me, they saved my life. Jake gave me my name and wouldn't give up on me. He spoke for me and convinced Angie and the others that I was safe. I owe him everything."

"Jake did that?" Cylus asked.

"You betcha," Melissa said. "He was really brave." She went back to crouching over and slicing the air with her one good foreleg. "I wonder if the First Queen will be much bigger than me."

"She's a lot older," Triana said. "I would think so."

"Oh," Melissa said softly. "Rats."

Astraea couldn't get over how much Melissa sounded like Jake. If she closed her eyes and listened, she heard a female version of him. Not the huge insect standing before her. "Don't worry, we'll all be facing her together. You won't be in there alone."

"Promise?" Melissa said.

"Yes, we promise," Triana answered.

That seemed to settle her some. She got up, walked to the roof edge, and peered down the street. Each of Melissa's footsteps caused heavy vibrations to run through the roof's surface. Considering the age of the building and what had happened with Lergo, Astraea wondered just how strong this old roof was.

When Tryn and the others returned, their arms were full. Old bedsheets had been carried up so that wounds could be cleaned and bandaged, and they'd found a jar to store fresh venom in. There was nothing they could use to make slingshots or bows, as there was no string that wasn't rotten. Their only choice was to use rocks they gathered along the way and covered in venom.

When the snakes had given all they could, everyone stood up. Without speaking, they knew it was time to move. There was still a lot of night left, and they couldn't waste it.

Tryn and Jake used their skateboards to get Triana, Cylus, and Darek off the roof and down to the street. Zephyr carried Astraea and her brother, and Melissa flew on her own.

When the mantis flew, Astraea was surprised by the fine graceful wings she'd kept hidden under the shell on her back. They were just like the insects' wings at home that were see-through and delicate.

They landed among the group of stationary Shadow Titans, but there were no signs of the Mimics that commanded them.

"How did they get here?" Astraea asked.

"I brought them down from the rubble," Melissa said. "I thought you might want them."

"We do, thank you," Jake said. "But what about the Mimics?"

"Those we don't need, so I sent them away," Melissa said. "The control things are over there."

The controllers for the Shadow Titans were gathered together, and the Shadows were ordered to follow behind the group as they started to walk.

Tryn and Jake rode their skateboards at street level, telling the boards to lead them to the First Queen. Without hesitation, the two boards moved them in the same direction.

Astraea and her brother stayed on Zephyr, while Darek carried Triana. As they followed the skateboards down the dark, empty streets, they remained silent. Lergo was still in the area, and they couldn't risk another encounter.

After several blocks, they entered another neighborhood. This area showed signs of damage from the monstrous snake, and they had to climb over the rubble. But unlike the area they'd hidden in, a lot of the undamaged buildings had lights shining brightly out the windows.

Mimics lived here.

Melissa walked beside Jake, looking at all the buildings. "They are here all around us. I can feel them," she said. She turned to Jake. "They know I'm here too."

"Don't be frightened," Jake said. "They won't hurt you."

"I'm not frightened. I just don't like them."

Zephyr turned to look back up at Astraea. "How can she hate her own kind?"

Astraea leaned forward. "Wouldn't you? They make you fight to the death, but when you don't die, they lock you in a cage until you starve. That's pretty cruel."

"That's Mimics," Vulturnus said.

The farther they traveled, the more buildings they saw with lights on. Astraea looked back in the direction where the sun rose and saw the first traces of light rising on the horizon.

"The sun is coming up," Astraea said. "We're going to need to find somewhere to hide."

"Not here," Cylus said softly. "How far does this city go?"

"Far," Tryn said. "By foot, I think it's going to take us several nights' walking to get to the queen."

"And these are really long nights," Triana said.

"Exactly," Tryn agreed.

"Let's go faster," Cylus said. "I don't want to be here when the sun rises."

They told the Shadow Titans to move faster as everyone entered a trot. Zephyr was limping a bit, but when Astraea asked, she insisted it was nothing. The way she snapped, Astraea knew Zephyr was in pain but wouldn't stop.

Keeping up the pace, they were able to cover more ground. But each moment saw more lights coming on in the buildings as the Mimics rose and prepared for their day.

"I think we're in trouble," Darek said. "They're getting up."

Melissa stopped and looked behind them.

Jake looked back at her. "What is it? Are Mimics coming?"

"No, it's not them. But I feel something," she said.

Cylus stopped and tilted his head to the side. "I feel it too. It's a kind of vibration, but not like footsteps."

"So do I," Darek agreed.

Everyone turned and looked back in the direction they'd come. Astraea listened closely but couldn't hear or feel anything. She was just about to comment when the worst thing imaginable happened.

Lergo slithered around the corner they'd just passed and was bearing down on them at speed.

"Fly!" Jake screamed. He ordered his skateboard off the ground and swooped closer to Cylus. "Grab hold!"

Tryn did the same to Darek and then looked at his sister. "Triana, hold on tight to Darek!"

Zephyr trotted and then entered a gallop. She was just about to launch into the air when her injured front leg gave out and she tumbled forward. Zephyr screamed as she started to fall.

Astraea and Vulturnus were thrown over her neck and crashed to the street several feet away. By the time Astraea stopped tumbling and was able to look up, Lergo was right in front of her and rearing up.

Astraea screamed as the gigantic snake opened its mouth, revealing its two immense fangs.

# 26

"JAKE, MELISSA!" A SMALL VOICE CALLED.

Lergo was looming above Astraea, Zephyr, and Vulturnus, but it wasn't attacking. It just hovered above them.

"Angie!" Melissa called. The Fallen Queen was perched on a roof directly above the massive snake. "Jake, look, it's Angie. She's alive!"

"Angie?" Jake cried. "Where is she?"

"I'm here," Angie cried.

"I see her!" Melissa called. "She's on the snake!"

Astraea was frozen on the spot, unable to comprehend what was happening. Melissa said Angie was alive, but Astraea couldn't see her. All she could see was the open mouth and sharp fangs of Lergo.

"Cylus, Darek!" Render galloped alongside the snake and then looked up, waving. "It's all right. Everyone, come down!"

Jake and Tryn ordered their skateboards cautiously down to the ground while keeping their wary eyes on Lergo.

Render ran up to the other centaurs, and they all noisily embraced.

"We thought you were dead!" Darek cried.

"I thought we were dead too when Lergo grabbed us. But it was going after Angie. I was just in the way and it took me too."

Jake used his skateboard to fly up just past the snake's head. He disappeared for a while. When he reappeared, Angie was on the skateboard with him and he had his arms around her tightly. "Look, everyone, she's alive!"

The reunion was noisy, and tear-filled as they all greeted each other again.

"How?" Zephyr cried. She was limping when she walked over. "How did you do it? How did you survive the attack on the roof?"

"It wasn't an attack. Lergo could feel me and wanted to get to me, but he was too heavy, and the roof collapsed."

"He?" Astraea asked.

"Yes," Angie said. "Lergo is a boy."

"I told you!" Cylus said.

Angie trotted over to the massive snake. Lergo lowered his head to the ground with only the tip of his forked tongue sticking out. Standing before him, Angie looked minuscule. She didn't even reach up to his nostrils. But still, Lergo stayed perfectly still as she petted his head. "He looks big and scary, but he's really very sweet."

"Oh no," Zephyr said. "That's the snake that nearly killed me on Zomos and tried to eat Astraea and me a couple of days ago. It is anything but sweet!"

"Not 'it.' 'He,'" Angie corrected. "And I'm sure he's sorry. But he's very old and hungry because he can't catch much food anymore."

"He's hungry?" Cylus said. "Meaning we'd be a good meal for him."

"No," Angie said. "He won't hurt you now that he knows you're with me."

"She's right," Render said. "He could have eaten me, but he didn't. All he wants is Angie."

Jake put his arms around her again. "Leave it to you to charm the biggest, deadliest snake in the universe!"

"I'm sorry we took so long to find you, but Lergo wanted to take us to safety. He knew we were in danger from the Mimics."

"How?" Vulturnus said.

Nesso hissed, *"Lergo may be very big and very dangerousss, and would even eat usss sssnakesss if he caught usss, but Lergo isss sssmart. He knew what wasss happening on Zzzomosss and hasss been here long enough to sssee. He jussst didn't care until he sssensssed Angie."*

When Jake translated, Cylus gasped, "So she can control him?"

"Not control," Angie said. "We're friends, that's all."

Jake looked up at the immense snake. "That is some friend."

"Are we going to stop the queen now?" Angie asked.

Astraea nodded. "Jake's and Tryn's skateboards are leading us there."

"Lergo wants to come too," Angie said. "He can help."

Everyone stood staring up at the snake. Lergo was black as the night as he sensed all the Mimics. But he just lay with his massive head on the ground before Angie, making no attempt to move.

"We can't take that big thing with us," Cylus said. "It'll eat us the moment we turn our backs."

"No, he won't," Angie said. "He's not going to hurt us. He can help keep us safe."

"But—but it's Lergo!" Cylus cried. "He's deadly."

"Yes, he is," Angie agreed. "But not to us anymore. Besides, if I go, he'll go. I can't stop him. Would you leave without me because of him?"

"No way!" Jake said quickly. "Where I go, you go."

"So, Lergo goes too," Angie said.

"I guess he does," Astraea said. "He's just like Belis. No matter how many times we told him to stay, he still wanted to follow us."

"Exactly," Angie said. She patted the snake's snout again. "You'll see, he can really help us."

Cylus raised his hands in the air in frustration. "I can't believe this. We came here to sneak into the queen's palace to get her. How are we supposed to do that now? It was bad enough with her." Cylus pointed to the Fallen Queen. "No offense, Melissa," he added.

"That's funny," Melissa said, "because I'm offended."

"I didn't mean it like that," Cylus said. "What I meant was, instead of going in quietly, we now have you and Lergo. What's next? A giant or two? How about the Hundred-handers? I'm sure they'd like to join us."

Astraea walked over to the angry centaur. "Cylus, calm down. I know it's not what any of us expected. But you know Melissa now, and she's wonderful. Lergo might be the same—look at Nesso, Belis, and my two in here." She patted her bracelet with the two snakes. "Besides, we don't have any choice. The only way we can stop him from following is to leave Angitia behind. But we're not going to do that. So you have to accept that Lergo is now part of your team."

Render nodded. "He didn't hurt me, Cylus, and I was actually in his mouth. If we're with Angie, he's with us."

The centaur crossed his arms over his chest. "Fine. But if he gets in my way, I'll—"

"You'll what?" Tryn said. "What could you possibly do against him?"

"I don't know; give me some time and I'll figure it out."

"Yes, you do that," Zephyr said. "But could you do it while we're moving? Have you forgotten the sun is rising? Mimics like to come out in the sun. But we don't like the Mimics because they want to kill us."

"Yeah," Cylus said. "Let's go."

They started to move again. But the mood had changed greatly since they'd found Render and Angie alive. There was a sense of hope that they might actually succeed.

Astraea and her brother stayed on the ground, despite Zephyr's protest that she was well enough to carry them. Her limp told Astraea that she wasn't. Instead they walked closely together down the street.

Astraea often looked back at the strange assortment of fighters moving together with the same goal. She had thought that nothing could ever be stranger than Melissa among them with all the Shadow Titans trailing behind. But Astraea had been wrong. Lergo was by far the strangest member of their team. Angie was seated on his wide back again, holding on to a bent scale. From the front, Astraea couldn't see her because the snake was just too big. But her occasional comment confirmed she was there.

Zephyr shook her head and snorted. "When I suggested we bring Lergo here, this was *not* what I meant." She glared back at the snake. "Despite what Angitia says, he's not a cute pet. He's a deadly monster."

"He's behaving like a pet with her," Astraea said. "If he's anything like the other snakes, he'll do whatever she asks."

"Maybe," Zephyr said. "But I agree with Cylus. I don't like him being here. Look at the size of him. I thought Melissa was big, but compared to Lergo, she's tiny. And we are just like ants walking in front of him."

"I just hope he'll help," Astraea said. She looked back at the snake, and then over to Melissa. "If the queen is Melissa's size or even a bit larger, Lergo should be big enough to get her."

Zephyr looked at the two as well. "Yes, but would he?"

Astraea shrugged. "We'll just have to see."

They fell silent as they continued on their journey. The sky above them was turning dawn gray as the sun rose slowly above the horizon. They were all feeling the pressure to find a place to hide that was large enough to hold Melissa *and* Lergo. But they were still in the city and surrounded by buildings. Buildings with lights on. Buildings filled with Mimics.

When daylight rose, there was nowhere to stop. They were in trouble and they all knew it. Every street they tried had buildings with lights on. Very soon, Mimics started to emerge.

"This is so bad," Zephyr said. "We're in big trouble."

Almost immediately things went from dangerous to really, *really* weird. The Mimics didn't attack or send out any tendrils. They just stood on their doorsteps and watched.

Once Lergo had slithered past them, they started to follow. They didn't speak or try anything violent. But from a few Mimics at first, there was soon a legion of them.

Jake looked back. "It's like some kind of demented parade."

"It sure is," Tryn said. He looked around at all the Mimics. "Is it because of Melissa?"

"Don't blame me," Melissa said as she glared at the Mimics. "They're not interested in me. I can hear them; they're calling others. They are saying we are moving. . . ." She stopped and looked at everyone. "They're telling my mother. The First Queen knows we are coming."

# 27

THE TERRIBLE PARADE CONTINUED throughout the day. When Astraea and her team stopped, the Mimics stopped. They didn't attack. They didn't speak. They just stood and waited.

"This is worse than when they try to kill us," Cylus said. He was standing at the side of Lergo, looking down the length of the snake to the mass of Mimics behind them. "At least then you know you can fight. But this . . . What is it?"

Melissa rose. "Stay here. I'm going to see what they're doing."

"Be careful, Melissa," Jake warned. "If the First

Queen knows about us, she knows about you. She might order them to kill you."

"They won't," Melissa said. "When I am near them, they do as I say."

Jake started to walk with her, but Melissa stopped him. "I said they wouldn't hurt *me*. I can't be sure what they'll do to *you*. Please stay here."

Jake waited with Astraea while Melissa walked back toward the growing army of Mimics. When she approached them, they parted to let her through.

"This is so strange," Tryn said. "I would never have believed this. It's like a game or something."

"This is no game," Vulturnus said. "It's deadly serious. Mimics are unlike any other species we've ever encountered. They have no compassion or feelings at all for our kind or even their own. They just exist."

"What makes Melissa different?" Astraea mused.

"I'm not sure," Jake said. "It could be because she's a queen and they are different from the Mimics that are like drones, or it could be because when she was very young, she touched me and learned about me, just like I learned about her."

"Whatever it is," Tryn said, "I'm glad of it."

After a while, Melissa returned. She looked back at the Mimics and they just stood there, watching and waiting.

"Well?" Jake asked.

"Let's keep moving," Melissa said softly.

"No, wait, tell us what they said," Jake said.

Melissa shook her triangular head. "If I do that, you will never trust me again. You'll hate me and won't be my friends."

"Just tell us," Jake insisted. "What happened? What did they say?"

Melissa gave the impression of a sigh. "You promise you won't turn against me?"

"Of course we promise," Jake said.

Melissa looked down at the ground. Despite being huge, she suddenly looked very small and vulnerable. "They told me if I kill you all right now, my mother will allow me to live and become a Risen Queen. She says I can have my choice of worlds—Titus, Xanadu, or Earth—and all these Mimics will be mine to take with me."

A heavy silence fell as everyone took in her words.

Finally Cylus said, "You're joking, right? This is a joke?"

Melissa shook her head. "I wish . . ."

Finally Tryn said, "What happens if you refuse to kill us?"

"If I refuse, when we reach my mother, she will call all the new queens together and they will kill you in front of me. Then my sisters will tear me to pieces."

"Wow," Jake said. "That is one very cold queen."

Melissa nodded. "She is. That's why she makes us fight. So only the most vicious queens survive."

Cylus took a step back. "So what are you going to do?"

Melissa bent down closer to him. "I knew you would hate me if I told you."

"I don't hate you . . . ," Cylus said.

"Yes you do; you're scared of me. I can tell."

Astraea approached the Fallen Queen and reached up to touch her leg. "I don't hate you, Melissa. None of us do. And I know you won't kill us because we're all friends. And friends don't hurt friends."

Melissa tilted her head to the side and peered long and hard at Astraea. "You mean that, don't you?"

"Of course I do," Astraea said.

"You already knew that," Jake said. "We're a team."

"Yes we are," Melissa said. "And I promise you all, I won't let my sisters hurt you. We will stop them." She turned and looked back at the Mimics. "We'll stop all of them."

They walked the entire day with the Mimics trailing behind them. By the time the sun started to descend, they'd left the area of dense buildings and started to see homes. Then they reached rolling hills of wild-flower meadows. There was even a slow-moving river that cut through the green hills.

After a long night and day of walking, they were grateful to settle down on the bank to rest. Zephyr and the centaurs entered the water and lounged in it. But they left it the moment Lergo came forward and slid into the water.

"No way," Zephyr said quickly. "Walking together is one thing. I am not swimming with that snake!"

The water washed Angie off Lergo's back, and she swam to shore. She watched the snake. "He's so old, everything aches," she said. "The water will help."

"Is it from eating Mimics?" Astraea stared warily at the gigantic snake rolling in the water.

"No, he's just very old. His bones hurt."

"He shouldn't be coming with us, then," Zephyr said. "If he stays here, we'll stop the queen and then take him back home."

"He won't," Angie said. "Not without me. It doesn't matter anyway."

"Why?" Tryn asked.

"He's dying."

"What?" Astraea cried. "Did we cause it by bringing him here?"

"*No,*" Nesso said. "*We live a very long time and grow very big. But then it isss time for usss to go into the nothing. Lergo isss going toward the nothing.*"

When Jake repeated the message, Astraea was surprised to feel a twinge of regret. Lergo should have been on Zomos to die in peace, and not here in this strange world, about to go into battle.

She looked at Tryn. "We should send him home."

"He won't go," Angie insisted. "Not without me."

"We have no right to expect him to fight for us," Triana said.

"*You will not be able to ssstop him,*" Nesso said. "*I would do anything for all of you. He feelsss the ssame for Angie. He will fight into the nothingnesss to protect her and you. But we had better hurry. I do not think he hasss much time left.*"

Jake repeated the message. Everyone looked at the gigantic snake in the water. He was so large; his body was wide enough to reach each bank.

"We still have a long way to go," Tryn said. "We can give him a while longer in the water."

They dozed and rested on the shore while the Mimics remained farther back. They didn't sit or lie down. They stood waiting.

"That is really disturbing," Zephyr said, watching the Mimics. "I hate them."

"So do I," Melissa agreed. "Part of me thinks I should care because I am kinda one of them. But I don't. They are just not nice."

In Astraea's life she had been exposed to all kinds of shapes and sizes of Titans and Olympians. She'd even met a few Nirads, the large four-armed rock-like people that were still good friends of the Olympians. But in all her life, she'd never met anything like Melissa. Titus had insects. Some could even be tamed, but Melissa was unique. She was intelligent and felt things deeply. Whatever happened, she had to be protected.

The sun started to set after the seemingly endless day. Everyone rose and prepared to get moving again.

When they did, the Mimics started to murmur.

"They're telling the queen we're moving again," Melissa said.

"Let them," Astraea said. "It's not going to stop us."

Angitia was the first into the water as she swam across the river in front of Lergo's head and made it to the opposite shore. When she walked farther inland, the old snake drew itself slowly out of the water and back onto land to follow her.

With the snake out of the way, the others entered the water and crossed the river. The Shadow Titans followed behind them, and soon they were all standing on the shore.

"Hey, look," Jake called. "The Mimics aren't following us."

The Mimics stood at the edge of the water but didn't go in.

"Ah, too bad," Zephyr said. "I kind of wanted to see them bobbing like sticks on a river."

"I say good riddance," Jake said.

Astraea said, "I wonder what would happen if they got really wet."

"Maybe they'd melt," Triana offered. "Should we try splashing them?"

"Triana!" Tryn cried. "You can't do that!"

"Sure I can," Triana said. "After everything they've done, I really can."

Astraea stepped between their growing fight. "Come on, children, we don't have time to play with the nasty Mimics. Let's just keep moving."

"I wasn't going to play," Triana muttered. "I was going to melt them."

Leaving the Mimics behind, they kept traveling in the direction the skateboards took them. Tryn would occasionally ask his skateboard to take him to Diana and the others. Each time he did, the board pointed them in the same direction they were already traveling. The group hoped they would all meet up before the others reached the queen.

The terrain around them changed, and they soon

entered woodland. As the full night descended, Jake couldn't see anymore and had to be carried by Render.

The walk was long and tiring. They stopped several times to rest. When they did, Melissa would disappear for a short while and then return. Sometimes she would bring back fruit for them to eat or tell them what was around.

The journey seemed endless, but no one complained or suggested they should stop. At some point during the following day, they left the trees and were faced with rolling hills of open grassland. When night returned, the hills flattened into smooth, even terrain. They were exhausted and out of food, but still they pressed on, feeling the pressure that each and every moment the queen was still spawning.

Late into the night, Melissa ventured out again. She returned a while later with a container full of ambrosia. "I found another camp full of people!"

She put the container down. "They were frightened of me, but then I told them about you and what was happening. I got them some food and then said I would bring you back so you can send them home with your ring."

Everyone was stunned as they listened to her story. "That's wonderful," Tryn said. "Where are they? How far?" He looked at the others. "Perhaps some are strong enough to join us."

"They're not far." Melissa pointed to the left. "Just that way."

"Did you see any Mimics?" Jake asked.

"Nope, the camp was quiet except for the people."

"How about Chiron, Diana, and the others?" Astraea asked. "Any sign of them?"

"Sorry," Melissa said. "Just the camp."

"If there's a camp, we must be near another town or city," Vulturnus said. "I wonder how far away the queen is."

"She's mega close," Melissa said. "I can feel her. If we stay on the ground, we'll reach her tomorrow. By air it would be much faster."

Tryn looked at Astraea. "Would you give me your Solar Stream ring? I'll go to the camp and use it to send the weakest prisoners to Xanadu and bring the stronger ones back here."

"I'll come too," Astraea said.

"No, please stay here and wait for us," Tryn said.

Astraea put her hands on her hips. "Tryn, I'm just as capable as you of rescuing those people."

"I know that!" Tryn insisted. "But for you to go, Zephyr has to fly, and she's still hurt."

"Hey, I'm fine," Zephyr said. "Don't bring me into your fight."

"No, you're not," Tryn said. "We all know you're still hurt from the building collapse. I've got my skateboard to use."

"So we all go," Astraea offered.

Tryn approached Astraea and lowered his voice. "Please stay, Astraea, and take care of him—" He pointed at Lergo. "Look at him, he's exhausted."

Astraea looked back at the snake. His head was down on the ground, and Angitia was petting his snout.

"You know how Cylus feels about him. You're the only one that has some control over that hotheaded centaur. Please, keep everyone here safe."

Astraea hated to be told what to do, but Tryn was right. Lergo was exhausted, and Cylus was ready to take the big snake on. Tryn was the best choice to go. But it didn't make it any easier to admit.

"Fine," she finally said. "We'll stay."

Tryn looked over to Vulturnus and said, "Some of them might recognize you. Will you come?"

"Of course," Vulturnus said. He gave Astraea a kiss on the forehead. "We will not be long. Stay safe."

Astraea nodded. "You too."

"Tryn," Angie called. "Will you look for my parents?"

Tryn nodded. "If they're there, I'll tell them you're with us and are safe."

When Vulturnus was settled behind Tryn on the skateboard, Tryn called, "We're ready, Melissa; lead the way."

"Coming," Melissa said. She looked back at Jake, Angie, and the others. "Later, dudes!" Opening her wing covers, she freed her wings and took off into the dark sky. "Follow me. The party's this way!"

Tryn ordered his skateboard to follow. "We'll see you soon!"

Astraea watched them in the sky until they were out of sight.

"Are they gone?" Jake called. "I can't see a thing."

"Yes, they're gone," Astraea said. "Since we have

to wait, how about we eat something and get some rest?"

They ate their fill of ambrosia. Against everyone's better judgment, Angie insisted on giving almost half the container to Lergo, arguing it would give him strength. The snake ate everything that she handed to him.

"Won't that make him, like, immortal?" Jake asked. "Tryn says ambrosia does that."

"It does," Astraea agreed. "But I don't know if it would work on Lergo. He's a big snake and didn't eat very much."

*"I eat it and I am immortal,"* Nesso said. *"You and I are forever."*

"Yes, we are," Jake agreed. He told the others what Nesso had said.

"At least it's made him feel a bit better," Angie said.

Cylus lay down in the grass and sighed. "Does anyone else still ache from the building falling on us?"

"Oh yeah," Darek said. "I don't think my back will ever be the same again."

"I'm sure I cracked a bone in my leg," Zephyr agreed.

"And my wings," Astraea added.

Render was still on his hooves. "Since I wasn't in the collapse and I'm not hurt, I'm going to take a quick look around. Maybe I can see how far we have to go."

"Be careful," Cylus ordered.

Render trotted off into the darkness.

"Look at him," Cylus complained. "Not a mark on him and he's trotting like he hasn't walked all this time."

"It's not fair." Zephyr yawned.

Jake was settled on the ground near Angie. He sat up. "Nope, I still can't see a thing."

"That's because you're a weak human," Zephyr teased.

"Zeph," Astraea said. "Don't start."

"What did she say?" Jake asked.

"Not much," Astraea answered.

"She said you are a weak human because you can't see Render," Angie said. "He's not weak, Zephyr; he just can't see in the dark."

"Which means he—is—a weak human," Zephyr muttered.

They all settled down, watching Render moving farther away. When he was nearly out of sight, they noticed him turn around and gallop back.

"Hey," Render panted. "There's a huge city just down a hill, not far from here. It's full of lights. It was too far for me to see details, but I think I saw movement down there."

Cylus got up. "Let's go check it out."

"We can't," Astraea said. "We promised to wait for the others."

"Tryn's got his board; he can find us," Cylus insisted. "I'm not saying we go in. I just think we should get closer."

Astraea looked at everyone in the camp. They were getting up and looked ready to move.

"All right," Astraea said. "We'll just get a bit closer. Then we stop and wait for the others."

Render offered his back to Jake again, and once he was seated, they started to move. The city was farther than they'd expected, but eventually, they made it to the top of the rise overlooking the brightly lit city.

"Hey, I can see the lights," Jake said.

"The queen is there?" Darek cried. "How are we supposed to get her in all of that?"

"It won't be easy, I know," Astraea said. "But we have to try. In the meantime, we go no farther. We'll stay here and wait for Tryn, Vulturnus, and the others."

They sat down again and waited. But as the long night passed, Astraea started to worry. "They've been gone a really long time. I hope everything is all right."

"Melissa wouldn't let anything happen to them," Jake said. "I'm sure they're fine."

"If there are prisoners with them, that will slow them down," Render offered. "We have time to rest; let's use it."

All they could do was wait.

Triana was lying on her back, looking at the sky. "This would be a nice world if it weren't for the Mimics."

"It does remind me of Earth," Jake added.

Astraea was lying on the ground and leaning against Zephyr. She combed her fingers through her best friend's mane. "Or Titus, without stars."

Angie was in front of Lergo and talking softly to the elderly snake. Astraea could hear her describing Titus and all the things she was going to show him when this was over.

"Lergo on Titus?" Zephyr said softly. "I don't think so."

"Maybe Xanadu," Astraea offered.

The insect sounds stilled as the air was filled with the hushing of Melissa's insectoid wings. "They're back," Triana called.

Melissa was gliding closer and touched down beside Astraea and Zephyr.

When Astraea rose, she looked for Tryn or her brother, but they weren't there. "Melissa, what happened? Where are the others?"

The tall mantis walked closer and tilted her head to the side as she looked at everyone in the camp.

"Melissa?" Triana called.

Lergo started to hiss. He rose and slithered toward Astraea at speed.

"Astraea!" Angie shouted. "Look, she has two forelegs! That's not Melissa. Run!"

The creature looked at the snake bearing down

on it and then charged. It smashed Zephyr with its triangular head, knocking her into the path of the snake. Lergo had to stop to avoid crushing her.

"Zeph!" Astraea screamed. She tried to run, but the queen moved with impossible speed and a sharp foreleg flashed out and caught Astraea around the waist. The grip was brutal and the sharp spines cut into her as it hoisted her off the ground.

The Risen Queen's wings opened and she launched into the air, taking Astraea away with her.

# 28

"WHAT'S HAPPENING?" JAKE CRIED. "SOME-one tell me what's happening!"

"Zephyr, stop!" Cylus shouted. "Stop!"

There was screaming and movement all around him, but Jake had no idea what was going on. "Nesso, talk to me!"

*"Assstraea hasss been taken,"* Nesso cried. *"It wasss a queen that looked like Melisssssa! It threw Zzzephyr at Lergo to ssstop him. Then Zzzephyr got up and flew after them."*

"Astraea, no!" Jake cried. "Can you see them?"

*"Not anymore. They are all gone."*

Jake cursed his inability to see. Though, if he had

been able to see, there was little he could have done to stop the queen.

"We have to go now!" Cylus said. "That monster isn't going to hurt Astraea or Zephyr!"

"We can't!" Triana said. "We have to wait for Tryn!"

"They could be all night getting back here," Cylus cried. "The queen's got Astraea! We have to do something!"

"Cylus, stop. Think!" Triana called. "What good would it do for any of us to go charging in there and get captured. We need more people!"

"Triana's right," Jake agreed. "I hate it, but she is."

They stood together looking down on the city. It took all their strength not to go racing there to try to find Zephyr and rescue Astraea.

After a while, Melissa landed among them as Tryn arrived with a large group of people. "Everyone, look how many came to help us."

"Tryn," Triana cried. "A Risen Queen came. She looked just like Melissa! She took Astraea. Zephyr chased her and we haven't seen her since!"

The moment Tryn and Vulturnus heard what had happened, they both shouted in rage.

"This is my mother's doing," Melissa said. "My sister wouldn't do anything without permission. The First Queen knew Astraea was our leader. So she arranged for Astraea to be taken to be used against us. I am sure there must have been more of my sisters hidden near the prison camp as well just in case Astraea went there."

"They set us up, and it worked perfectly," Jake said. "We walked right into it."

"I am going to tear that queen apart!" Tryn cried. "If she touches one hair on Astraea's head . . ."

"You will have to do it after me," Vulturnus said. "No one touches my little sister!"

Triana was beside Jake. "I have never seen my brother so angry before."

Jake still couldn't see her, but he said, "We both know why. If anything happens to Astraea, he's going to be unstoppable."

"There will be no stopping any of us," Render added. "That queen will feel our wrath."

There was only the briefest discussion about the camp rescue. They did not celebrate the fact that they had managed to send over a hundred prisoners to Xanadu while at least fifty had joined in the fight against the queen. There was only the fear for Astraea and what the queen was going to do to her.

"I had hoped Diana, Apollo, and the other fighters would be here by now," Tryn said. "We can't wait for them. We must get to the queen before she hurts Astraea."

Melissa said, "It is a trap. They are going to be waiting for us. We must be prepared."

"We will be," Tryn said darkly.

They pressed on in the night. After walking slowly down the hill toward the city, they stopped on the outskirts to prepare as best they could. When Astraea had been taken, the two snakes were taken with her in her bracelet, leaving Nesso as the group's only source of venom.

Jake turned to Angie. "Do you think Lergo could give some venom?"

"I don't know, but I could ask. . . ."

When Lergo let Angie know that he still had venom, the gathering of rescued prisoners divided into groups to go out searching for pebbles, sticks, and anything else they could use as weapons to cover in venom.

"We're still going to need something for him to bite on," Angie said. "I don't think there's a jar big enough for his fangs."

"I got this. Leave it to me," Melissa said as she took off into the night sky.

After a time, a large pile of pebbles and rocks were gathered before the massive snake.

Melissa returned with a fallen tree larger than any of them could have ever hoped to carry. She laid it beside Lergo. "It's up to you now, dude!"

Angie stood before the tree and asked Lergo to bite it. The snake moved forward and lifted the tree in his mouth. When he bit down, a large fountain of venom poured from each fang, covering the rocks, filling their venom jar, and leaving a pool all around.

"That's a lot of venom," Cylus commented. He directed the prisoners to start dipping their sticks into the deadly liquid.

Despite the urgency, they had to spread out the rocks to let them dry before they could be safely touched. When they were ready, Cylus, Render, and Darek called everyone forward.

"Take as many rocks as you can carry," Cylus said.

"It only takes one to bring down a Mimic, so use them sparingly."

The filthy, starving prisoners came forward and collected a share of the pebbles. Many used part of their tattered clothes to make sacks to carry even more.

"I hope that's enough," Triana said.

"We don't need a lot," Tryn said. "We have him."

Jake couldn't see where Tryn was looking, but he had a pretty good idea. They were going to use Lergo to kill the First Queen.

# 29

ASTRAEA FELT EACH AND EVERY SPINE ON the queen's foreleg as they cut into her back and abdomen. She tried to brace herself against them, but each time she did, the queen tightened her grip. There was no point begging her to stop; the queen was purposely hurting her.

They flew toward the bright lights. The city streets were much like in the other city they had been staying in. There were homes on the outskirts and then larger buildings with their lights on. But this city showed no damage from Lergo.

That would soon change.

Astraea knew the others would come, and when

they did, Lergo would be with them. This would end, once and for all.

The queen slowed and started to descend. They were approaching a building much like the one that contained the Mimic nursery. The one that was now deep underwater thanks to Pegasus and Zephyr. But this one gave Astraea chills.

There were thousands and thousands of Mimics standing outside it. Streetlights blazed brightly, and away from the streetlights, Mimics held torches.

The young queen hovered above the masses, and they parted to allow her room to land. When she did, the air was filled with clicking and Mimic language.

Outside the main building were lines of Shadow Titans three and four deep. Without being told, Astraea knew this had to be the palace of the First Queen.

They walked forward and the Shadow Titans parted. Up three steps, and then the young queen approached the doors as two large Mimics opened them.

There was more chatter as the two Mimics glowered at Astraea. Entering the building, the young queen could not stand up, as she was much taller than the ceiling. Crouched over, she put Astraea down and used her deadly forelegs on the marble floor to balance herself.

Astraea lifted her tunic and inspected the wounds caused by the queen's spines. The sharp points had broken the skin, and a line of blood drops dotted her abdomen.

The queen pushed her forward, forcing her to walk. Astraea turned sharply. "This won't end, even if you kill me. My friends are coming and will stop you from ever hurting anyone else again."

The queen screeched and whacked Astraea with her triangular head, throwing her back against the wall. Astraea slid down to the floor with the wind knocked out of her. Everything hurt, but her wings had taken the brunt of the impact and protested in pain.

Astraea scowled and stayed down. In the light of the corridor, she wondered how she could have ever mistaken this queen for Melissa. Not only were their forelegs different, but this insect queen's face showed rage and menace, while Melissa's somehow managed to convey innocence and friendship. It was hard to imagine they were sisters.

The queen motioned for Astraea to get up and go down the hall. For a moment Astraea considered defying the order. But when the queen opened her forelegs to reveal the spines again, Astraea thought better of it.

"All right, all right, put those things away!" Astraea climbed to her feet.

The queen motioned again for her to walk forward, and Astraea did as she was told. She felt the bracelet on her arm and hoped the queen didn't realize that Frick and Frack were hidden inside. It had never been discussed whether snake venom was deadly to queens, but it was to the Mimics, which made Astraea feel a bit reassured.

They moved down the long corridor. Toward the end, two large Mimics stood before another set of doors. A Titan stood with them. A Titan that Astraea hated. Tibed, the traitor. The last time she'd seen him was at her grandparents' house. She'd thought the Mimics would have killed him by now. She was wrong.

"Well, look who's here," Tibed said. His face was

flushed with excitement. "Astraea, you would have done better to never get involved. At least you might have lived—a bit longer."

"You're a traitor, Tibed, and everyone in Titus knows it."

"No," Tibed said. "I am an opportunist. They were going to invade whether I helped them or not. At least now I will survive, and your grandfather and all your family will be destroyed." He leaned closer as malice rose in his voice. "And you, Astraea, you will be first to go."

"You're such a fool, Tibed. Do you actually think these Mimics will let you rule Titus? You're going to end up in one of those camps just like everyone else."

Tibed's face turned red with rage and he raised his hand to strike her, but the queen lowered her head and clicked at him.

Tibed nodded. "You are right; it is not my place to deny the First Queen her pleasure. I just hope she lets me watch your death."

One of the Mimics stepped forward and spoke to Tibed. "This is Astraea of Titus? The spawn that has caused us so much trouble?"

"It is," Tibed said.

The Mimic leaned closer to Astraea. "I shall enjoy witnessing your end."

A sharp retort was on Astraea's lips, but with the violent queen standing right behind her, she held it in. "I wouldn't have been any trouble to you if you hadn't invaded Titus."

"We go where we please," the Mimic said. "Titus is ours now. As are Xanadu and many other worlds. Our queen has spawned. There are many new, powerful Risen Queens, and we shall spread even farther."

Again Astraea withheld a comment that would surely have resulted in a blow from the queen, or a tendril from the Mimic. Neither option held any appeal.

"Nothing to say?" Tibed taunted.

"No," Astraea said firmly.

"That is probably the first intelligent thing you have said." The Mimic pushed open the door and stood back. "Both of you go in; she is waiting for you."

Astraea peered in and gasped. But her shock was short-lived, as the Risen Queen shoved her brutally in the back.

The room before her was much bigger than Astraea had imagined. It had been built by knocking out the ceiling and all the walls of the building, creating a chamber that was at least three stories tall and as big as the whole building.

But that wasn't what stole her breath. The chamber was filled with young queens. They all turned and stared as she and Tibed walked in.

Astraea had never felt so small and insignificant in her entire life. All the queens loomed above her as she was pushed forward. Hissing and spitting sounds rose louder all around her. She didn't have to understand their language to know they were threats.

"Come forward," a voice called.

The mass of queens parted, giving Astraea a clear view of what lay ahead. The First Queen.

Astraea stopped and stared, horrified by the sight before her. She couldn't speak. She couldn't breathe. She had never seen anything so terrifying in all her life. The queen was impossibly large. Easily three or four times larger than Melissa. Her front half did look like Astraea's insect friend, but the other half was completely different. The queen's distended abdomen was grotesquely long and swollen and seemed to ripple as though there were something moving inside. Astraea couldn't see what was happening at the back end because of all the Mimics hovering around. But if she had to guess, Astraea thought the queen was laying eggs.

"You have been looking for me?" the First Queen asked. "Well, here I am, Astraea."

Once again Tibed looked back at her and grinned. "This is going to be wonderful. Your death will start the end of your family's rule."

He strutted forward until he reached the First Queen. He bowed. "Your Majesty, I am Tibed, the one who has given you Titus."

The First Queen bent down until her head was just before him. "You are the one that betrayed your people." Her purple eyes narrowed.

"I serve only you."

The First Queen rose again. "I hate traitors of any kind." A large foreleg shot forward with lightning speed and caught Tibed in a brutal grip. She hoisted him off the ground.

"Your Majesty," he cried. "Please, I helped you!"

"We did not need your help, Titan!" She tossed Tibed across the chamber and screeched.

Astraea watched in horror as several queens charged at Tibed. She couldn't see what happened next, but she could hear Tibed screaming, and then there was silence.

Astraea turned away, looking only at the queen.

"Bring her forward."

The young queens started to shove Astraea forward. Each step brought her closer to the First Queen. Finally she arrived and had to look up almost to the ceiling to see the First Queen's head.

"Your turn," the First Queen hissed.

Astraea started to scream.

# 30

AS JAKE AND THE OTHERS PREPARED TO attack the city, Zephyr returned to the group. She touched down, covered in a film of foamy sweat.

"Are you all right?" Triana cried.

"No!" Zephyr cried. "I'm as far from all right as you can get! We're in so much trouble! There are Risen Queens everywhere! I mean everywhere! Not to mention all the Mimics and Shadow Titans! Although it's nighttime, the city is lit up like it's day. There had to be thousands of Mimics, all gathered outside a big building. It was surrounded by Shadow Titans at least four rows thick. Then some more queens arrived. I thought for sure they would see me, but they were focused on getting into the building."

"What did she say?" Jake asked Render. "Please tell me."

While Render translated Zephyr's words, Vulturnus started to pace. "That building must be where the First Queen is."

Zephyr nodded. "Before the other queens arrived, I watched the queen that took Astraea carry her into it." Zephyr shook her head in pain. "She looked so small and so scared. I wanted to slam down on the ground and drown them all! But I couldn't risk the queen killing Astraea."

"If all the surviving Risen Queens are gathering together, then the spawning is nearly finished," Melissa said. "Soon they will be old enough to move to their own worlds. They will be given a number of Mimics to take with them, and then they will spread."

"If they do that, there will be no stopping them," Vulturnus said. "World after world will be overrun by them. Millions of innocent people will die."

"Billions," Jake said. "More than that. Earth has just over seven billion people. I don't know about

Titus or Xanadu, but that is a lot of people. All enslaved or worse."

"We must get Astraea out of there," Zephyr said.

Darek looked at the freed prisoners. "Maybe some of them should go back to Xanadu or Titus to plead with Jupiter to help us. We have to tell him what we've seen and what is happening. It must be stopped before it's too late."

"He won't listen to them," Cylus said. "Pegasus left ages ago. He would have found Jupiter and told him what we've discovered. Plus all the prisoners we've freed and sent back. Jupiter and the others know what's happening here, but they still haven't come. It's just us."

"We can fight," one of the prisoners called. "We may not be many, but we are ready to stop the Mimics."

"And," Jake added, "Chiron and the others are around here somewhere."

"Plus there's me," Melissa added. "And that big guy over there." She indicated Lergo.

"There are enough of us if we are careful," Cylus said. "So let's stop talking and get moving."

They started toward the city. Lergo moved forward

and was slithering beside them instead of behind them. As they got closer, the light from the city made the area bright enough for Jake to see by. But with the passing of each step, they knew they were heading into a slaughter. The kind that deep down they knew they couldn't possibly win.

"Even if we only stop a few queens, that's still a few worlds that we can save," Jake said.

"At least until my mother spawns again," Melissa said. "Or my sisters."

"That isn't helping, Melissa," Jake said to the Fallen Queen.

"Oh, sorry," Melissa said. "Yes, let's stop my sisters."

They picked up more stones as they walked and used the last of their venom to coat them. Nesso tried to give more, but she was out.

*"I'm sssorry,"* she said softly.

"Don't be," Jake said, stroking her softly. "You've been awesome."

Just before they reached the first houses, they stopped and huddled together. "I've been thinking," Tryn said. "If we go charging in, they will get us fairly quickly. I suggest we try to sneak in."

"You're kidding, right?" Jake cried. "Have you seen all of us? We can't sneak in. How do you expect to hide Lergo?"

"I don't," Tryn said. "But what if Angie asks Lergo to go in first and he does his Lergo thing of smashing buildings and squishing Mimics and Shadow Titans?" Tryn looked over to Cylus. "Would you, Render, and Darek take charge of the prisoners? Divide them up and from hidden places start taking out Mimics. The rest of us will try to find another way into the First Queen's building."

Cylus nodded. "Good plan." He looked at the other centaurs and then the prisoners. "All of you, come with me. We'll distract everyone while they go for Astraea."

Zephyr snorted. "You do all realize that they already know about us, right? I mean, that queen came into our camp and took Astraea. She saw Lergo; she saw the centaurs and me. They will be expecting us."

"We don't have much choice," Tryn said. "We must get Astraea away from there."

"Yes, we must," Zephyr agreed. "All I'm saying is, ours won't be a surprise attack."

Vulturnus nodded. "But they don't know what we're capable of. Let's go get my sister!"

As agreed, Angie sat high on Lergo and directed the snake to go first. When it slithered past everyone, Jake felt sick about asking a girl his sister's age to lead a monster into battle. But with everything at stake, they didn't have much choice.

"Angie, hold on tight!" Jake called before they moved off.

"I will. Go get Astraea!"

The rest of them followed closely behind the slithering snake. When they moved past homes and entered a more built-up area, they parted. The centaurs galloped ahead with their groups of rescued prisoners running with them, and moved into positions around the palace.

Tryn and Jake used their boards, and Triana and Vulturnus rode Zephyr. "Follow me," Zephyr said as she climbed higher above the brightly lit city. "The palace is just ahead."

Melissa was flying with them. When Jake looked over, he was sure he could somehow detect fear on the Fallen Queen's triangular face.

"I don't think we stand much chance," he said softly to Nesso.

*"But we will be together to the end,"* Nesso said.

"Yes, we will."

Up ahead was a building that looked much larger than the palace he'd seen on Titus, or any of the libraries or universities from home. He doubted even Brutus the giant could do much damage to it. "It's a fortress!" he called.

"Every fortress has a weakness," Tryn said. "This place was built by the indigenous people, and we know they didn't believe in locks. So there must be plenty of ways in."

The sky around them was free of the flying queens as the group neared the palace. Zephyr flew to the rear of the building. "I found a place that's sheltered. Follow me."

They touched down in the treed area. The back of the palace loomed, immense before them. Windows lined the wall, and light shone out from within.

"Why aren't there any Shadow Titans back here?" Jake asked.

"I don't know," Vulturnus said. "Perhaps they didn't think we'd ever get this close."

"That," Jake said darkly as he looked around. "Or this is a trap."

Crossing a narrow path, they reached the wall of the building. When they approached the nearest window and peered in, they received the shock of their lives.

"Look how many queens there are," Zephyr cried. "I saw a few, but not that many!"

Jake didn't need to understand Zephyr to realize what she said. They were all shocked at the number of Risen Queens in the building.

"Look, there's Astraea!" Triana pointed to the middle of the room. "Right there; you can see her just between those queens. . . ."

It was difficult to see Astraea because of all the tall queens around her. But occasionally they could catch glimpses of her being shoved forward by the queen directly behind her.

"She's bleeding," Jake said.

"Yes," Melissa said. "That's because of these. . . ." She showed the sharp spines on her praying mantis foreleg. "My sister would have carried her in these."

They followed Astraea as best they could as she was pushed forward. When she stopped, they all heard her screams through the glass.

Melissa's head was taking up most of the window as she and Jake peered into the room. She turned to him. "I think she just saw my mother."

Tryn looked at Melissa. "What will the First Queen do to her?"

Melissa lowered her head. "You don't want to know."

"I will tell you," a voice said lightly. "But you won't like the answer, spawn."

They all turned and saw that they were surrounded by hundreds of Mimics and Shadow Titans.

Jake looked up at Melissa. "Tell them to stay back."

Melissa gave the order, but the Mimics didn't follow. They kept advancing. "We're too close to my mother; they won't listen to me."

"That's right, you filthy fallen failure. You will die here with these spawn." The Mimic looked at the others around him. "It is time to end this."

# 31

"SILENCE!" THE FIRST QUEEN SCREECHED.

The young queen behind Astraea smashed her in the back and knocked her to the floor.

"That's better," the First Queen said. "I am Langli, and you have come to kill me."

Astraea turned to look where Tibed had been tossed, but there was no sign of the traitor. All the queens that had attacked him were standing again.

"Tibed served his purpose and is now gone," the First Queen said. She lowered her head closer to Astraea. "You have come to kill me. Isn't that so?"

Astraea remained silent as the First Queen's head hovered before her.

"You have much to answer for, young Titan," Langli continued. "You have repeatedly killed my children, denied them their food, and destroyed two precious queens. That is unforgivable."

Astraea heard herself talking back to the queen and had no idea where the words were coming from. "You have invaded my world and taken my people. You have even more to answer for!"

The First Queen's head rolled back, and she screeched loudly enough to rattle the glass in the building.

The Risen Queen behind her pounced on Astraea and picked her up in her sharp forelegs. She carried Astraea forward and lifted her up until she and Langli were face-to-face, only a hand's breadth apart.

"You will die, Astraea of Titus. Not like Tibed, whose death was quick. You will die slowly and it *will* be painful. But not before you witness the end of one other." The queen looked up and screeched.

The young queen placed Astraea down on the floor at Langli's legs. Then she backed up as one of her sisters entered. She was holding someone in her forelegs. Astraea dreaded finding out who it was. But then her horror became complete when she saw it was Riza. The Xan was unconscious and limp in the Risen Queen's vicious grip.

"Riza!" Astraea tried to run to her, but Langli's sharp foreleg caught hold of her in its tight, insectile grip and lifted her off the ground.

"You are going nowhere, foolish spawn. I told you, you will bear witness to the end of the last powerful Xan. And then you too will follow her into oblivion."

Astraea was held firmly in Langli's foreleg as the young queen carried Riza forward. The Xan had lost her pearlish glow and was covered in slime that Astraea recognized as the same slime from a Mimic nursery. Riza had been used like Emily, to feed grub queens.

Langli's purple eyes thinned to slits as she peered at Astraea. "Did you really think you could defeat us? The powerful Xan couldn't, and countless others before you couldn't. What makes you think you were so much better than them?"

This time Astraea said nothing. The grip around her waist warned that if she said one thing wrong, she would be crushed without hesitation.

"Nothing to say, spawn?" Langli taunted.

Astraea looked at Riza and said, "Why do you need to hurt the Xan? Can't you spawn on your own?"

The queen gave a strange impression of a laugh. "Of course I can spawn without them. But with the Xan's power, I can produce many more strong eggs. Then, being the generous mother that I am, I feed what's left of the Xan to my young queens. We all share in the banquet of power. This time, I was fortunate to have two Xan at my disposal. This has been the biggest spawning ever, and we will now spread across the universe."

The First Queen focused on Riza. "It is time for me to regain my strength so that I may bear even more queens." With her free forearm, she reached out and lifted Riza's limp body from her daughter's grip.

Langli looked sideways at Astraea, as though challenging her, as a tendril came out of her chest. It moved slowly forward until it landed on Riza's arm. The Xan let out a soft whimper.

"Ah," Langli sighed. "Delicious . . ."

Astraea watched in horror as Langli's tendril pulsed and drained power from Riza. She had to do something. Had to stop the queen from killing Riza, even if it meant the loss of her own life.

Astraea started to shout and struggle. This caused the queen to laugh with a sickening, squeaking sound. While she shouted, Astraea carefully moved her arm to her bracelet. She slid open the cover, freeing Frick and Frack.

"Stop! Please, you're killing Riza!" Astraea prayed the two snakes understood her message. "Pull your tendril back!"

"Why would I do that?" Langli said as she started to close her forearm slowly on Astraea.

Astraea howled as the sharp points cut deeper into her abdomen. The pain drove all thoughts from her mind while the spikes cut into her. She prayed for darkness and an end to the suffering. But it wouldn't come. She was trapped in the foreleg as the First Queen killed her slowly.

"Please, stop," Astraea cried weakly.

The First Queen started to laugh, but then a choking sound started. "Wha-what is happening?"

The grip on Astraea loosened and she fell to the ground at the queen's insectoid feet. Riza landed in a clump beside her. Looking up, Astraea saw her two tiny snakes biting into the tendril.

Langli's pupils widened until the purple iris could no longer be seen. The queen's front end started to quiver, and she staggered. She started to screech in twisting agony and sway on her legs as the snake venom took hold.

Astraea caught Riza by her thin wrist and hauled her back just as the First Queen shrieked a final time and crashed down to the floor. She thrashed and convulsed before becoming still.

The young queens in the chamber started to shriek and rock their heads back and forth when they realized their mother was dead. Finally they all turned to Astraea and started to click and hiss.

With her body hurting from the dead queen's sharp foreleg, Astraea pulled Riza farther away and drew her dagger. She stood no chance against the room full of Risen Queens. Almost in unison, they started to flutter their wing covers and hiss even louder.

"This is it, Riza. I'm sorry I couldn't save us."

The queens took several steps forward, and the hissing turned to full, angry-sounding clicks.

In the little time she had left, Astraea thought of all the things she would miss in her life. Her parents, her brothers, and most of all, Zephyr. Her wonderful, funny, and sarcastic four-legged sister. She regretted not seeing Tryn and his beautiful eyes again, or seeing Jake finally make it home to Earth.

So much would be lost in the next minute. All she could do was stand up slowly, hold her head up high, and face whatever came next.

But the attack she expected didn't happen. Instead, the queens in the chamber turned from her, looked at each other, and started to fight.

# 32

JAKE WAS FROZEN IN FEAR AS THE MIMICS advanced on them. Any minute now they would send out their tendrils of death. He looked over at Triana and saw the fear on her face.

They had made it so close, but not close enough.

With a rock in his hand, Jake pulled back his arm. This might be the end, but he was going to take a Mimic or two with him.

Just before he released the rock, the Mimics paused and started to howl. He looked at them in confusion, and then back into the window. The scene inside was pure chaos.

"Look," Jake cried. "The queens are killing each other."

The others peered in and gasped at the terrible fight. "What's happening?" Triana asked.

"My mother just died," Melissa explained, "and my sisters are fighting to select the next First Queen. The winner will stay here; the others will have to leave to start their own colonies."

"You did this!" one of the Mimics howled. "You killed our queen!"

They started to charge again.

Melissa rose to her full height and flapped her wing covers. She screeched louder than Jake imagined possible. It halted the Mimic attack as they looked up at her and then lay down on the ground. "I'll take care of all these creeps," she shouted. "Get inside and save Astraea!"

Zephyr charged at the Shadow Titans and started stomping. "You heard her—go!"

Tryn hauled back his arm and used all his force to punch through the window. The glass shattered and rained down. "Get inside!"

Jake, Tryn, Triana, and Vulturnus crawled into the palace. The sights and sounds were horrifying as the fight escalated. The floor was becoming littered with limbs and even some wings and heads cut from the battling queens.

They moved between tall insect legs as they made their way toward the front of the room. Just ahead, they came face-to-face with a young queen. She bent down, hissed, and opened her forelegs to catch Tryn and Triana, but before she could strike, she was cut down by one of her sisters.

"This is insane!" Jake cried.

"Let's hope it lasts long enough for us to get Astraea out of here!" Vulturnus called.

Pressing on, they reached the dead First Queen. Jake figured she would be large, but he'd never imagined she would be this monstrous.

A queen's legs stomped down in front of Jake. He looked up at her as she loomed above him. She opened her pincerlike mouth and came down to bite him.

Jake jumped onto his board and darted between her legs. He flew up behind her and started throwing venom-covered rocks at her. Most bounced off the insect exoskeleton without doing any harm. But when the queen turned, a rock struck her in the soft eye. Despite her size, the venom on the rock started to work, and she thrashed around the room, hitting her sisters, before she collapsed to the ground and became still.

"They work!" Jake shouted to the others. "The rocks kill queens! Aim for their eyes!"

The group started to use their rocks as they pressed on. But for each queen that went down, another replaced it.

"There are too many," Jake cried. "Let's get Astraea and go!"

"Jake?" Astraea shouted.

"Astraea?" Jake called. "Where are you?"

"I'm back here. I've got Riza!"

The group darted around the body of the First Queen and found Astraea huddled against the back wall, cradling Riza in her arms.

Tryn charged forward and embraced her. "I was so scared when Zephyr told me what happened." He looked at the blood on her tunic. "You're hurt!"

"I'll be fine."

"What happened to you?" Vulturnus said as he hugged his sister.

"It was awful," Astraea said. "The queen hurt Riza. We have to get her out of here."

Vulturnus reached for Riza and lifted her out of Astraea's arms. "Come on, before it is too late!"

Astraea climbed to her feet and they started to move. They had gone only a few steps when the sounds in the room changed. The fighting slowed and then stopped. The floor was littered with the bodies of dead queens, but there were at least twenty survivors. Some had horrendous injuries. But among them was one queen with no injuries at all. She rose tall above the others, and her insect legs clicked on the floor as she approached.

She hissed and lowered her head as she peered at them. Turning back to the other surviving queens, she screeched. They lowered their heads and backed away.

The new First Queen faced Jake and the others. She opened her spined praying mantis forelegs, drew them back, and prepared to strike.

# 33

A TREMENDOUS CRASH SOUNDED BESIDE them as Melissa broke through the palace wall. "Back off, bug-face! These are my friends!"

The new First Queen screeched and charged at Melissa.

Melissa tore through the debris of the wall and started to fight with her sister. The sound was sickening as the two queens battled. Melissa was at a distinct disadvantage because of her deformed limb. But somehow she was moving in ways the other queen didn't.

Melissa rose on one back leg and kicked her sister with the other. Then, as her sister fell back, Melissa spun around quickly and struck the First Queen with her long abdomen and wings, tossing her across the room.

Jake watched the incredible fight and realized he knew what Melissa was doing. "She's using kung fu!"

"What?" Vulturnus called.

"Kung fu. It's a kind of martial art from back home!" Jake shook his head in disbelief. "Melissa must have learned it from me during our mind-link."

"You fight like that?" Tryn asked.

"No," Jake cried. "I just watch a lot of kung fu movies!"

The fight was the strangest thing Jake had ever seen. The new First Queen was losing ground against Melissa's unfamiliar fighting style. It wasn't long before the vicious queen was driven to the ground.

Facing defeat, the new First Queen screeched, and the other queens in the room responded. They started to charge, but not toward Melissa—they clicked and ran at Jake and the others.

# 34

"RUN!" MELISSA SHOUTED. "GET OUT NOW!"

Astraea felt Tryn's hand slip into hers as they faced the queens. "Everyone, separate!"

Tryn hauled Astraea forward as the group ran in different directions. They tried to reach the doors, but they were blocked by queens. Turning quickly, they saw that the only other way out, through the broken wall, was also blocked.

"We're trapped!" Tryn cried.

Whichever way Tryn and Astraea ran, there were queens after them with slicing forelegs and snapping mouths.

The friends found each other and huddled together,

fearing the worst as they faced the room of queens. Suddenly the building started to shudder. Sounds of crashing rose louder and louder. Everyone looked toward the doors as Lergo broke into the chamber. The queens hesitated for a moment and looked back at Astraea and the others. But then they charged at the massive snake.

Watching the monsters fight was surreal. Lergo caught two in his mouth at once and bit down. The dose of venom must have been massive, as the queens were dead before he cast them aside.

A queen struck Lergo across the snout with her sharp forelegs, cutting deeply into his scales. The snake rose higher and his head smashed down on her.

Angie could barely be seen on the snake's wide back, but she was there, holding on tightly and encouraging him to go on.

"Angie, be careful!" Jake shouted.

"I am," her small voice called back.

"Everyone, use your rocks!" Astraea cried.

While the queens focused on Lergo, those with rocks started to hurl them at the distracted queens.

Most of the rocks hit their outer shells and bounced off. But a few struck their eyes and brought them down.

As the fight continued, a tremendous boom sounded outside the palace. This was followed by another and then another.

Astraea thought she recognized the sound but didn't dare to hope. Could it be?

"Jupiter?" Tryn called. "Is that Jupiter?"

The queens were oblivious to the sounds outside and continued their attack on the snake. One opened its wings and flew up and landed on Lergo's back. It moved forward, going for Angie.

"Angie, look out!" Jake swooped up on his skateboard to Lergo's head and scooped Angie up in his arms moments before the vicious queen could strike.

With Angie safely away, Lergo started to spin. He knocked the queen off his back and crushed her before she could rise and get away.

Jake flew back to the group. "Let's get out of here before they kill us!"

"I have to stay with Lergo," Angie cried as she tried to pull away from Jake. "He needs me."

"He needs you to live," Jake said, struggling to hold on to the strong Titan. "Please, come with me!"

Angie stopped resisting and reluctantly went with Jake as they ran toward the hole in the wall.

Right before they crawled through, Astraea looked back and saw Lergo coiled tightly around two queens while fighting several more.

Across the room, Melissa was still fighting with the First Queen.

"Melissa, come on!" Jake called as he helped Angie through the rubble.

"No, you go!" Melissa shouted back.

Astraea helped her brother pass Riza out to Tryn and Triana. Then she climbed through, and Jake and Angie followed behind her.

After making it outside the building, they were faced with a full-on war, as thousands of Titans and Olympians were taking on the Mimics. The sky was filled with fliers using slingshots to shoot venom-covered rocks, while on the ground, others used spears, arrows, and slingshots.

Somehow Jupiter had managed to get hold of his chariot and winged horses and was soaring across the dawn sky, shooting lightning bolts at the queens that flew up to attack him.

Pluto had his own chariot with skeletal horses, peeling across the sky and firing rocks at the Mimics.

There were more sounds of crashing, and Astraea looked over to the left to see Brutus and several other giants storming through the area and stomping on Mimics with their thick black boots.

"Astraea!"

Astraea looked up and saw Zephyr in the sky. She was covered in cuts and signs of battle but looked magnificent. Zephyr landed on the ground before her. The two embraced like they hadn't seen each other in eons.

"Are you all right? You're bleeding," Zephyr cried.

"Me? What about you? What happened?" They both laughed and cried as they embraced again.

Zephyr finally said, "I've stomped so many Shadow Titans!" She looked at the building. "What happened in there?"

"Astraea killed the First Queen," Tryn said. "You should have seen her; she was enormous."

"Are you calling Astraea enormous?" Zephyr

demanded. Then she laughed. "Only I can say that!"

"No," Tryn said. "The First Queen was enormous. But Astraea defeated her anyway."

"I didn't do it; Frick and Frack did," Astraea corrected. "We owe them so much."

"We owe them everything!" Zephyr said.

Jupiter soared across the sky just above them, still using his best weapons, the lightning and thunderbolts.

"Oh, and guess what. Jupiter's here," Zephyr said. Then she laughed again. "Actually, I think half of Titus is here. Diana and her fighters arrived just after the others went in to get you. There are Titans, Olympians, and even Nirads! Plus some kinds of beings I've never even seen before—all fighting. Get on my back. You need to see this."

Astraea shook her head. "We have to take care of Riza."

"Go on," Tryn said. "The fighting has moved away from here. We'll keep Riza safe."

Astraea was thrilled to climb back up on Zephyr. Even before she was settled, Zephyr was taking off. She soared over the battle, ducking and dodging the queens that were escaping the palace. Astraea saw her mother holding a spear and chasing a queen across the sky.

Astraea had only ever known her mother to be gentle and accepting. But the woman she saw in the sky, Aurora, daughter of Hyperion, was a masterful flier and powerful warrior. She darted and dove at the queen while masterfully keeping clear of her deadly forelegs. Holding her spear high, Aurora swooped in on the queen and struck her at the base of her skull. The queen fell to the ground, and Astraea's mother flew away, ready to take on another.

"I can't believe this," Astraea cried. "They actually came."

"Look who else is here," Zephyr called.

Farther ahead Astraea saw Emily Jacobs seated on Pegasus. The two were soaring elegantly together. Emily's long hair was billowing out behind her, and her eyes blazed with excitement as she used a sling-shot to shoot at Mimics on the ground. When Emily saw Astraea, she waved excitedly.

Astraea could see the pure joy on Pegasus's face as he carried Emily into battle. "Why isn't she using her powers?" Astraea asked Zephyr. "She's a Xan; she could end all this in a moment."

"Diana told me her powers are gone," Zephyr said. "The queens drained her like all the other Xan. Emily is just like an Olympian now."

Cupid was also in the sky using his slingshot against Mimics.

Astraea sat up higher on Zephyr, peering down on a battle she'd never imagined would happen. Tears rose to her eyes as she watched her people fighting for their freedom and the freedom of so many more.

"Are you all right?" Zephyr asked.

Astraea sniffed and leaned forward on Zephyr's neck, holding her tightly. "I am now."

# 35

ASTRAEA WAS EAGER TO JOIN THE BATTLE, but Zephyr refused to carry her farther until she agreed to have her wounds tended.

As a healer applied potions to the cuts on her abdomen from the queen's spines, Astraea saw a young Titan satyr she recognized from Xanadu being treated for a head wound. When the healer left to gather more bandages, Astraea leaned closer to the satyr. "What happened on Xanadu?"

"Yeah," Zephyr said. "Was Jupiter really angry at us?"

The satyr nodded. "Jupiter was furious when Arious told him where you went—his face turned bright red, and I thought for sure his head was going to explode." She grinned impishly. "But he was set on his plan to free Titus, and we left Xanadu for home. We took a load of snakes with us, and using our slingshots, we were able to drive back the Mimics. We went into the prison and found it had been refilled with more Titans. Once they were free, the main battle for Titus started. The Mimics could not stand against the snake venom, and in two days, it was mostly over. Then Pegasus arrived and told Jupiter what was happening. He insisted the Mimics could only be defeated here, and Jupiter agreed. While some fighters remained on Titus, the rest of us came here and . . ." The satyr paused, and terror rose on her face when Melissa was escorted into the treatment area.

"Don't worry," Astraea said to her. "She's on our side."

Melissa had several deep wounds from the fight with her sister. Despite the handicap of her useless foreleg, her strange battle style had seen her defeat the new First Queen.

Two healers came forward and started to work on

her, but their movements were cautious and fearful until Melissa spoke in her strange, Jake-like style and thanked them for their help.

"You are all done," the healer said to Astraea as he returned and finished bandaging her abdomen. "Just lie back and let the potions and ambrosia work."

The moment he left to treat others, Astraea threw back her covers. "I have to get up."

"You aren't going anywhere," Zephyr said, tossing the blanket back over her. "You are still healing."

"I'm fine." Astraea got up despite Zephyr's warning. "Besides, they need us out there. Tryn and Triana are fighting; so are Jake and Angie; I have to help them."

Melissa also rose, knocking over several treatment trays as she stood. "I have to help them too."

"I thought you didn't want to fight," Astraea said to her as she pulled on a clean tunic.

"I don't," Melissa said. "But this isn't about me. We are in an especially dangerous time. There is only one Risen Queen left. She will be looking to defeat me to become the true First Queen and gain complete control. The best way to do that is to go after those I love. Jake and Angie are targets. So are you. Until my sister is stopped, this war won't end."

As they left the treatment area, several of the healers shook their heads in disappointment. But nothing could stop Astraea from joining the battle.

On their way to the weapons store, Zephyr stopped. "Let me just say, I am doing this under protest. You should be resting, not fighting. And to be honest, I'm a bit of a wreck too."

"I know, and I'm sorry," Astraea agreed. "But we haven't won this fight yet." She picked up a slingshot and two large bags of venom-covered rocks, which she draped over Zephyr's neck.

Astraea climbed up gingerly onto Zephyr's back. "Let's end this, Zeph, and then we can finally go home."

"Fine . . . let's do this." Zephyr galloped and then launched into the air.

The fighting was a short flight away. Titan and Olympian warriors fought the Mimics and the Shadow Titans they controlled. Jupiter and his brothers were still flying across the sky, using their powers to blast the Shadow Titans.

"Don't they ever sleep?" Zephyr commented.

Astraea shrugged. "I guess that's why they're called the Big Three. They just keep fighting."

Melissa joined them in the sky. She looked over at Astraea and Zephyr. "If my sister shows up, things will get really freaky really quickly. I don't want you to hang around. Leave her to me. Do you understand?"

Astraea nodded and continued to fire rocks at the Mimics. Farther ahead, they spied Pegasus and Emily soaring across the sky.

Zephyr changed direction and joined them.

"How are you?" Emily called.

"Better," Astraea answered. "And you?"

"Fantastic!"

Emily's face glowed with joy at being reunited with Pegasus as they swooped down into the battle.

As the long day progressed, Jupiter whished past Astraea and Zephyr and invited them to follow. When they did, he pointed down to a large building. "Our fighters have found where the Mimics are making the Shadow Titans. They have been using

Riza's power to make them move, but they couldn't give them life!"

Astraea looked down on the gray, unassuming building. When Jupiter's two brothers, Pluto and Neptune, arrived, the Big Three merged their powers and fired at the building. The blast was so large, it sent rubble and pieces of Shadow Titans flying high in the air. Within moments, the large building evaporated, leaving only a large hole in the ground.

Jupiter turned his chariot around. "They will never trouble us again!"

The sun finally descended in the sky as dusk arrived. Astraea and Zephyr stopped to eat and rest. The area around them had been cleared of Mimics. Seated in the recovery area, they saw fighters being carried in that had been struck by tendrils, as well as others that had been wounded by Shadows.

"The Mimics aren't giving up easily," Astraea said.

Zephyr nodded. "I just hope it ends soon. My wings are killing me!"

Before long they were joined by Jake and Angie, Tryn, his sister, and Vulturnus.

"Have you seen the centaurs?" Astraea asked.

Tryn nodded. "They've joined up with Chiron and his group of warriors. I never realized there were so many centaurs on Titus. It's quite a sight."

Not far from where they ate, Lergo rested on the ground.

"He's too old for this," Angie said. "But he won't stop."

Astraea looked at the tired old snake and still felt regret for bringing him into this. "Hopefully, it will be over soon and we can take him home. I would think—"

Her words were cut off when an alarm sounded with loud shouts and calls.

"Now what?" Jake said as he and everyone else rose.

The Olympian Mercury swooped in to the recovery area using his winged sandals. "Everyone, arm yourselves. The last Risen Queen is coming, and she has a legion of Mimics with her!"

Melissa landed outside their area. "Jake, Angie," she called urgently. "This is it; my sister knows she's losing. She's here to kill me and our leaders." She looked back to where the queen was approaching. "Please, keep everyone here. This has to end once and for all."

"Melissa, no!" Jake cried. He ran up to the mantis. "Please, you've been fighting all day. You're too tired to take her on."

Melissa lowered her triangular head down to him. "Jake, I know this queen. She is my close sister, the one I fought when I was a grub. She hurt me then, and I was frightened. I'm not frightened now—I have all of you to fight for."

"No, she'll kill you," Jake cried.

Melissa pressed her big head against him. "Back then I was a child and believed that the only way to stop them was to show them peace. They didn't understand then, and they don't now. She has come to hurt you. But I won't let her. I love you, Jake. I love all of you, and that is what makes us different. That is why I must fight. I fight for you. This is my destiny. I must go to her and end this."

Before anyone could speak, Melissa opened her wings and took off.

Jake ran back to the others and grabbed his skateboard and slingshot. "I'm not going to let her fight alone."

"We're coming too," Astraea said.

"We are?" Zephyr cried.

"Yes!" Astraea replied. "Come on, Zeph. It's Melissa; we have to help her."

The group of friends were soon in the sky, following behind Melissa. Beneath them, the battle raged as Titans and Olympians continued to fight the Mimics. Everywhere Astraea looked, there seemed to be a limitless number of Mimics marching on them.

Up ahead, the second mantis zoomed toward Melissa. They met in the sky with an aerial battle filled with more violence than Astraea had witnessed throughout the whole war.

The two large queens cut and bit into each other as they fought for supremacy. Once again, Melissa's mangled foreleg put her at a disadvantage, and she was struck several times by her sister's two.

"Melissa, get down to the ground!" Jake shouted. "Fight her on the ground!"

They could see that Melissa was trying to get her sister to go down, but it was as though she knew Melissa was the better fighter on the ground.

"Wait," Astraea cried, as she clung to Zephyr. "Remember what happened on Zomos? We can destroy her wings and force her down!" She called to the others, "Go for her wings! Use your rocks and let's down her!"

At Astraea's suggestion, Jake with Angie on the back of his board and Tryn with Triana, pulled out their slingshots and aimed carefully at the attacking queen's cellophane wings.

One rock couldn't do much damage, but a lot of rocks could. They tore holes through the fine wings until the First Queen could no longer fly. While still fighting Melissa, the queen made it down to the ground. It was here that Melissa pressed her advantage with her strange back kicks.

The sounds and sights of the fight were sickening as the two queens screeched and squealed at each other. At one point, the Risen Queen had Melissa pinned down. But before she could bite Melissa's head off, Melissa twisted around and kicked her sister away with a brutal blow.

The Risen Queen lay on the ground, moving slowly. She rolled over and tried to rise, but she collapsed to the ground again.

"That's what you get for being so mean!" Melissa shouted at her. "Stay down! It's over!"

The Risen Queen screeched and struggled to rise. Just as she regained her feet and turned on Melissa again, Lergo slithered in, and before anyone could stop the immense snake, it attacked the Risen Queen.

"No!" Melissa shouted at Lergo. "Bad snake, bad snake. Let her go!"

Instead of releasing the Risen Queen, Lergo threw back his head and swallowed her whole.

"Not cool, Lergo," Melissa chastised as she waved her foreleg at him. "Not cool at all!"

When everyone landed, Melissa looked at them. "I told you to stay back; it was too dangerous."

"We're a team," Astraea said. "And we fight as a team."

"Speaking of fighting," Jake said as he looked around. "Um, everyone, look . . ."

They were soon completely surrounded by Mimics.

Melissa nodded tiredly. "Okay," she shouted at the Mimics, raising her one foreleg. "Who's next?"

The Mimics lowered their heads and started to click.

Jake climbed off his board and approached her. "I don't think they want to fight you."

Melissa looked around. "No?"

"Nope," Astraea said. "Melissa, you're the First Queen. You're their ruler!"

"Oh no!" Melissa said. "No way, no how. I'm no First Queen. I'm just Melissa!"

# 36

ASTRAEA, ZEPHYR, AND THE OTHERS accompanied Melissa as she limped back to the recovery area to have her fresh wounds from the fight seen to. As they moved, Mimics by the thousands tried to get close to her. With a hiss, she drove them back.

Within a short time, reports were coming in from all over Tremenz that the Mimics had stopped fighting.

"It's over, Zeph," Astraea said as she patted Zephyr. "I can hardly believe it. It's finally over. We can all go home."

"I *don't* believe it," Zephyr said. She looked around at all the Mimics trying to get close. "I mean, look at them. They're not doing anything. I'm sure they're waiting to pounce on us when we least expect it."

"They won't," Melissa promised.

"How can you be so sure?" Zephyr asked.

"Trust me, I'm a queen," Melissa said. Then she started to chuckle, with a strange sound coming out of her insectoid mouth.

Jake patted her tall back leg. "I knew you could do it. So much for being a Fallen Queen. You're a hero; you beat them all!"

"I don't feel like a hero," Melissa said. "In fact, I kinda hurt all over. Heroes don't hurt."

"Sure they do," Tryn said. "You're the biggest hero I know. You ended this. You freed us all."

Melissa looked at him and lowered her head. "No, Tryn, we all did."

Their emotions were running wild as it finally sank in that the struggle with the Mimics was over. All around them Titans were putting down their weapons and embracing the Olympians they'd fought beside.

Before they reached the recovery area, Melissa stopped. "Jake, what do I do now?" She looked up and saw the mass of Mimics waiting just outside the camp. They weren't trying to fight—they just stood staring at her, waiting for her to command them. "They want me to be their First Queen, but I don't want to."

"You don't have to," Jake said. "You're free. You can be anything you want to be and do anything you like."

"Can I come to Titus?" Melissa asked.

Astraea nodded. "Of course, and there's Xanadu and anywhere else you want to go."

Days later everyone was still too tired to celebrate when reports came in from Titus and Xanadu that all the Mimics had stopped fighting. It would only be a matter of time before they melted into nothingness.

Now that the conflict was over, the real work could begin. Tremenz didn't belong to the Mimics—it had been stolen a very long time ago. But the few survivors from the camps that had originated there had only known slavery. It was their ancestors that had built the cities, the parks, and all the art. Jupiter promised to help them, but they had a long way to go.

Astraea was joyously reunited with her whole family. Her two missing brothers had been found in another camp, and with Aquilo recovered from his ordeal, their reunion was loud and filled with love.

Tryn and Triana met up with their parents and embraced excitedly.

Astraea saw Jake standing back with Angie as they watched all the reunions. When Angie left to check on Lergo, Jake approached Jupiter. Astraea didn't hear their conversation, but the expression on Jake's face saddened as he walked away.

"Jake." Astraea trotted over to him. "What is it?"

Jake looked at Angie. "I've been asking everyone about Angie's parents. Jupiter just told me they didn't make it. He said they were killed in one of the camps some time ago."

Astraea gasped. When she did, Zephyr came up to her, and Astraea told her what had happened.

"She's alone?" Zephyr said.

"She doesn't have any family," Astraea said. "No brothers or sisters or aunts or uncles."

Jake shook his head. "You're wrong," he said. "She has me."

The journey back to Xanadu felt even longer than it had been to come to Tremenz. But then again, Astraea had never been more anxious. She hadn't had the chance to speak at length with Emily during the fighting or after it ended, as she and Pegasus had raced to bring Riza home to Arious.

When they arrived on the glass lake, they walked through the jungle and emerged in the clearing outside the temple. Melissa was with them and gazing around in wonder. "Oh wow, this place is totally awesome! It smells so pretty. I want to stay here forever!"

Jake was walking with his arm around Angie. He had told her about her parents and promised she would never be alone and that if she wanted, she could come to Earth with him. But that didn't help with the pain. Lergo was slithering close beside her, as though he too felt her pain. For the first time in ages, the snake's colors returned to normal and he looked just like Nesso. An enormous version of her, but still the same.

Outside the temple, they saw a large gathering of Xan who had been rescued from multiple camps around Tremenz. They welcomed Astraea and her team with much gratitude.

"Do you remember your home now?" Jake asked Mila.

The stunning, eight-foot-tall Xan smiled calmly. "After a visit to Arious, we had our memories restored. We are indeed home and grateful to be."

"How is Riza?" Astraea asked.

The Xan turned and swept her arm open to invite them into the temple. "Go see for yourself; she is just inside."

Everyone ran forward and entered the temple. As Mila had promised, Riza was at the entrance standing with Emily, Pegasus, Joel, and Paelen. Brue was also pressed inside, licking Paelen enthusiastically with her two tongues.

When Emily saw Astraea, she ran at her and embraced her tightly. "You did it! You beat the Mimics!"

Astraea shook her head. "Not me, it was all of us." She looked back at Zephyr, Tryn, Jake, and the centaurs. "We all did."

Riza came forward. "I am so grateful to you all," she said softly. "We owe you so very much."

Jake was staring up at Riza with his eyes and mouth wide open.

"Close your mouth. You're letting the flies in," Joel teased as he approached and patted Jake on the back.

Riza looked at Jake and smiled radiantly. "Jake," she said. "I am so pleased to meet you. Arious has shown me how special you are. I am eternally grateful. Thank you." She bent down to kiss his cheek.

Astraea laughed as Jake turned bright red. "Breathe, Jake, breathe."

Riza's eyes landed on Melissa standing just outside the entrance. She walked forward. When Melissa saw her, she stepped back and turned to walk away.

"Melissa, wait, please," Riza said softly. "Why do you turn from me?"

Melissa stopped but wouldn't look back. "I know what my mother did to you. I'm so sorry. I understand if you don't want me here."

"Oh, child, you are most welcome here. I want to thank you."

"You do?" Melissa turned around and faced the Xan.

"You have done the most for us," Riza said. "You stopped the Mimics, and we are in your debt. We would be honored if you chose to stay with us on Xanadu."

"Really?" Melissa said. "I'd love to, but—but I can't. I'm going to stay with Jake and Angie and we're going back to Earth."

Astraea looked over to Jake, and he shook his head.

"I understand," Riza said. She looked at Angie. "Ah, Angitia . . ." Her eyes held great sadness as she knelt before the Titan. Even so, Riza was still much taller than Angie. Riza took her hands. "I am so sorry to hear about your parents. I wish I could bring them back for you, but my powers have not yet returned—if they ever do. We have all lost so much during this struggle, but it's over now. Soon we will all rebuild our lives."

Angie sniffed. She looked back at Lergo waiting outside the temple. "If you can't bring my family back, can you help Lergo? He's in so much pain."

Riza rose and walked toward the snake, still holding Angie's hand. Lergo's body stretched from the temple all the way through the clearing and into the jungle on the opposite side.

Riza reached out and touched the snake's snout and then looked down on Angie. "We Xan have had the power to move worlds, enlarge this one if needed, and cross the universe with a single thought," she said softly. "But stopping the natural end of life was never within our reach and not something we or anyone should ever do. Lergo is so very old; he has earned his rest. But I promise you this: We will all care for him here. There are herbs that we can give him to ease his pain and help heal his wounds. We will make a special place just for him. Lergo will want for nothing. And when his time comes, he will not be alone."

The snake closed his eyes as Riza stroked his damaged head. "Sleep now, old friend."

Moments later, Belis slid out of the temple over to Astraea. He pressed against her and raised his head to be petted.

"Oh great," Zephyr said. "Look who's back. . . ."

Astraea excitedly kissed the top of the snake's head. "I'm so glad to see you again!"

"Please, Astraea," Zephyr said. "I just ate."

# 37

THE VAST MAJORITY OF TITANS AND Olympians returned to Titus to retake their home and clear up the mess. Before long, the last Mimic melted into oblivion and their threat in the universe went with them.

Jake stayed with his friends on Xanadu working with Emily, Joel, Paelen, and all the others to build an area that would become Lergo's final home.

Melissa settled in easily and was a great help with lifting heavier logs out of the way. She was included in all the fun and was learning to play, as Joel brought out his soccer ball and they all joined a game.

Finally the time came when Jake and Nesso had no

more excuses to stay. It was time for them to return to Earth.

After rising early in the morning, Jake was holding Angie's hand as he called his friends together. They'd all known this time was coming, though no one had spoken of it. Astraea could barely look at him.

Jake inhaled deeply. "We knew this day would come," he started. "When the fight was over and everyone was safe. It's time for Nesso, Angie, and me to finally go home."

He looked over and saw tears sparkling in Astraea's and Triana's eyes. Tryn was shuffling around and wouldn't meet his glance, and the centaurs pawed the ground.

"I don't know how long I've been gone because time is messed up between our worlds. But my mom must be thinking I'm dead."

"Let her think it," Cylus said. "Then you can stay here with us. You're part of our herd now, you stupid human. You can't go. I forbid it."

Jake shook his head. "I have to. I can't leave her thinking I'm dead any more than you could with your mother. But I need to ask you guys a favor. . . ."

"When are you leaving?" Astraea asked weakly.

"Today," Jake said. "It would be cruel to let them wait any longer. But would you—"

"You haven't given us any time to prepare?" Triana said. Her voice was breaking. "You can't go, not now."

"I know, and maybe it's easier this way. But I have to tell you all something—"

"You can't do it," Tryn said. "You just can't. You're my best friend, Jake. I can't lose you."

"Would you all shut up and let me speak?" Jake cried.

"Fine," Tryn said. "But if you expect me to say good-bye, you're crazy."

"I don't expect that," Jake said. "What I've been trying to ask is, would you come with me to help explain to my mom why I can't live on Earth anymore and need to stay here with all of you? My family will never believe me unless they see you for themselves."

"What?" Tryn cried.

Jake looked up to the sky and sighed. "When I lived in California, all I did was skateboard and cause trouble with my sister. I was just a dumb kid that didn't know or care about anything. But I've changed. I've seen things that I'll never forget and been places and done things that no one would believe. I could never give that up and live a boring life on Earth, knowing you're all here."

"You—you want to stay with us?" Triana asked.

"Yes," Jake said. "Besides"—he smiled at Angie— "I really can't take you from here. You're a Titan and would be in too much danger on Earth. But I won't leave you alone—we're family now." He looked over to Melissa, who was playing with Brue. "Not to mention that crazy Fallen Queen. How could I give her or all of you up? I—just can't. I've spoken with Riza and with Jupiter; they said I could stay either here or on Titus. It's up to me. I have found a place here, a home with all of you. I just can't leave it."

"Now he wants to stay. Isn't that a surprise . . . ," Zephyr said.

Astraea looked back at her and then to Jake. "She can't believe you want to stay. But she's thrilled."

Zephyr snorted. "Astraea, will you ever tell him what I actually say?"

"Never." Astraea grinned.

* * *

Jake held up the Solar Stream ring and called out his home address, finishing with his bedroom in the early morning. The blazing light of the vortex opened, and Jake looked back at all his friends. "Mom is going to freak when she sees you, so please don't be offended by anything she or Molly say."

"Would you please stop talking and just go?" Cylus said impatiently.

Jake grinned at Cylus, and the centaur smiled back and nodded as they all walked into the blazing light.

They emerged together in Jake's small bedroom and were treading on each other in the tight space.

"Stop shoving me," Render said to Darek.

"I'm not, but there's no room in here."

"It's too small. I can't breathe," Zephyr complained.

"Zeph, you're on my foot!" Astraea cried.

Jake moved to his door and struggled to open it. He made it to the hall, and the others poured out behind him.

"I'm stuck!" Zephyr whinnied as she tried to get through the doorframe.

454

Astraea was behind her and had to push while Tryn and Triana pulled from the front. With a bit of straining, the doorframe broke and Zephyr made it through.

"Of all the indignities . . . ," Zephyr complained.

When they were all in the hallway, Jake turned and saw Molly emerging from her bedroom. Her eyes were wide and she was mouthing silent words. Finally she managed, "Mom . . . ?"

"Moles," Jake cried as he ran up to her and embraced her tightly. "Boy, have I missed you! Look how you've grown! You're almost as tall as me! How old are you now?"

Jake looked back at the others. "Molly is younger than me, but now she looks older! This time difference thing is awesome!"

Molly couldn't speak as she looked past him to the odd assortment behind him. She pointed at Cylus and the centaurs. "Wha . . . ?"

"What?" Cylus said, crossing his arms over his chest. "Haven't you ever seen a centaur before?"

"Molly?" a voice called.

"Mom?" Jake cried.

"Jake, is that you?" His mother charged into the hall but stopped dead in her tracks when she saw everyone standing with him.

Jake ran up to her and threw his arms around her. "I have missed you so much! You wouldn't believe what I've been through."

A toddler waddled up to Jake's mother. "Is that Billy?" Jake asked as he smiled at the little brother he'd never met.

Jake's mother was still glued to the spot but nodded.

Billy looked at everyone and then pointed at Zephyr. "Horsey . . ."

Zephyr looked at Astraea and sighed heavily. "Here we go again. . . ."

"Mom," Jake said proudly. "I have some friends I really want you to meet."

# ACKNOWLEDGMENTS

I think these will be the hardest acknowledgments I've ever written. Of course, I want to thank Anna Parsons, my wonderful editor at Simon & Schuster, and always, Veronique, my great agent. And everyone else who helped make this book a reality.

But the real thanks go to my dad.

So many of us are blessed with amazing fathers. I was lucky enough to be one of them. My dad was delightfully insane. We did the wackiest things while my brothers and I were growing up, and somehow he made everything fun. When I became an adult and moved away, as most do, I started my own life. But when my wonderful mom died, my dad and I came back together, and he moved in with me. But our relationship changed. We went from father/daughter to being roommates and the best friends ever.

From the day my first Pegasus book came out, my dad used to laugh and call Pegs that "crazy talking horse"—I laughed too and always told him Pegasus didn't speak. But now, in the Titans books, Pegasus does. So I guess Dad was right.

This book was written just before the Covid-19 lockdown of 2020. We all saw this terrible year unfold and never imagined that there could be so much heartache and so many changes for all of us, all around the world. I didn't think it could get worse. I was wrong. In September, just two weeks before writing this, I lost my best friend and father. Not from Covid, but another illness.

I am telling you this not to make you as sad as I am, but to ask a favor of you. When you finish this book and put it down, please go to the ones you love and give them enormous hugs. If they ask you why, tell them that Pegasus told you to.

Let them know just how much they mean to you. That's all I ask. Just to give them a hug.

And I send a hug out to each and every one of you. Stay safe, stay strong, my dear friends. Things will get better for all of us . . . one day.

RILEY GAZED OUT OVER THE SEEMINGLY endless ocean. The water was calm as their sailboat, the *Event Horizon*, cut smoothly across the surface. Above them the sky was cloudless and the kind of blue she never saw at home. She inhaled the clean, salty air and felt a sense of peace wash over her. This was the start of their second week out on the boat with one more week facing them.

"Lunch!" Her father appeared at the hatch that led down to the lower deck.

"Coming." Riley walked confidently along the smooth deck and made it to the hatch. She paused long enough to call to her aunt, who was at the helm. "Aunt Mary, I'll eat quickly and then take over, if you like."

"Thanks, Riley. Go enjoy yourself."

When she reached the small galley, her father said, "I don't know where your cousin is."

"He's probably in his cupboard."

"Cabin," her father corrected. "Go get him before the food gets cold."

Riley nodded and walked toward the back of the boat where the cabins were. She liked to tease her father and call them cupboards because that was about the size of them. She knocked on Alfie's door but heard no response. "Alfie, it's lunch."

Riley walked down to her own cabin and opened the door. There she saw her cousin sitting on her bunk, reading her diary.

"What are you doing in here, Creep? Give that back!"

Riley rushed at her cousin as he held her diary aloft. His teasing smile broadened farther as he climbed on her bunk and held the book high above her head.

"Alfie, give it back!"

"Oh, poor little Shorty isn't having any fun. . . ." He opened the diary to her last entry and started to read aloud. *"I hate my life. I hate this boat and I hate the ocean. I just want to go home and be with my friends. . . ."*

Riley snatched at her diary, but Alfie kept pulling it away and taunting her with it. Finally, her frustrations got the better of her, and she hauled back and punched her cousin in the stomach as hard as she could.

Alfie dropped the diary, collapsing onto the bunk, gasping for breath.

Just as Riley picked the book up, her father burst into her cabin. "What's going on in here?" When he saw Alfie lying on Riley's bunk, he rushed over. "What happened? Alfie, what's wrong?"

Her cousin's face was red as he tried to regain his breath. He pointed a shaking finger at Riley. "Sh-she p-punched me in the stomach."

Her father's eyes flashed to her. "Is that true?"

"He started it!" Riley cried. "Dad, he came in here and stole my diary. He was reading it and everything!"

Her father helped Alfie sit up on the bunk and lower his head between his knees to ease the pain. Then his ice-blue eyes landed on her. "We don't hit people—ever. Do you hear me?"

"But, Dad . . . ," Riley cried.

"No buts," he spat. "Your mother and I raised you better than that. Now, I want you to apologize to your cousin."

"What? That's not fair! He snuck in here and went through my stuff. Why should I apologize?"

"It doesn't matter what he did. You don't hit people! Apologize to Alfie."

Riley looked from her father to her despicable cousin and back to her father again. The expression on her dad's face said he wasn't going to back down.

Riley gritted her teeth. "Okay, I'm sorry. . . ." She turned and ran out of her cabin and up the small steps to the upper deck, muttering, "I'm sorry I didn't push you off the boat . . . !"

Bitter tears of frustration were stinging her eyes as she sat down at the pointed front end of the boat with her legs dangling over the side. This was as far away from the others as she could get, but it wasn't far enough.

"You okay up there, Riley?" Mary called.

Riley had her back to her aunt and didn't want to answer. She didn't want Mary to see her tears.

"Riley?" Mary called.

"I'm fine!" Riley snapped. But she wasn't fine. She wanted to go home. Instead she was trapped on the boat for another two weeks with her father, aunt, and cousin.

This was meant to be a family-bonding trip, since she hadn't seen her relatives in over a year. She loved her aunt Mary very much but hated Alfie. He was twelve, making him just a year younger than her. But he was already taller and stronger and took every opportunity to prove it.

When the trip was first announced, Riley thought her mother and brother, Danny, would be going. But her mother couldn't leave her job at the hospital. She was a doctor with a lot of patients that needed her. Danny didn't want to go. At sixteen, he was given the choice. Riley wasn't. So instead of spending her spring break at home with her friends, she had to go on this stupid trip.

Aunt Mary was recently divorced and going through a hard time with Alfie. The voyage around the Bahamas was meant to clear things up between them. Maybe it was working for Mary, but being stuck on the sailboat with Alfie was ruining Riley's life.

From the moment they left their home in Denver,

Colorado, Riley had a bad feeling about the trip. By the time they'd flown to Miami, Florida, and made it to the port and their sailboat, her premonition came true.

The first thing Alfie did when he saw her was pat her on the head and call her *Shorty*. Since then, the teasing had been nonstop—but only when her father or aunt weren't around.

Gazing into crystal clear ocean, Riley wondered how things could get any worse. As tears trickled down her cheeks, she saw the sunlight glinting off something reflective in the water. It was there, and then it wasn't. She watched the spot, and again the sun caught the silvery sparkle of fish scales. It was a tail. A long one. As the fish moved, Riley gasped. The silver tail trailed up to what looked like a torso with stubby arms and a round head covered in shaggy dark hair. As she watched, the head turned. The face was gray like the body, with two holes where a nose should be and large deep-set eyes that were as black as night. When it opened its mouth, it revealed a row of sharp, pointed teeth.

Riley was too stunned to scream. She pulled her legs in and moved back from the edge. A moment later, the creature darted down into the depth.

"Riley?"

Riley jumped at her father's voice. Her heart was pounding ferociously in her chest, and she opened her mouth to tell him what had just happened. But then she looked back at the water and saw only the ocean. Had the creature been real? What was it? Some kind of mermaid? If it was a mermaid, it wasn't anything like the ones she'd read about in books. This was a terrifying monster. Or worse, maybe it wasn't there at all.

Riley was still shaking as she looked from the water to her father and back to the water again. Would he believe her if she told him? Considering he spent most of his life in water as a marine biologist, she doubted it.

"If you're thinking about going for a swim before lunch, forget it. That water looks pretty, but don't be fooled, it's cold and deep."

Did her father think she would actually go into the water with that sharp-toothed monster swimming around? "I—I wasn't going to," she stammered.

He sat down on the deck beside her and scooted up to the edge until his legs were dangling over the side.

"Bring your legs in, Dad," Riley warned. She may have been angry with him, but there was no way she'd let him endanger himself if that creature was still around.

"It's fine," he said. "I won't fall in."

"What about being pulled in?" Riley said.

He smiled at her and shook his head. "I doubt anything out there would be interested in me."

"Don't be too sure," Riley warned.

He gazed into the water and sighed heavily, but then said nothing. After what seemed an eternity of silence, he said, "Did I ever tell you that humpbacks are the only whales that sing a long, complicated song that they change as they move around the world? And a male's song can be heard for hundreds of miles?"

Riley did know that because her father had told her a million times before. And when he wasn't telling her, he was listening to whale songs at full volume in his study. That's when he was home and not on some expedition. As a marine biologist, his specialty was cetaceans and he was especially obsessed with humpbacks. She figured that was why he wanted to go on this trip. Yes, for Mary and Alfie, but also to study the humpbacks during their spring migration from the Caribbean to far up north. What she really resented was her father dragging her along with him. Whales were his thing, not hers.

He continued, "Also, humpbacks are—"

"Dad, enough about the stupid whales," Riley said. "I know you love them and the ocean and all that, but I don't. To me, they're just big stinky fish."

Her father gasped. "Whales are not fish!"

"I know," Riley sighed tiredly. "They're mammals, just like us." She turned and saw the hurt her comments had caused shining in his eyes. "Dad, I'm sorry. I just don't understand why you like them so much. They're kinda pretty if you're into barnacles and stuff like that. But you spend more time on the ocean with your whales than at home with us."

He looked away and stared into the deep blue waters. Finally, he said, "You're right. I'm sorry. It was unfair of me to bring you on this research trip. But since I spend so much time away from home, I just thought it would be extra special for you and me to spend some time together."

"But we're not spending time together," Riley said. "You're always on deck with your binoculars looking for whales or you're photographing them or writing notes about them. Aunt Mary is always busy steering the boat—that leaves me stuck with Alfie. Dad, he hates me and he's doing everything he can to annoy me. You don't see it because he stops when you're around. Even today, you only noticed when I hit him and not before when it was him tormenting me."

He was still staring into the water but nodding his head. "I'll talk to him."

"Why bother? He's not going to stop no matter what you say. He's a spoiled brat, and Mary is letting him get away with everything."

"I know," he agreed. "That's why Mary asked to go on this trip. She's hoping I might be a good influence on him. . . ." He chuckled softly. "But you're right. I haven't been much of a role model for him." He turned and looked at her. "Or you."

It was Riley's turn to gaze into the ocean.

"So when did you start keeping a diary?"

Riley shrugged. "Mom gave it to me for this trip. She said writing things down on paper is different than putting them on my phone or laptop. She said a diary should be about experiences and my personal feelings—just for me to write and read."

"Is that what it is?"

Riley nodded. "Yeah, I guess it kinda is. I write

down where we've been, what I've seen, and what I'm feeling—even if what I am feeling is anger at Alfie."

"So when you caught him reading it . . ."

"I lost it and hit him—just as hard as I could."

"How did that make you feel?" he asked.

Riley shrugged. "I guess it was good at first because he felt just as bad as I did. But then I started to feel guilty because I'd really hurt him."

"So no more hitting?"

"No more hitting . . . ," Riley agreed. "But I won't make any promises about kicking or maybe biting!"

He smiled at her. "Good enough."

There was another long period of silence, but this time it was a good silence. It was the silence of being comfortable and not angry anymore. Riley pulled out her cell phone from her pocket, but there was still no signal.

"We're too far out," her dad said.

"I know, I just keep checking anyway."

He laughed. "Your mom said it'd be a nightmare getting you off that thing."

"I'm not on it all the time," Riley said defensively.

"No, just most of it," he teased. "Even when there isn't a signal."

"Well, I like to stay current."

"Current?" he laughed. "You mean keeping track of what your friends are saying on that Facie . . . thingy?"

"Facebook," Riley said. "I don't use it. I was hoping to look up more about the Bermuda Triangle and the creatures that live in it. You know, like . . . mermaids?"

"Mermaids?"

Riley nodded. "My friend Lisa says that when boats or planes go into the Bermuda Triangle, they see really weird things and sometimes they even disappear completely. She says aliens live in there and destroy ships.

"When I told her where we were going, she said to be careful and not go into the Bermuda Triangle. I wanted to look it up to see how far away from it we are."

He chuckled again and shook his head. "Well, honey, I hate to tell you this, but technically speaking, we've been in the Bermuda Triangle for most of this trip." He pointed out over the water. "It spans from Miami down to Puerto Rico and over to Bermuda. But you don't have to worry. In all the times I've been in here, I haven't seen anything unusual at all—including mermaids or aliens."

Riley's eyes went big and she gasped. "We're in the Bermuda Triangle? Really?"

"Uh-huh."

"That explains it."

"Explains what?"

"Just before you came on deck, I saw something weird in the water, right here off the bow. It might have been a mermaid, but not a nice-looking one."

Her father started to laugh. "Oh, so you only like nice mermaids?"

"Dad, I'm serious. I swear I saw something in the water right before you arrived. It had a long silver tail, a gray body, and a head with big black eyes and two slits for a nose. Its mouth was full of sharp teeth. It looked right at me."

He frowned. "From what you describe, it could have been a barracuda. They have a nasty mouth full of teeth and can look very threatening. Though there aren't many cases of attacks on humans. Believe me, we are more dangerous to them than they are to us."

"No Dad, it wasn't a fish. It was a—a . . ."

Her father shook his head. "Riley, you're too old to believe in mermaids. If they existed, with all the time

I've spent in water, I'm sure I would have seen one by now. Trust me, there are a lot of strange creatures out there, but mermaids aren't one of them."

Riley looked back at the water. She had seen something there and it *had* seen her.

Her father tapped her on the end of her nose. "Now, how about you and I go into the galley and have some lunch?" He winked. "Though I don't think Alfie will be hungry for a while."

Riley started to get up. "I guess I should go say sorry again."

"Maybe," he agreed. "But not for a while yet—let him think about what he's done and your response to it. I've sent him to his cabin for the rest of the day as punishment for going through your things. So the rest of the day is for you and me."

"And the humpbacks," Riley added.

He rose up beside her. "Well, maybe a few humpbacks—or mermaids, if we're lucky."